Arkell's Endings
Keith Arkell

GINGER GM
gingergm.com

First published in 2020 by Ginger GM Ltd

Copyright © 2020 Keith Arkell

The right of Keith Arkell to be identified as the author of this work has been asserted in accordance with the Copyrights, Designs and Patents Act 1988.

All rights reserved. No part of this work may be reproduced, stored in or introduced into a retrieval system, or transmitted in any form or by any means, electronic, mechanical photocopying, recording or otherwise, without prior permission of the publisher. In particular, no part of this publication may be scanned, transmitted via the Internet, or uploaded to a website without the publisher's permission.

British Library Cataloguing-in-Publication Data
A catalogue record for this book is available from the British Library.

ISBN: 9 781527 265592

Distribution: Chess & Bridge Ltd,
44 Baker Street, London W1U 7RT
Tel: +44 (0)207 486 7015. Email: info@chess.co.uk
Website: www.chess.co.uk

Production: Richard Palliser
Cover illustration: Pete Mitchell
Printed and bound in England by TJ International, Padstow

Ginger GM Ltd – Chess Grandmaster Simon Williams
www.gingergm.com

Contents

Foreword	Jonathan Speelman	7
Introduction		8

Opponent

1. Suba [B]   Watson, Farley & Williams, London 1991   *12*
Double-rook endgame

2. Vachier-Lagrave [W]   European Union Championship, Liverpool 2008   *17*
Bishop against knight

3. Kosten [B]   Montpellier Open 2002   *22*
Rook and bishop versus rook and knight

4. Kotronias [B]   Gausdal Classic 2002   *28*
Same-coloured bishop endgame

5. Rodshtein [W]   Hastings Masters 2014/15   *32*
Rook and pawn endgame

6. Koneru [B]   British Championship, Street 2000   *36*
Bishop and knight against bishop and knight

7. Hebden [B]   British Rapidplay Championship, Leeds 1998   *40*
Double-rook endgame

8. Zak [B]   Lewisham International 1983   *44*
Two bishops versus bishop and knight

9. Milliet [B]   London Chess Classic Open 2015   *47*
Bishop and knight versus bishop and knight

10. Kulaots [W]   Gelsenkirchen International 1995   *51*
Rook and knight against rook and bishop

11. Holland [B]   High Wycombe Open 2002   56
King and pawn endgame

12. Houska [W]   Mindsports Olympiad, London 1999   60
Two bishops versus bishop and knight

13. Certek [W]   Vienna Open 2016   63
Two bishops versus bishop and knight

14. Wadsworth [B]   Gatwick International 2016   68
Rook and knight against rook and bishop

15. Ledger [B]   British Championship, Eastbourne 1990   72
Rook and knight against rook and knight

16. Ilfeld [W]   London Chess Classic Open 2013   77
Double-rook endgame

17. Ernst [B]   HZ Open, Vlissingen 2007   82
Bishop and knight versus bishop and knight

18. Spreeuw [B]   British League (4NCL), West Bromwich 2003   86
Rook and bishop against bishop and knight

19. Palliser [B]   Monarch Assurance Open, Port Erin 2000   89
Rook and bishop against rook

20. Ward [B]   British Championship, Aberystwyth 2014   93
Rook and pawn endgame

21. Bradbury [B]   EACU Open, Newmarket 2019   97
Rook and knight against rook and knight

22. Toma [B]   British Championship, Hull 2018   102
Knight versus bishop

23. Bruno [W]   European Senior Championship, Eretria 2015   107
Two rooks against rook and bishop

24. Zakarian [B]   British League (4NCL), Hinckley 2014   *111*
Two rooks and bishop against two rooks and knight

25. Franklin [W]   British League (4NCL), Telford 2019   *113*
Knight and pawn endgame

26. Orr [B]   Edinburgh Open 1988   *118*
Knight against bishop

27. Panzer [W]   Hastings Challengers 1990/91   *121*
Queen and pawn endgame

28. Groves [B]   Jersey International 1985   *125*
Bishop and knight against knight

29. Webb [W]   Hastings Masters 2009/10   *130*
Double-rook endgame

30. Sugden [W]   British Championship, Canterbury 2010   *134*
Rook and pawn endgame

31. McDonald [B]   Southend GM 2009   *139*
Rook and knight against rook and bishop

32. Granda Zuniga [B]   Isle of Man Open, Douglas 2014   *142*
Rook and bishop against rook and knight

33. Byrne [B]   Watson, Farley & Williams, London 1991   *145*
Rook and bishop against rook

Afterword – Simon Williams pays homage to Keith Arkell's talent   *149*

Index of Opponents   *159*

Foreword by Jonathan Speelman

In this fascinating work, Keith Arkell adds to his earlier autobiographical collection with a new book dedicated to the phase of chess in which he truly shines: the endgame.

The initial position of the game of chess could in theory have three possible outcomes with 'perfect play': a win for White, a draw, or, if for some strange reason White is in absolute zugzwang, a win for Black. Nobody seriously believes the last, though as far as I know it hasn't been mathematically proven and most strong players believe that while White can get some 'edge' from the opening – a human concept of a position easier to play – that if God played God then the game would end in a draw.

This implies that in order to defeat a strong player you have to induce significant error(s), and there are a number of ways to do this. With enough opening theory and a lucky or well targeted hit against a weak point, you may be able to deliver a knockout blow even against a strong opponent very early on. Sometimes you can create sufficient problems in the middlegame, either through positional pressure or some vicious attack (sound or not) to topple the enemy. However, if neither succeeds then normally the game will eventually liquidate to an endgame.

This is the aspect of chess in which the difference between stronger and weaker players is most marked. Precisely because there are far fewer pieces on the board, it is crucial that you handle them well. Strong endgame play demands underlying knowledge, precise calculation, good nerves to keep yourself together for hours on end and, above all, patience.

Keith's endgame play demonstrates all of these in spades and his whole approach to chess is to aim for endgames – they should be playable, but don't have to start advantageously – in which he can slowly outplay the enemy.

In this collection, he has explained his very practical mindset in both the earlier phases of the game – in which, in contrast to time-trouble addicts, he tries to make sensible decisions reasonably quickly – and in the endgame itself.

Keith is the man one would least like to face with three pawns versus four on the same side in a rook endgame or, much worse, with a rook against a rook and bishop. Like a python, once he has hold of an opponent he is a master of slow strangulation and playing through this fine collection will help you to develop this ophidian skill yourself.

Introduction

It has long seemed to me that as the standard of play rises, so does the overall percentage scored by White. Taken to its logical conclusion, this might suggest that with perfect play, chess is a win for White. However, I think that most of us don't believe this, and that at some rarefied level the curve goes the other way.

We tend to assume that with ideal play, chess is a draw. When we speak of a player having the 'advantage', we may simply mean that he has a very clear plan at his disposal for putting his opponent under pressure. While the player with the slightly worse position may stand OK from an objective perspective, from a practical perspective they can have some difficult problems to solve: for example, having to find a string of 'only moves' in order to stay afloat.

Such issues have always guided my thinking. I rarely look to create unfathomable complications, I don't carry around an armoury of opening traps, and I don't concern myself with trying to force a win from the earliest stages. Instead, my opening repertoire and subsequent play are all about creating a framework from which I can try to acquire the tiniest of advantages, and then, inch by inch, convert that into something tangible. Unsurprisingly, I win many of my games in the ending. Very often I am not sure at what point my opponent's position has deteriorated from what was difficult but tenable, to a forced loss.

The Arkell Hierarchy of Pawns

I should introduce 'Arkell's Hierarchy of Pawns'. Carry this philosophy to the board and you will rarely be stuck for a plan! It is not an absolute set of values, but can readily be applied to most so-called normal positions, i.e. those in which both players castle kingside. When the opponents both castle long, you can usually reverse the hierarchy, and when the kings aren't opposite each other, other considerations usually come to the fore.

Arkell's Hierarchy of Pawns is based on:

i. The b-pawn is slightly less valuable than the c-pawn. That is why, for example, Black is prepared to give his opponent a lead in development in the Adorjan 'Black is OK' variation of the Queens Indian, 1 d4 ♘f6 2 c4 e6 3 ♘f3 b6 4 g3 ♗a6 5 b3 b5!?.

ii. The c-pawn is slightly less valuable than the d-pawn. Very strong players understand these matters intuitively, without even the need to verbalise them. Bent Larsen, for instance, didn't like to play the white side of the Open Sicilian because he regarded 3 d4 as an anti-positional move. Of course, it isn't as simple as that because White has an early initiative and attacking chances. Likewise, in the Symmetrical English with d4 cxd4; ♘xd4 White gains space in compensation for the unfavourable pawn exchange. Taken in isolation, however, the exchange ...cxd4; ♘xd4 (rather than a pawn recapture) is a gain for Black.

iii. More subtly, I believe that this also applies to the e- and d-pawns. When Black exchanges with ...dxe4, he makes a minuscule gain. His king will be fractionally safer than White's and the opposing d-pawn will be a target – either directly or in conjunction with a plan of ...c5. Meanwhile Black will remain super solid with his pawns on e6 and f7. You will probably have heard it said that when Black achieves the move ...d5 in the Sicilian, he not only equalises, but stands better.

iv. The same goes for the e- and f-pawns. It is no accident that when White successfully achieves the break e2-e4 (or e3-e4) against the Dutch Defence, he is usually doing well. The situation vis-à-vis the f- and g-pawns is less clear, as it depends on specifics such as king safety.

v. Back to the other side, it's pretty obvious to most players that swapping your a-pawn for a b-pawn is a positional gain, all else being equal.

So there you have it. My hierarchy of pawns states that as you work your way across from the a- to the f-pawn, the value increases. This philosophy has a huge bearing on how I play chess. By contrast, traditional thinking simply dictates that you capture towards the centre.

Choice of Games

Another favourite of mine is the so-called 'Carlsbad Structure'. I have probably played more than a thousand games in which my c-pawn and my opponent's e-pawn are absent after an early exchange on d5. The resulting plan for White is to push the b-pawn up the board to create weaknesses, as part of a 'minority attack', the full impact of which may not be felt until the endgame.

Also in these pages are many rook and pawn endgames. In their wonderful book *Chess for Life*, Natasha Regan and Matthew Sadler conclude that as a percentage of all games played, I have more of these than any other chess player!

Other games highlight the power of two bishops, and the advantage of bishop over knight in general. However, there are also a few games where the knight proves to be the more valuable piece. There are conversions to a full point from material superiority, as well as a few wins from theoretical draws, including rook and bishop versus rook, and even bishop and knight versus knight and pawn. I have also selected one queen and pawn and one king and pawn endgame.

Thought Processes

With the exception of Rodshtein-Arkell, in which the engines and tablebases throw up some very beautiful variations, I have approached this book in an unusual way. My intention has been to reproduce my thoughts at the board – sometimes with analysis, including where flawed, and other times with assessments, judgements and uncertainty. With a few exceptions, I have avoided objective assessments or computer-generated variations. Where words are appropriate, I've used them, and where variations are appropriate, I've given the lines which I saw at the board.

Although I have never done more than browse endgame books, my favourites being those by John Nunn and Jonathan Speelman, I have always taken pleasure in the games of Rubinstein, Miles, Salov, Karpov and, of course, the current world champion, Magnus Carlsen. However, my favourite grinder, particularly during the 1980s, was Ulf Andersson. I was mesmerised by how he would typically extract win after win, often in rook and knight endgames arising from the Exchange Slav.

Chess openings have never really interested me, but around the time I was nearing IM standard I began to realise that I gained significantly in strength as the material on the board was reduced. I was seeing and managing to pull off unusual mating patterns, and finding that I had a good feel for piece coordination. Reaching plenty of endgames really can work wonders for your chess.

Regarding the development of my own style and preferences, I have always had a fondness for a favourable pawn structure, or some other long-term advantage, such as the two bishops, even should this allow my opponent an initiative in compensation. In these circumstances it is usually desirable to trade queens, hence the reputation I have gained for doing just that!

Acknowledgements

After trimming down what could have been a very long list of people to whom I am indebted in one way or another, I would like to express my very great appreciation to Peter Griffiths for invaluable suggestions in tightening up and generally improving the prose of this work, and to Richard Palliser for his skill and speed in shaping it into a format for printing, while contributing one or two tweaks along the way.

I would like to offer my special thanks to Simon Williams for approaching me about this project in the first place, and for his positivity (and patience!) throughout. I also greatly appreciate the closing chapter Simon has contributed to these pages, and through which the abundance and generosity of his friendship shines.

As I write, I am touched that legendary endgame expert Jonathan Speelman has agreed to write a foreword to these pages. In my early days as a professional player I was regularly inspired by how often Jonathan would outplay some of the world's best with subtle endgame play.

Thank you as well to my first hero, Ulf Andersson, for showing four decades ago what can be achieved with limited material. In more recent years, David Howell has inspired and impressed with his endgame prowess. In many ways it feels as if David has received the chess grinder's baton from me and runs with it at speeds barely imaginable. For every 2350-rated player I grind down in 80 moves, it seems that David does the same to a 2550 player in 120 moves. So, thank you, David for inspiring me by doing what I do, only much better.

And, finally, I am particularly grateful to another great friend of mine, Jonathan Hawkins. Jonathan is the only player with whom I really discuss chess at any length away from tournaments, and he is an exceptionally strong endgame player who has taught me a lot and continues to do so.

Keith Arkell,
Paignton, June 2020

1. Arkell-Suba

Our first encounter features a then very strong GM, and I was up against Suba's favourite Benoni. This endgame lasted more than 11 hours and caused a long delay to the prize-giving. After a slow start I was hoping to finish with a hat-trick of wins, having just defeated GMs Hector and Khalifman.

Keith Arkell - Mihai Suba
Watson, Farley & Williams, London 1991
Modern Benoni

1 d4 e6 2 c4 ♘f6 3 ♘f3 c5 4 d5 d6 5 ♘c3 exd5 6 cxd5 g6 7 g3 ♗g7 8 ♗g2 0-0 9 0-0 ♘a6 10 ♘d2 ♘c7 11 ♘c4 ♘fe8 12 a4 b6 13 ♕c2 f5 14 e3 ♗b7 15 ♖d1 ♘f6 16 ♖b1 ♔h8 17 b3 ♕d7 18 ♗b2 ♖ad8 19 ♖d2 ♕f7 20 ♕d1 ♗a8 21 ♗a1 ♖d7 22 b4 cxb4 23 ♖xb4 ♖c8 24 a5

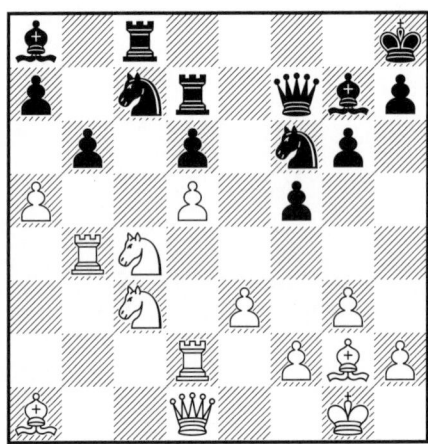

Using the hidden vulnerability of Black's bishop on a8 to increase my positional advantage.
24...b5
No self-respecting Benoni player would cede the c6-square for free by 24...bxa5 25 ♘xa5, so Black reluctantly seeks some activity at the cost of a pawn.
25 ♘xb5 ♘xb5 26 ♖xb5 ♖xc4 27 ♖b8+ ♘g8 28 ♖xa8 ♖dc7 29 ♗f1 ♖c1 30 ♗xg7+ ♔xg7 31 ♕a4 ♘f6 32 ♕d4 g5 33 ♔g2 g4 34 a6 ♖7c5 35 ♖b2 ♔g6 36 ♗e2 ♕xd5+

37 ♕xd5 ♘xd5 38 ♖xa7 ♖a5 39 e4

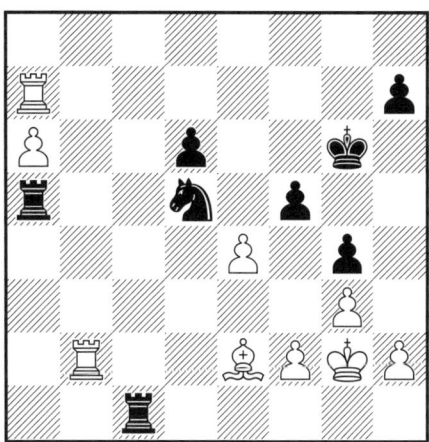

Despite the time-trouble we were in, I would shudder today at making such a move since I now appreciate the value of maintaining the e3 and f2 structure deep into the game. Instead, I should be targeting d6.

39...♖aa1 40 f3 ♘e3+ 41 ♔f2 ♘d1+ 42 ♗xd1 ♖xd1 43 exf5+

Somewhere around here we slowed down, realising we had made the time control at move 40. There were no increments back in 1991.

43...♔xf5 44 fxg4+ ♔xg4 45 ♖g7+ ♔f5 46 a7 h5 47 ♔g2 h4 48 ♖f2+ ♔e6 49 ♖f8

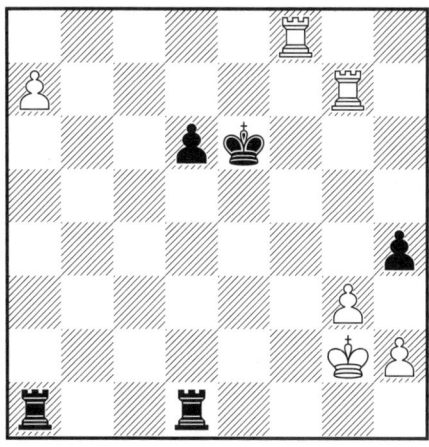

49...hxg3

One line I was aware of was 49...♖g1+ 50 ♔h3 hxg3 51 hxg3 (definitely not 51 a8♕? ♖xa8 52 ♖xa8 gxh2) 51...♖h1+ 52 ♔g4 ♖a4+ 53 ♔g5 ♖ha1 54 ♖f6+ ♔e5

55 ♖e7+ ♔d5 56 ♖d7 ♖a6 57 a8♕ ♖xa8 58 ♖dxd6+, with excellent winning chances.
50 hxg3 ♖a2+ 51 ♔h3 ♖da1 52 ♖ff7 ♖a4 53 ♖b7 ♖h1+ 54 ♔g2 ♖ha1 55 ♖h7

To alter the status quo I wanted the maximum checking distance in order to push Black's king around a bit. Bear in mind that one special aspect of a four-rook ending is the increased vulnerability of both kings...
55...♔f5 56 ♖h5+ ♔g6 57 ♖d5 ♖xa7 58 ♖xd6+ ♔f5

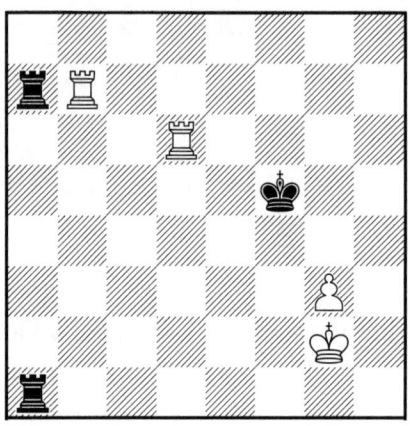

...And here is a case in point: 58...♔g5? 59 ♖b5+ ♔g4 60 ♖d4# clearly won't do.
59 ♖b5+

I'd never seen anything like this, but two things seemed obvious: to drive Black's king as far from the g-file as possible, and to protect my own king from harassment.
59...♔e4 60 ♖e6+ ♔d4 61 ♖b2 ♔d3 62 ♖f2 ♖a8 63 ♖f4 ♖8a2+ 64 ♔f3 ♖f1+ 65 ♔g4 ♖g1 66 ♖f3+ ♔d4 67 ♔f4 ♖a8 68 ♖e4+ ♔d5 69 ♖d3+ ♔c5 70 ♖c3+ ♔d6 71 ♖d3+ ♔c5 72 ♖e5+ ♔c4 73 ♖f3 ♔d4 74 ♖g5

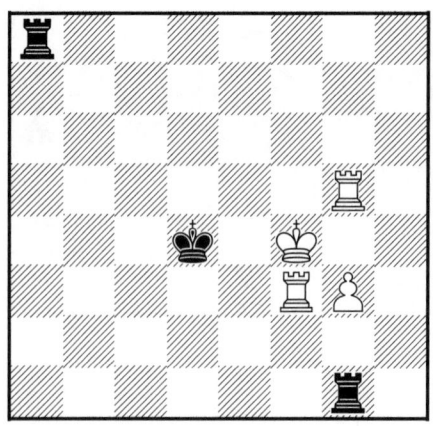

To win the game, I must get my pawn moving. Eventually I formulated a plan to set up a fortress of rooks on the sixth rank, both protecting my king and creating an umbrella under which I could safely achieve g3-g4.

74...♖f8+ 75 ♔g4 ♖a8 76 ♖g6 ♔e4 77 ♖b3 ♖a4 78 ♔h5 ♖a5+ 79 ♔h4 ♖h1+ 80 ♔g4 ♖a8 81 ♖b4+ ♔e3 82 ♖e6+ ♔d3 83 ♖bb6 ♖g1 84 ♖bd6+

Another advantage of my connected rooks is their ability to spoil the coordination of Black's king and rook on a8, as becomes clear in the following notes. At the same time Black must avoid an exchange at all costs.

84...♔c4 85 ♔f4 ♔c5 86 ♖c6+ ♔b5 87 ♖b6+

This sequence of moves is designed to deny Suba the option of checking on my fourth rank, so that I can finally get going with g3-g4.

87...♔c5 88 ♖a6 ♖f8+

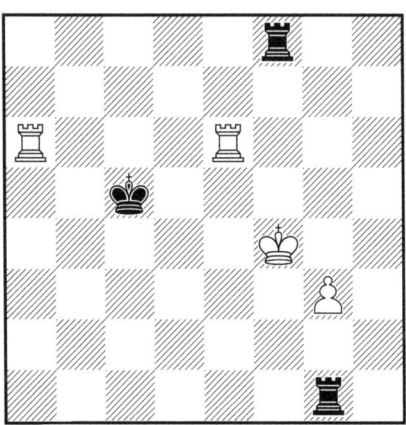

As an example of the obstruction motif, 88...♖b8 would be met by 89 ♖ac6+ ♔b5 (and not 89...♔d5? 90 ♖ed6#) 90 g4.
89 ♖f6 ♖d8 90 ♖ac6+ ♔d5
Alternatively, 90...♔b5 91 ♖b6+ ♔a5 92 ♖bd6 ♖c8 (or 92...♖g8 93 ♖g6 ♖f8+ 94 ♖df6 ♖d8 95 g4) 93 ♖a6+ ♔b5 94 ♖fb6+ ♔c5 when again I can finally play 95 g4, with my rooks having continual access to g6 and f6 to neutralise the black rook on c8.
91 g4 ♖f1+ 92 ♔g5 ♖g1 93 ♖a6 ♖g8+ 94 ♖g6 ♖e8 95 ♖a5+ ♔e4 96 ♖g7 ♔d4 97 ♖a4+
Long games are no recent habit of mine, and only here do we exceed the length of my successful effort against the American legend Robert Byrne from the fourth round of this tournament – see Game 33.
97...♔d5 98 ♖f4 ♔e5 99 ♖ff7 ♔e6 100 ♖f5 ♖a8 101 ♖g6+ ♔e7 102 ♔h6 ♖a4 103 ♖e5+ ♔f7 104 ♖f5+ ♔e7 105 g5

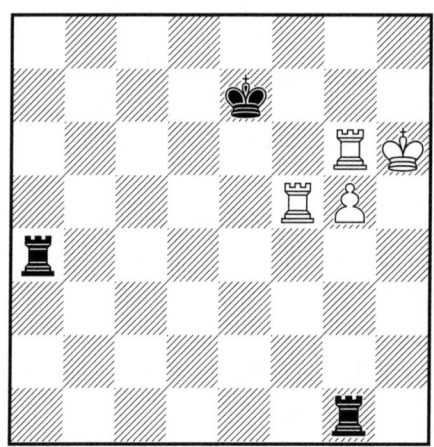

In the worst case scenario I would have been obliged to repeat the process to force through g4-g5. The task becomes noticeably easier as my pawn advances, because Black both doesn't have so much space to work with at the top of the board and has mating threats to contend with.
105...♖h4+ 106 ♔g7 ♖hg4 107 ♖e5+ ♔d7 108 ♔f7 ♖4g2
Allowing mate in two, but if 108...♖f4+ 109 ♖f6 ♖fg4 110 g6 ♖4g2 111 ♖e7+ ♔d8 112 ♖d6+ ♔c8 113 ♔e8! and mate soon follows.
109 ♖e7+ 1-0

2. Vachier-Lagrave-Arkell

I included this game because of an unusual missed opportunity and because of the skill of my prominent opponent in extracting blood from a stone.

> **Maxime Vachier-Lagrave - Keith Arkell**
> European Union Championship, Liverpool 2008
> *Caro-Kann Defence*

1 e4 c6 2 d4 d5 3 e5 c5 4 dxc5 e6 5 ♘f3 ♗xc5 6 ♗d3 ♘c6 7 0-0 ♘ge7 8 ♗f4 ♘g6 9 ♗g3 0-0 10 ♘bd2 f5

It's always a relief when I reach a playable position with my own variation against the Advance Caro-Kann.

11 exf6 ♕xf6 12 c4 ♘b4 13 ♗xg6 ♕xg6 14 ♘e5 ♕c2 15 cxd5 ♕xd1 16 ♖fxd1 ♘xd5 17 ♘e4 ♗e7 18 ♖ac1 b6 19 ♘c6 ♗f6 20 ♗d6 ♖e8 21 ♗e5 ♗xe5 22 ♘xe5 ♗a6 23 h4 h6 24 ♔h2 ♖f8 25 f3 ♖ac8 26 ♘c6 ♖c7 27 ♘d4 ♖xc1 28 ♖xc1 e5 29 ♘c6 ♖c8 30 ♖d1 ♖xc6 31 ♖xd5 ♖c2 32 ♖d8+ ♔h7 33 ♖d2 ♖xd2 34 ♘xd2

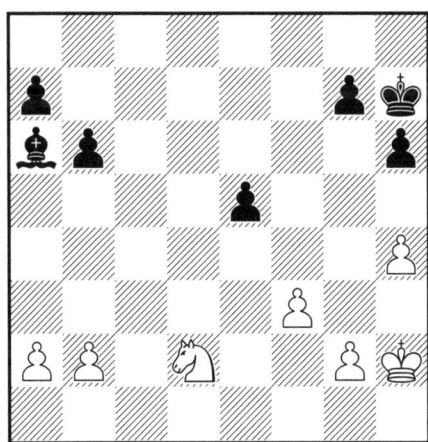

White has the tiniest of advantages, but with a bit of care I felt I ought to be able to draw the game.

34...♔g6 35 ♔g3 ♔f5 36 ♔f2 ♗b7 37 ♔e3 h5

From a practical point of view this is the first in a series of tiny errors, allowing White an extra option. It would have been better to wait with, for instance, 37...♗c6.

38 ♘f1 g6

Missing his next move. Today I would have a serious look at 38...g5.

39 g4+

The first minor jolt to my psychological stability. The position should still be manageable, but this move unsettled me.

39...hxg4 40 ♘g3+ ♔f6 41 fxg4 ♗d5 42 ♘e4+ ♔e7 43 a3 ♗e6 44 h5

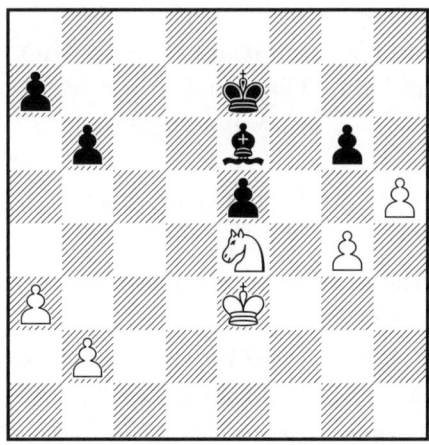

44...gxh5

This is the second minor error. There is no reason at all why I shouldn't play 44...♗xg4 followed by ...♔f8 when we will soon reach a level position.

After losing such a game it is easy to convince yourself that you would never make these errors against a weaker opponent. I think there are two possible explanations for what is really going on:

i. When there is a bit of fear and some negative emotions are whirling around, your brain works less well.

ii. Your opponent is using his higher level of skill to create problems for you.

45 gxh5 ♗f5 46 ♘c3 ♔f6 47 ♘b5

Having originally had some margin of error, it was disconcerting to realise that I now needed to tread very carefully. One danger is that Maxime will penetrate on the queenside while I go after the decoy on h5.

47...a6

I should label this move the third minor error. Better is 47...a5, not only putting the pawn on a dark square, in harmony with my bishop, but also avoiding a passive queenside structure.

48 ♘d6 ♗h7 49 b4 ♔e6

After 49...♔g5 50 ♘c4 the alarm bells would really start ringing.

50 ♘c4 b5 51 ♘d2 ♔d5

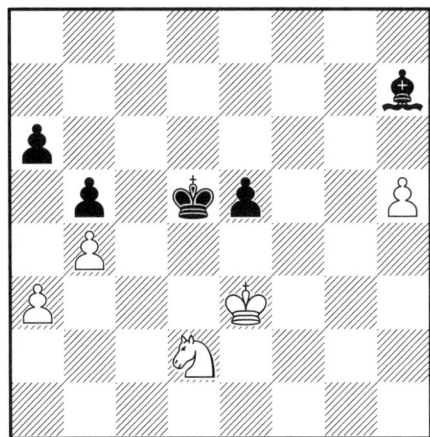

I still hoped that with due care I might be OK, but felt very uneasy. Until now there has been no need to analyse any long variations – it has all been about making micro-decisions.
52 ♘f3 ♝f5?

There is something more subtle going on here than either I or even my illustrious opponent fully grasped at the time. Since the position is so interesting I'm going to break my rule (sticking with 'live' thoughts), and try instead to sum up the position objectively.

As is often the case, it's all about the 'z word'. In the position with the white pawn on h6, knight on g5 and king on f4, and the black bishop on g6, pawn on e4 and king on d5, if it's my move, I lose.

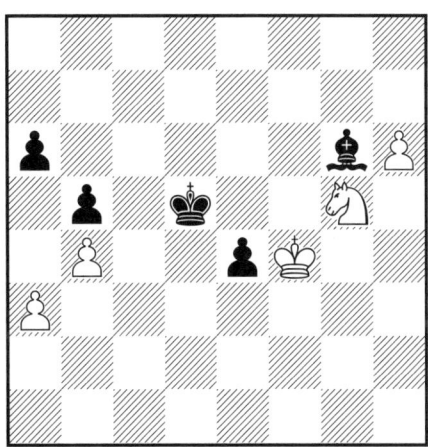

That's because 1...♔d4 allows 2 ♘e6+ ♔d3 3 ♘f8 e3 4 ♘xg6 e2 5 ♘e5+ followed by 6 ♘f3. White to play, however, has no useful move: for example, 1 h7 ♗xh7 2 ♘xh7 ♔c4 and he can't get his knight to c6 in time to prevent my removing all his pawns.

The reason why 52...♗f5 is a blunder is because that valuable square will be needed later by the bishop. It would not there get cut off by ♘e4, as when on b1 or c2, nor forked as my king dashes off to c4, as when on g6.

The problem, then, is that after my opponent's next move (53 h6), I have to move my bishop from its idyllic square because I am in zugzwang. Therefore, I should have preferred 52...♗b1 or 52...♗c2.
53 h6 ♗g6

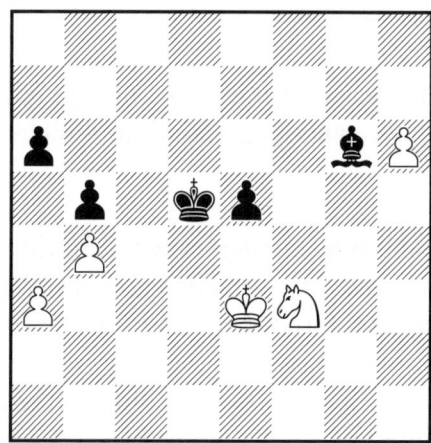

Had I played 52...♗c2 (or 52...♗b1), then here 53...♗f5 would have placed MVL in zugzwang, because after 54 ♘g5 I can play 54...♔c4 under the most favourable circumstances, and draw easily.
54 ♔d2?

After 54 ♘g5! there are more zugzwangs, with the bottom line being that I am losing. Let me give an example: 54...♔c4 55 ♘f7 ♔d5 56 ♔d2 e4 (56...♔d4 57 ♘g5 e4 58 ♘e6+ ♔c4 59 ♘c5 also wins) 57 ♔e3 ♔e6 58 ♘g5+ ♔e5 59 h7 ♗xh7 60 ♘xh7 ♔d5 61 ♘f8 ♔c4 62 ♘d7 ♔b3 63 ♘c5+ ♔xa3 64 ♘xa6 and White is just in time.
54...e4 55 ♘g5 ♔c4

Now I am fine, so long as I find one difficult move under time pressure.
56 ♘e6 ♔b3 57 ♘f8 ♗f5 58 ♔e3 ♔xa3 59 ♔f4

A few years later I showed this position to the legendary Swedish Grandmaster and endgame maestro Ulf Andersson.

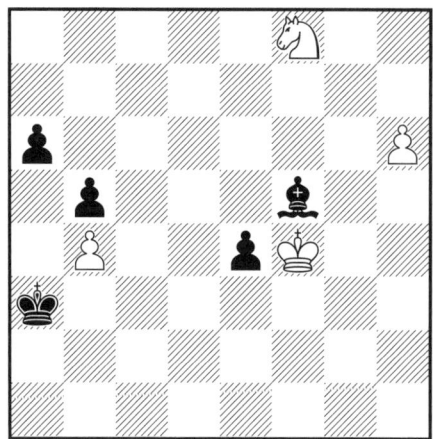

After seconds rather than minutes, Ulf put the black king on a2. This is, indeed, the only square which prevents a vital tempo gain by the white knight. If instead 59...♔xb4? 60 ♔xf5 e3 61 ♘e6 e2 62 ♘d4 e1♕ 63 ♘c2+ wins, or if 59...♔b2? 60 ♔xf5 e3 61 ♘e6 e2 62 ♘f4 e1♕ 63 ♘d3+ with the same outcome. After 59...♔a2!, though, the position is drawn. What I find fascinating is that after each minor error the draw became that little bit more tricky to achieve until, exhausted and in time-trouble, 59...♔a2 was beyond me.

59...e3? 60 ♔xe3 ♔xb4 61 ♔f4 ♗c2 62 ♔g5

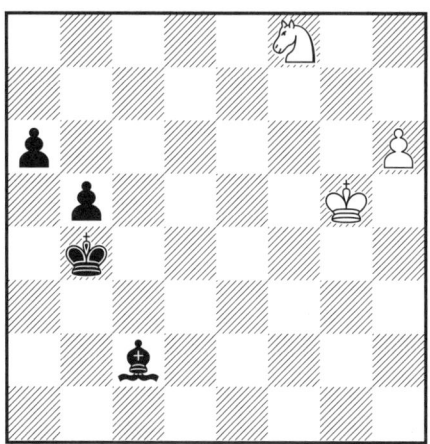

62...♔a3 63 ♘g6 b4 64 h7 b3 65 h8♕ b2 66 ♕c3+ ♗b3 67 ♘e5 b1♕ 68 ♘c4+ 1-0

3. Arkell-Kosten

Against English GM Tony Kosten I was able to win the ending of rook and bishop versus rook and knight, without pawns, by exploiting his poorly placed pieces, and vulnerable king.

Keith Arkell - Tony Kosten
Montpellier Open 2002
'Speckled Egg' System

1 d4 ♘f6 2 ♘f3 g6 3 b4 ♗g7 4 ♗b2 0-0 5 ♘bd2 d5 6 e3 c6 7 c4 a5 8 b5 ♗f5 9 ♗e2 cxb5 10 cxb5 a4 11 0-0 ♘bd7 12 ♗a3 ♖e8 13 ♖c1 ♕a5 14 ♘h4 ♗e6 15 ♕c2 ♗f8 16 ♘hf3 ♗g4 17 h3 ♗xf3 18 ♘xf3 e6 19 ♗xf8 ♔xf8 20 ♗d3 ♖ed8 21 ♕c7 ♕xc7 22 ♖xc7

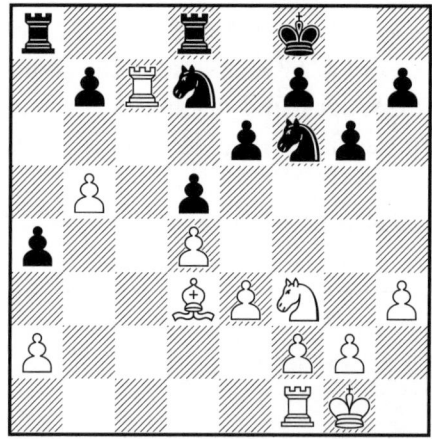

With control of the only open file, I thought I must be a little better in this late middlegame.
22...♖ab8 23 ♖fc1 ♘e8 24 ♖7c3 ♘b6 25 g4
It made sense to gain space wherever I could.
25...♖bc8 26 ♔f1
While Black was busy challenging me on the c-file, I began to dream of getting my king to b4.
26...♖xc3 27 ♖xc3 ♘d6 28 ♖c5 ♔e7 29 ♔e2 ♖a8 30 ♘e5
Objectively I should have played 30 g5, as the following note indicates.

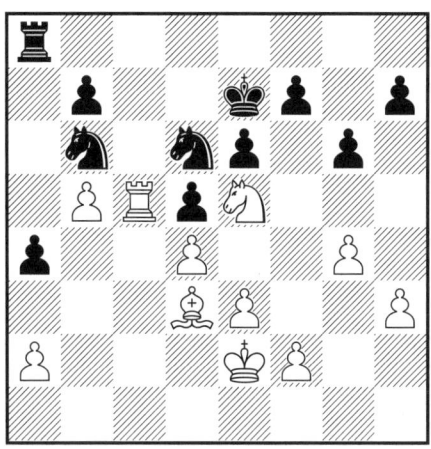

30...♔d8

I can understand Tony not being interested in 30...f6 31 ♖c7+ ♔d8 32 ♖xh7 fxe5 33 dxe5 when b7 and g6 are both *en prise* and I've already got two pawns for the piece, but I was far from sure what was happening in this line.

31 g5 ♘d7 32 ♖c3 ♖a5 33 ♖c1 ♘xe5 34 dxe5 ♘c8

Against 34...♘c4 I think the best I could have obtained would have been a rook ending with only a minuscule plus.

35 ♖b1 ♘b6 36 f4 ♘d7 37 ♖c1

I didn't want his king coming to b6, when I risk being worse.

37...♖a8 38 ♔d2 ♘b6 39 h4 ♔d7 40 h5

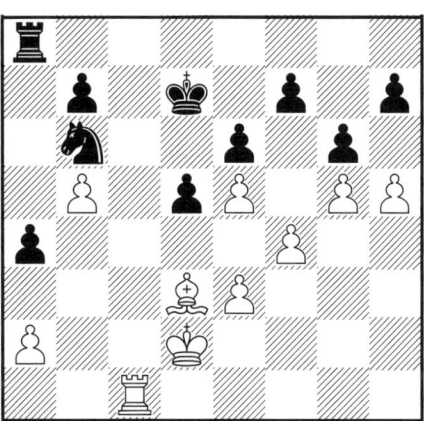

These moves are obviously the logical consequence of 31 g5. If I'm lucky, I might distract him enough to get my king to the much sought after b4-square.

40...♖a5 41 ♔c3 ♖a8 42 ♔b4 ♔d8 43 ♖h1

Black is really on the ropes now, and I probably should have won the game more easily than I did.

43...♔e7 44 hxg6 hxg6 45 ♖h7 ♖g8 46 a3

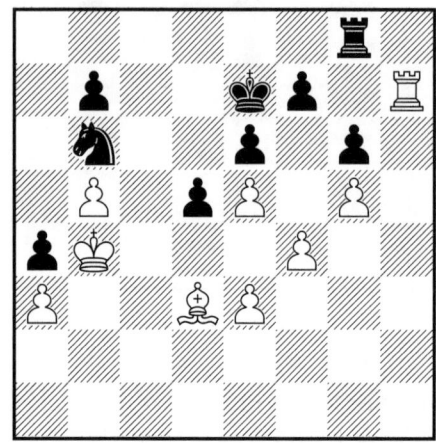

Frustratingly, I couldn't quite finish matters with 46 ♔a5 as Tony has 46...♘d7 47 ♗c2 (not 47 ♔xa4? ♘c5+) 47...♖a8+ 48 ♔b4 ♘f8 49 ♖h2 a3. Obviously I'm doing well here, but I wanted something cleaner, and the text move puts him in zugzwang.

46...d4

There is no waiting move which doesn't damage his position further.

47 exd4 ♘d5+ 48 ♔xa4 ♘xf4 49 ♗e4 b6 50 ♖h4 ♘e2 51 ♗f3 ♘g3 52 d5 exd5 53 ♗xd5 ♖d8 54 ♗c4 ♘h5 55 ♔b4 ♖d1

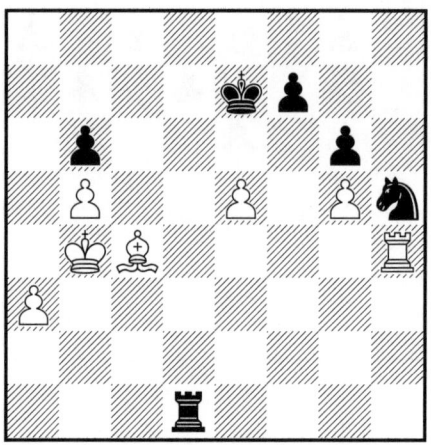

Black has found all the right moves to keep the game going, but now I messed about a bit too much and soon regretted not simply playing 56 a4. It was the move my hand wanted to play, and common sense suggests that I ought to be able to quickly play a4-a5 and utilise my passed b-pawn while his knight is still on the other side of the board.

56 ♗b3 ♖e1 57 ♖c4 ♖xe5 58 ♖c7+ ♔d8 59 ♖b7 ♖xg5 60 ♗xf7?

I can still win pretty much by force with 60 ♖xb6, but it was the last move before the time-control and I wanted to mop up all his pawns.

60...♖g4+

Oops, that's a bit of a nuisance! It quickly dawned that I had given away most of my advantage with 60 ♗xf7. Realistically I've now got to shed my a-pawn.

61 ♔c3 ♖g3+ 62 ♔d4 ♖xa3 63 ♔e5

Played quickly and hoping to set up some mating ideas, such as with, for example, ♔d6 and ♗d5.

63...♘g3 64 ♗xg6 ♔c8 65 ♖xb6

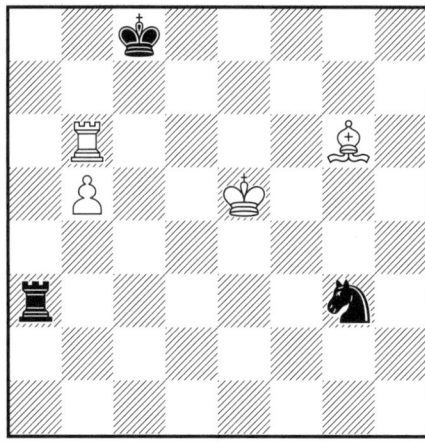

Three factors gave me hope here:
 i. That I can somehow queen my b-pawn (very unlikely).
 ii. That I can make him sacrifice his knight for my b-pawn (slightly more likely).
 iii. That I can force or persuade him to give up material to prevent a mating attack (most likely of all).

65...♔c7 66 ♖c6+ ♔b7 67 ♖d6 ♖b3 68 ♗d3 ♘e2 69 ♗e4+ ♔c8 70 ♖c6+ ♔b8 71 ♔d6

Played after using up most of my remaining time (we didn't have increments in those days). I analysed many lines which would result in rook and bishop versus rook, an ending which I have won umpteen times (see Games 19 and 33), and also lines with

a rook against his stranded knight. I wasn't sure whether I had covered everything, but this aggressive king move was extremely tempting.
71...♖xb5 72 ♖a6 ♔c8
He stops the mate, but I'm now after his knight.
73 ♗c6

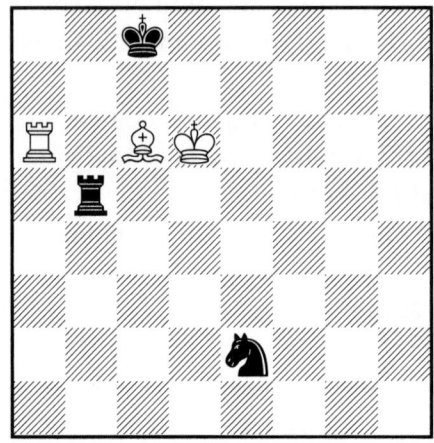

First improving the bishop.
73...♘d4
Chatting with Tony afterwards, he had also seen 73...♖b2 74 ♖a8+ ♔b8 75 ♖a2 ♘d4 76 ♖h2 ♘b5+ (76...♘xc6 77 ♔xc6 amounts to the same thing).

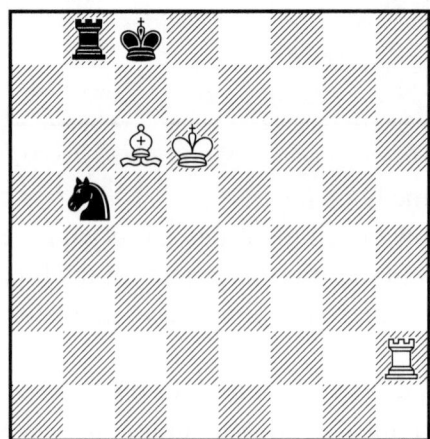

For many moves White's bishop has dominated the knight, but now that Black manages to exchange them, he is losing with just rook against rook: 77 ♗xb5 ♖xb5

78 ♔c6 and the combined threats end the game. In this line I saw that 77...♔b7 was possible, but would have been happy to play a promising rook and bishop versus rook position, especially with us both short of time.

74 ♗xb5 ♘xb5+ 75 ♔c6

It was impossible to calculate all the ramifications here, but it must be winning.

75...♘d4+ 76 ♔c5 ♘f5 77 ♖f6

Strangely enough, I had seen this exact position when giving up my last pawn with 71 ♔d6, so I already knew that 77...♘e7 would be met by 78 ♔d6 ♔d8 79 ♖f8#.

77...♘g3 78 ♖f3

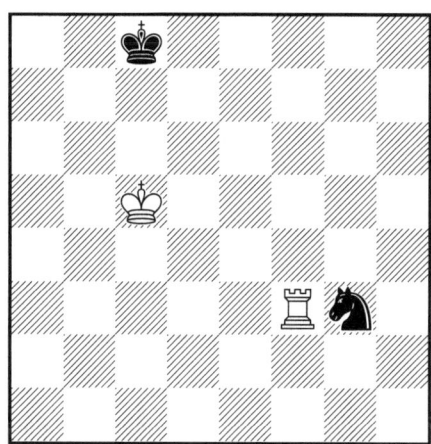

Rounding up the knight is fairly straightforward now. Years earlier, at the Thessaloniki Olympiad of 1988, I was actually standing next to Karpov's board watching him convert the same ending against Ftacnik.

78...♘h5 79 ♔d6 ♔b7

Or 79...♘g7 80 ♖f8+ ♔b7 81 ♖f7+, etc.

80 ♔e5 ♔c6 81 ♖h3 ♘g7 82 ♖h6+ ♔c5 83 ♖h8 1-0

The knight-snaring ♔f6 will follow.

4. Arkell-Kotronias

After a long trip to Gausdal, in the north of Norway, I was plunged straight in at the deep end against a very strong, likeable and well-known grandmaster.

Keith Arkell - Vasilios Kotronias
Gausdal Classic 2002
'Speckled Egg' System

1 d4 ♘f6 2 ♘f3 g6 3 b4

With this opening, nicknamed 'The Speckled Egg', I managed to down four GMs in 2002, the other three being Tony Kosten, Ketevan Arakhamia-Grant and Luke McShane. It's a kind of Polish reversed, and can be a useful tool to take King's Indian players out of their theory.

3...♗g7 4 ♗b2 0-0 5 ♘bd2 d6 6 e4 e5 7 dxe5 ♘g4 8 ♖b1 ♘xe5 9 ♗e2 ♘bc6 10 b5 ♘xf3+ 11 ♘xf3 ♗xb2 12 ♖xb2 ♕f6 13 ♖b1 ♘e5 14 ♘d4

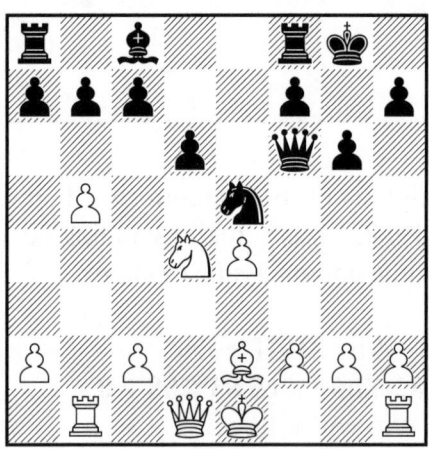

Of course, Black's position is already very comfortable, but at least I have engineered my favourite structure: four pawns versus three on the kingside.

14...♘d7 15 0-0 ♘c5 16 f3 ♗d7 17 ♕d2 ♖ae8 18 c4 ♕e5 19 ♖fe1 ♔h8 20 ♗f1 g5 21 ♘b3

Ideally I would like to manoeuvre this piece to d5, but didn't think there was enough time in view of possible counterplay by ...f5 or ...g4.

21...b6 22 ♘xc5 ♕xc5+ 23 ♔h1 ♕e5 24 a4 ♖e6 25 a5 ♖fe8 26 axb6 axb6 27 ♖a1

♖h6 28 h3 ♗e6 29 ♖ed1 ♔g7 30 ♔g1 ♖g6 31 ♖a7 ♖c8 32 ♕d4

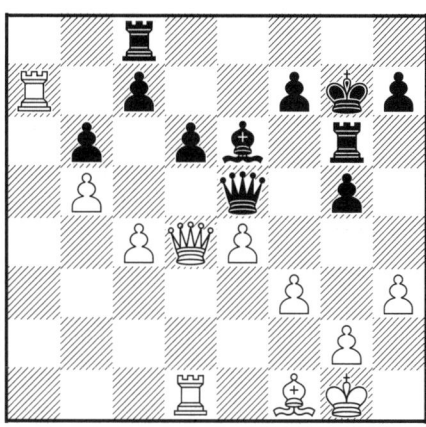

Without the queens, I have a better chance of realising White's long-term strategic aims, obtaining flexible pawns on the kingside while keeping Black's queenside under lock and key.

32...♕xd4+ 33 ♖xd4 ♔f6 34 ♖d2 ♔e7 35 ♔f2 f6 36 ♔e3 ♖gg8 37 g3 ♖gf8 38 ♖h2 f5

A strong player will rarely sit back in such a position and wait patiently for White to organise h3-h4 or f3-f4 at his leisure.

39 exf5 ♗xf5 40 h4

There won't be a better moment to make this break – if I wait, ...h5-h4 will take some of the sting out of my plans.

40...gxh4 41 ♖xh4 ♔f6 42 g4 ♗b1 43 f4

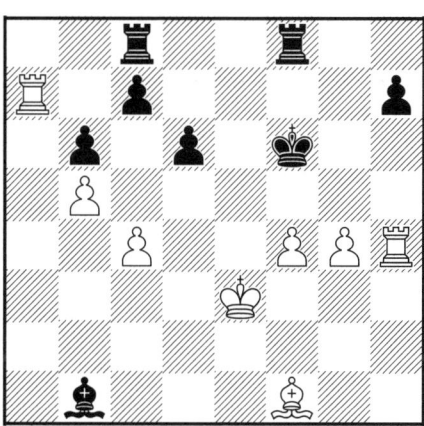

I have achieved my aim in creating a flexible pawn majority. In addition,

Arkell's Endings

Black's bishop is looking a little concerned.
43...♖ce8+ 44 ♔f3 ♖e7 45 ♖h2 ♔g7 46 f5 h6 47 ♖a1 ♗e4+ 48 ♔f4 ♖e5 49 ♔g3 ♖fe8 50 ♖e1 ♗b7 51 ♖xe5 ♖xe5 52 ♖a2 ♖c5 53 ♖a7 ♗e4 54 ♔f4 ♗c2 55 ♖a3

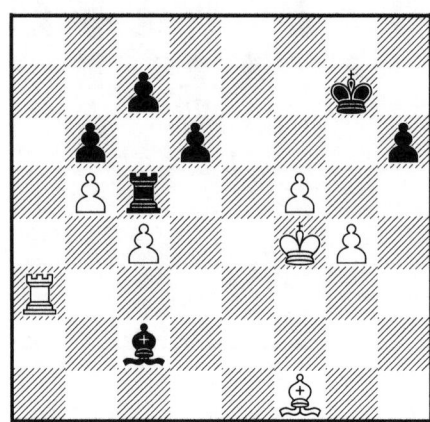

Black now hasn't much choice. If he waits, the answer is 56 ♖c3, intending ♗g2-d5, tying him in knots. As played, the subsequent bishop ending favours White, but not decisively so.
55...d5

Alternatively, if 55...h5 56 ♖c3 ♗b1 57 ♖c1 ♗a2 58 g5 with connected passed pawns.
56 cxd5 ♖xd5 57 ♖c3

Maybe 57 ♖e3 would provide better chances, eyeing up e6 and e7, but over the board I rather fancied the bishop ending.
57...♖c5 58 ♖xc5 bxc5 59 ♔e5 ♗d1 60 f6+ ♔f8 61 ♔f5 ♗c2+ 62 ♔e6 ♗d1 63 ♔d7

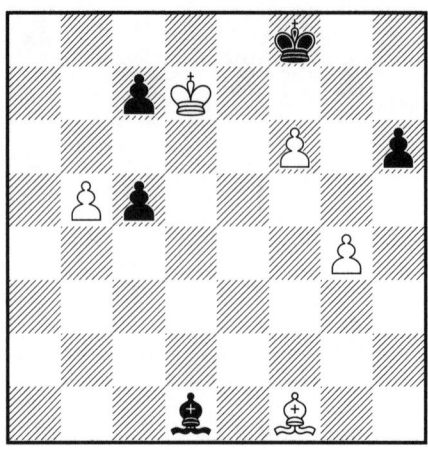

The last roll of the dice...
63...♗xg4+?
...And he obliges. After 63...♗a4 64 ♗c4 ♗xb5+! 65 ♔xb5 ♔f7 66 ♗e2 h5 only a bishop and wrong-coloured rook's pawn would remain.
64 ♔xc7 ♗f3
If 64...♔f7 65 b6 ♗f3 66 ♗b5 (threatening ♗c6) 66...c4 67 ♗xc4+ ♔xf6 68 ♗b5 h5 69 ♗c6 ♗xc6 70 ♔xc6 h4 71 b7 and White queens first.
65 b6 h5

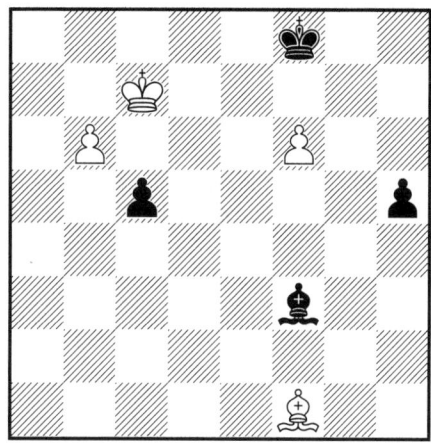

66 ♗e2
Necessary, otherwise both players queen at the same time.
66...♗e4 67 ♗xh5 c4 68 ♗g6 ♗f3 69 ♔d6 c3 70 ♔e5 1-0
I can now collect his c-pawn, go back to c7 to win his bishop with b7, and, finally, decide the game with my f-pawn.

5. Rodshtein-Arkell

Exceptionally for this book, I have annotated the following game in the traditional way. There are a number of beautiful lines and ideas which would never see the light of day were I to only relay what I saw and thought about at the board.

Maxim Rodshtein - Keith Arkell
Hastings Masters 2014/15
Caro-Kann Defence

1 e4 c6 2 d4 d5 3 e5 c5 4 dxc5 e6 5 a3 a5 6 ♘f3 ♗xc5 7 ♗d3 ♘e7 8 0-0 ♘g6 9 ♗g5 ♗e7 10 ♗xe7 ♕xe7 11 ♘c3 ♗d7 12 ♕d2 0-0 13 ♖ae1 ♘a6 14 ♘d4 ♘c5 15 f4 ♘xd3 16 cxd3 ♕c5 17 ♕e3 f6 18 exf6 ♖xf6 19 g3 ♖e8 20 ♘f3 ♖c8 21 ♖f2 b6 22 ♖fe2 h6 23 ♕f2 ♖cf8 24 ♕d4 ♗c8 25 ♕xc5 bxc5

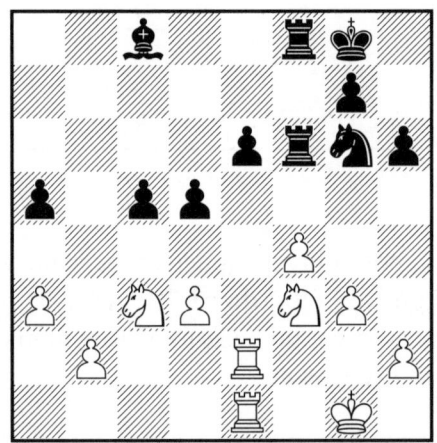

My pet variation (3...c5) against the Advance Caro has given way to a French-type middlegame, in which Black's doubled rooks on the f-file don't appear overly useful, but just watch what happens next.

26 ♘a4? ♘xf4! 27 gxf4 ♖xf4 28 ♘xc5 ♖xf3 29 ♖e3 ♖3f4 30 h3 ♖8f6 31 ♖1e2 ♔f7 32 ♔g2 ♔e7 33 ♔g3 ♔d6 34 ♘b3 a4 35 ♘a5 d4 36 ♖e4 ♖f3+ 37 ♔g2 ♖xd3 38 ♖c2 ♗d7 39 ♘c4+ ♔e7 40 ♘b6 ♔d6 41 ♘c4+ ♔e7 42 ♘b6 ♔d8 43 ♖c4 e5 44 ♘xd7 ♔xd7 45 ♖xe5 ♖c6 46 ♖d5+ ♖d6 47 ♖xd6+ ♔xd6 48 ♖xa4 ♔d5 49 ♖b4 ♖e3 50 ♖b7 ♔c4 51 a4 d3 52 ♔f2 d2 53 ♖c7+ ♔b3 54 ♖d7 ♖xh3

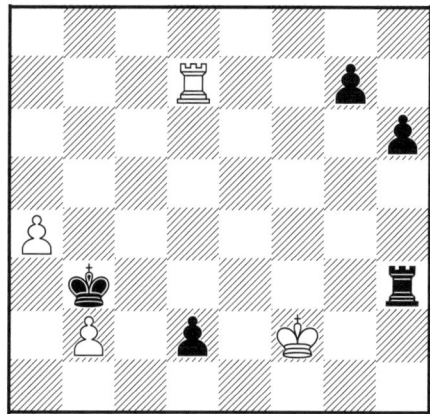

Having won a pawn through an unusual blunder, I reached this fascinating rook and pawn endgame. My gut feeling was that 55 ♔g2 ought to draw with best defence, whereas after the move played I would either be winning, or at least have excellent practical chances.

55 ♔e2?

Having examined the ending with all the tools available to the modern chess player, I'm now certain that 55 ♔g2 would have drawn, although the defence is far from straightforward. Here is a sample line: 55...♖h5 56 ♖xd2 ♔xa4 and now 57 ♔g3 and 57 ♖f2 both lose, whereas 57 ♖e2 and the counter-intuitive 57 ♖d4+ draw. Difficult stuff for a human to understand, and therefore it's very easy for White to go wrong in practice.

55...♖h2+

From here until the end I am always winning by force, but I don't always take the most expedient route.

56 ♔d1 ♔xa4 57 ♖xg7 h5 *(see diagram top right)*

Clearly forced, as White threatened to play 58 ♖d7 followed by ♖xd2. At the time I thought mostly in terms of concepts, rather than concrete variations, and quickly grasped the following:

i. When my pawn gets to h3, my opponent must keep his pawn on b2. If he loses it or moves it, I will win simply by playing ...♖h1+; ♔xd2 h2, when both ♔e2 and ♔c2 lose to ...♖a1. On the other hand, if he keeps his pawn on b2, he will have ♔c2 after those moves.

ii. If he puts his king on c2 to prevent my going after his b-pawn with my king (he can't defend the pawn with his rook, which needs to stay on the h-file to prevent the winning ...♖g2), then I can rush my king to e1, threatening to queen my d-pawn. A check on the e-file will then be met by the decisive ...♖e2.

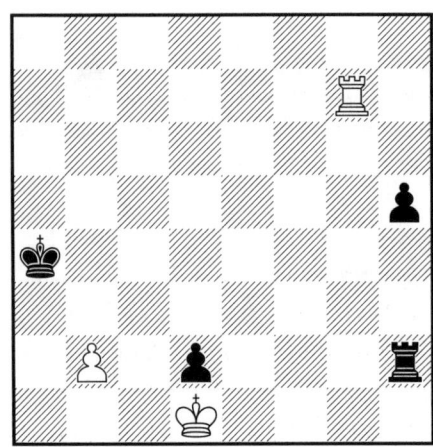

As such, I concluded that I must be winning because his king needs to be on both c2 and d1 at the same time. These concepts are basically correct, but there are some very nice variations if White defends optimally.

58 ♔c2 ♚b5 59 ♖c7 h4 60 ♖c8 ♚b6 61 ♖c4 h3 62 ♖h4 ♚c5 63 ♔d1 ♚d5 64 ♔c2 ♚e5 65 ♖h8 ♚e4 66 ♖e8+

If he tries to keep my king away from e1, he must play 66 ♔d1 when best play goes as follows: 66...♚d3 67 ♖d8+ ♚c4 68 ♖c8+ ♚b3 69 ♖c3+ (at the board I didn't see this idea, only considering the variation 69 ♖b8+ ♚a2 70 ♔c2 d1♕+! 71 ♔xd1 ♖xb2 72 ♖a8+ ♚b1 73 ♖h8 h2 74 ♔e1 ♖g2, winning) 69...♚b4!, and not 69...♚xb2?, after which there is a study-like draw: 70 ♖b3+ ♚a2 71 ♖e3! ♖h1+ 72 ♔xd2 h2 73 ♖e2! and with accurate defence there is no way for Black to win.

66...♚f3 67 ♖f8+ ♚e2 68 ♖e8+ ♚f1 69 ♖e3 ♚g2

The then German number one GM Arkadij Naiditsch attempted to annotate this difficult ending for *Chess Evolution*. He wrote that my opponent missed a draw here with "70 ♖d3!!". In reality this just adds two moves to the game by forcing me to repeat the position with 70...♔f1 71 ♖e3 (there is nothing better) before, hopefully, finding either of the winning moves 71...♔f2 or 71...♖h1.

After the latter, best play would result in something like: 72 ♔xd2 (other moves again lose more quickly) 72...♔f2 73 ♖e2+ ♔f3 74 ♖e3+ ♔f4 75 ♖e2 h2 76 ♔c2 ♔g3 (the queen versus rook and b-pawn ending after 76...♖c1+ is winning, but takes far longer than the text move) 77 ♖e3+ ♔f2 78 ♖h3 ♔g2 79 ♖h8 ♖g1 when White will have to give up his rook, and I will get back in time to stop his b-pawn.

Ironically, Naiditsch summed up his annotation thus: "So, finally it was a winning endgame for Black, but both players managed to exchange presents. Again we can see how hard it is to play rook endgames well!" I would add: or indeed to annotate them!
70 ♔xd2 ♖h1 71 ♖e8 h2 72 ♖h8 ♖b1 73 ♔c3 h1♕ 74 ♖xh1 ♖xh1 0-1

6. Arkell-Koneru

The following game revolves around a single strategy: my manoeuvres against Black's exposed b-pawn.

> **Keith Arkell - Humpy Koneru**
> British Championship, Street 2000
> *Queen's Indian Defence*

1 d4 ♘f6 2 ♘f3 e6 3 c4 b6 4 g3 ♗b7 5 ♗g2 ♗e7 6 0-0 0-0 7 ♘c3 ♘e4 8 ♘xe4

White normally fights for an advantage with either 8 ♗d2 or 8 ♕c2, but as usual I aim for a position I like rather than an objective edge.

8...♗xe4 9 ♘h4 ♗xg2 10 ♘xg2 d5 11 cxd5

I have scored well with 11 ♕a4, when the recommended reply 11...♕d7 allows a minority attack with 12 ♕xd7 ♘xd7 13 cxd5. It is, however, a bit more difficult to play for a win after 11...dxc4.

11...♕xd5 12 ♘f4 ♕b7 13 ♗e3 ♘a6 14 ♕b3 c5 15 ♖ac1 ♖ac8 16 ♖fd1 cxd4 17 ♗xd4 ♖xc1 18 ♖xc1 ♖c8 19 ♖c3

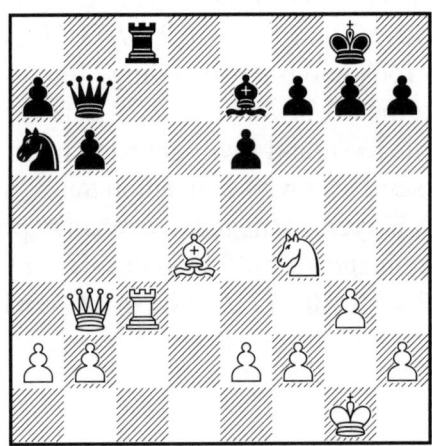

It's not my normal style to look for an advantage with symmetrical pawns, but I felt I had a little something here. Not much, but the just slightly better placed pieces.

19...♖xc3 20 ♕xc3 ♗b4 21 ♕e3 ♗f8 22 ♕e5 ♘b4 23 a3 ♘c6 24 ♕e4 ♕c7 25 ♗c3 h6 26 h4 ♗d6 27 ♔g2

Today I would probably play 27 ♘d3, avoiding 27...♗xf4 28 gxf4 ♕d7 when the queen will sit happily on d5.

27...b5 28 ♘d3 a5

There's not much to analyse here, but there may be some lines in which those queenside pawns start to feel exposed.

29 g4 ♕b6 30 g5 hxg5 31 hxg5 b4 32 axb4 axb4 33 ♗d2 ♕b5 34 f4

Alternatively, 34 g6 releases a bit of tension, but slightly damages Koneru's pawn structure.

34...g6 35 ♘f2 ♔f8 36 ♕d3 ♕xd3 37 ♘xd3

I was very happy to have got this much out of such a harmless opening. My plan now is to frighten the straggler on b4 while avoiding too many pawn exchanges.

37...♔e7 38 ♔f3 ♔d7 39 ♔e4 ♔c7 40 ♗e3 ♗f8 41 ♗d4 ♔c8 42 ♗f6 ♔c7 43 ♘f2

To make way for my king.

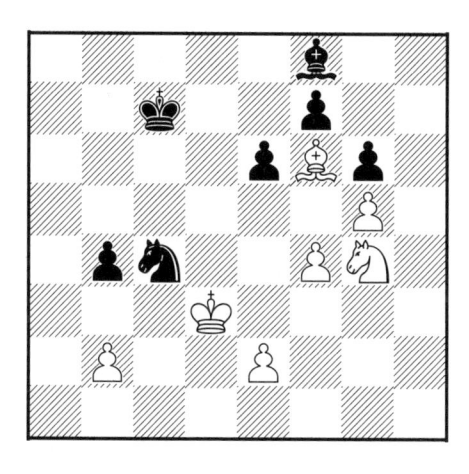

43...♘a5 44 ♘g4 ♘c4 45 ♔d3

The situation has improved: not only is b4 a target, but I've also fixed its colleague on f7.

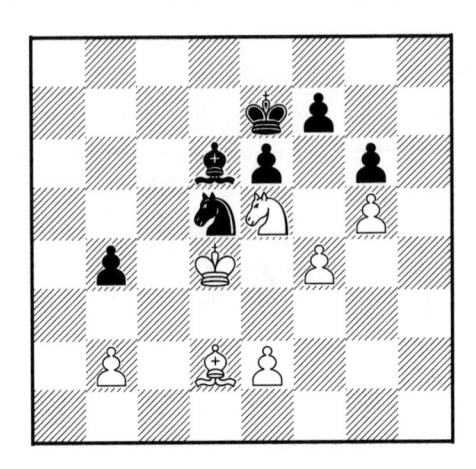

45...♘d6 46 ♗e5 ♔d7 47 ♗d4 ♘f5 48 ♘e5+ ♔e8 49 ♗f2 ♗d6 50 ♔e4 ♘e7 51 ♗e1 ♘d5 52 ♗d2 ♔e7 53 ♔d4

If left alone, I'll play ♘d3 and ♔c4 when e2-e4 will lead to the capture of Black's b-pawn.

53...f6 54 gxf6+ ♔xf6 55 e4 ♘e7 56 ♘d3 ♘c6+ 57 ♔c4 ♗e7

Black would have preferred 57...e5?, but it drops a piece to 58 ♔d5. Meanwhile the b4-pawn is becoming more and more worried for its safety.

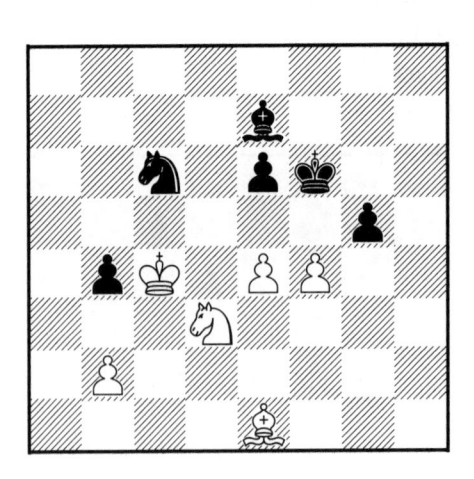

58 ♔b5 ♘d4+ 59 ♔c4 ♘c6 60 ♗e1 g5

61 ♗f2

I was a bit uncomfortable about capturing on g5 then on b4 because of the reduced material, but perhaps that was the best way: for example, 61 fxg5+ ♔xg5 62 ♗xb4 ♘xb4 63 ♘xb4 ♔f4 (63...♗xb4 leads to a lost king and pawn ending – by one tempo) 64 ♘c6 followed by ♔d3.

61...♘a5+

On 61...gxf4 I intended 62 ♗h4+ ♔f7 63 ♗xe7 ♔xe7 64 ♔c5 ♔d7 65 ♘xf4 and soon I will pick up the b-pawn.

62 ♔b5 ♘b3 63 ♗e3 gxf4 64 ♗xf4 ♘d4+ 65 ♔c4 ♘c6 66 ♔b5 ♘d4+ 67 ♔a5 ♘b3+ 68 ♔b5 ♘d4+ 69 ♔a4 ♘c6 70 ♗e3

I've still not quite rounded up that pesky pawn, but at least my opponent is a long way from menacing mine on e4.

70...♗d6 71 ♔b5 ♘e7

71...♘e5? 72 ♗d4 obviously won't do, but now at last I'm ready to collect my spoils, while still keeping a grip on the centre.

72 ♗c5 ♘c8 73 ♔xb4

It's because my pieces are so well coordinated that there is nothing Black can do to prevent my extra passed pawn winning the game.

73...♗e5 74 ♔a4 ♘d6 75 ♗xd6 ♗xd6 76 ♔b5 ♔g5 77 ♔c6 ♗f8 78 ♘c5 ♗e7 79 ♘xe6+ ♔f6 80 ♔d5 ♗b4 81 e5+ ♔e7 82 ♘d4 ♗d2 83 b4 ♔e8 84 b5 ♗a5 85 e6 ♗b6 86 ♘c6 ♗c7 87 ♔c5 ♔f8 88 b6 ♗xb6+ 89 ♔xb6 ♔e8 90 ♔c7 1-0

7. Arkell-Hebden

My long-time friend and rival Mark Hebden complained, not without a little whimsy, that I hadn't included any of our 150 or so encounters in my autobiography *Arkell's Odyssey*. Here, to restore the balance, is one of our countless struggles in the razor-sharp King's Indian, Panno variation – a game which helped me to win the British Rapidplay Championship in 1998.

Keith Arkell - Mark Hebden
British Rapidplay, Leeds 1998
King's Indian Defence

1 d4 ♘f6 2 ♘f3 g6 3 c4 ♗g7 4 g3 0-0 5 ♗g2 d6 6 0-0 ♘c6 7 ♘c3 ♖b8 8 h3 a6 9 e4 b5 10 cxb5 axb5 11 e5 ♘d7 12 ♘g5 ♘xd4

Mark and I used to play out this position regularly, and while on the whole I scored well, he believes that the piece sacrifice should lead to equality.
13 ♕xd4 ♘xe5 14 ♕h4 h6 15 ♘f3

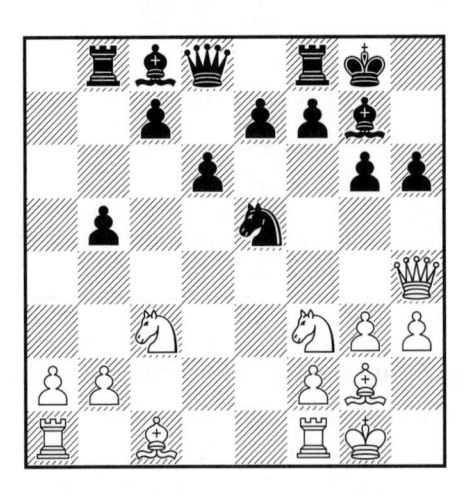

15...♘xf3+

In future games Mark began to rely on 15...e6, trusting in his phalanx of central pawns to neutralise my extra piece. Let's now proceed quickly to the endgame, which, after all, is the topic of this book.
16 ♗xf3 g5 17 ♕h5 b4 18 ♘e4 ♗f5 19 ♗g2 d5 20 ♖d1 e6 21 ♗e3 ♕e8 22 ♘c5 ♗g6 23 ♕e2 ♕b5 24 ♕xb5 ♖xb5 25 ♗f1

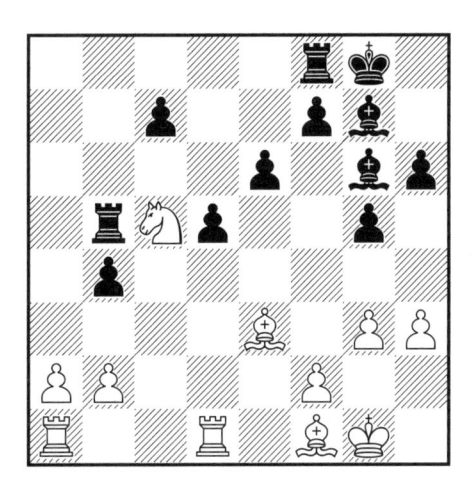

I would nearly always prefer to have the extra piece in such endgames, even if the objective assessment is equality. Unless the pawns become really threatening, you have a kind of initiative which enables you to dictate the course of the game. Giving his rook a nudge here is the only way of dealing with the twin threats of ...d4 and ...♗xb2.
25...♖a5 26 ♘b3 ♖aa8 27 ♗d4 ♗xd4 28 ♖xd4 ♖fb8 29 ♗d3
There was also an argument for 29 ♘c5.
29...♗xd3 30 ♖xd3 ♖b5

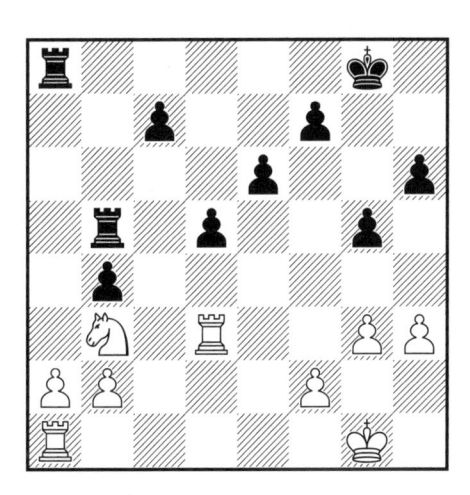

Mark must fight for the c5-square before I get time to play ♖d2 and ♖c2. With my next move I decided to put piece activity above all else, and was already planning to ensnare his king.

31 ♖c1 ♖xa2 32 ♖xc7 ♖xb2 33 ♖f3

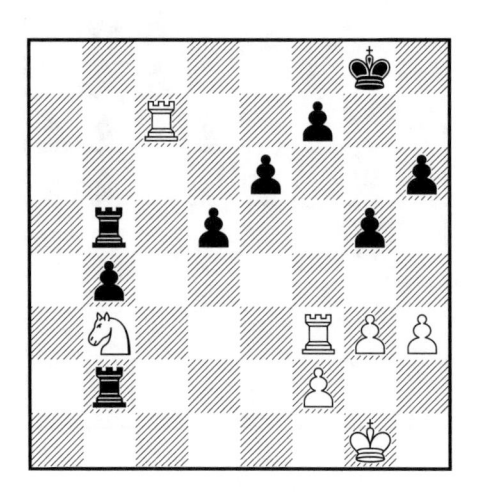

With more time to think, I might have first gone 33 ♘d4.
33...♖b8

Even though this game was played more than 20 years ago, I still remember thinking that Black could probably have forced a draw here by 33...e5, squeezing my knight out of the game. After he missed this chance, however, I was able to rectify my mistake.

34 ♘d4 ♖f8 35 ♖b7 b3

Mark would be more than happy to give up this pawn if he could swap off a pair of rooks, removing the danger to his king and obtaining some drawing chances.

36 ♘xb3 ♖d8 37 ♖e7

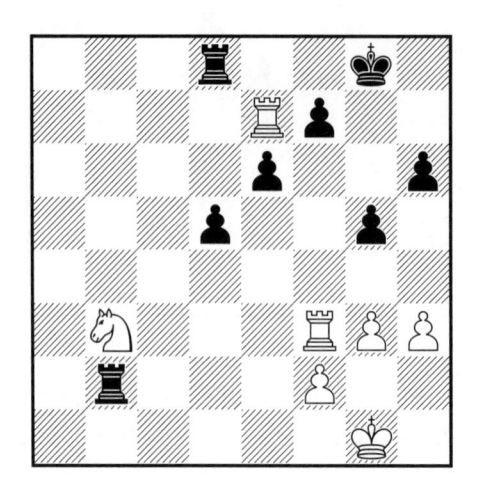

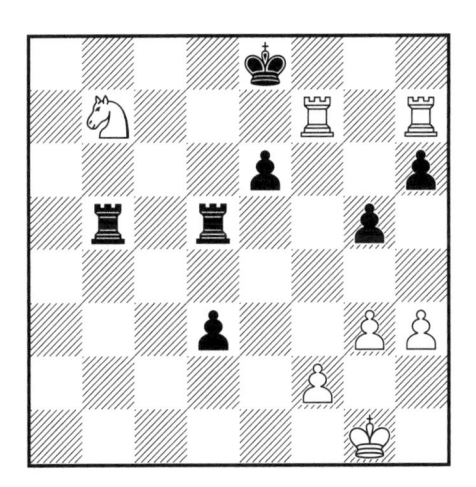

My plan now is to aim everything at f7. Give my knight enough time to start jumping around and Black is finished, so he is pretty much reduced to putting all his eggs in one basket, relying on his d-pawn.

37...d4 38 ♘c5 ♖b5 39 ♘b7 ♖dd5

Black can't allow ♘d6, but even with my time running low, it wasn't too difficult to work out the final combination.

40 ♖fxf7 d3

Black's rook suffocates after 40...♖f5 41 ♖g7+ ♔f8 42 ♘d6 ♖b1+ 43 ♔g2 ♖f6 44 ♘e4 ♖f5 45 g4 ♖f4 46 ♘c5.

41 ♖g7+ ♔f8

If 41...♔h8 it would have taken me four more moves to force the same position as in the game: 42 ♖h7+ ♔g8 43 ♖eg7+ ♔f8 44 ♖c7 ♔g8 45 ♖hg7+ ♔f8 (45...♔h8 allows a quick knockout with 46 ♖ge7) 46 ♖cf7+ ♔e8 47 ♖h7.

42 ♖ef7+ ♔e8 43 ♖h7

This is the key move and a concept worth remembering. There is no defence against ♖c7, threatening mate on h8, as well as c8.

43...d2 44 ♖c7 d1♕+ 45 ♔h2 ♕d4 46 ♖c8+ ♖d8 47 ♖xd8+ ♕xd8 48 ♖h8+ ♔e7 49 ♘xd8 1-0

8. Arkell-Zak

A mediocre first half leads here to a fascinating endgame in which I played for mate with my lone two bishops against my opponent's knight and two pawns. Afterwards the inimitable Jim Plaskett quipped, "Arkell, you would be an IM easily if you didn't play so many stupid games!".

Keith Arkell - Vladimir Zak
Lewisham International 1983
Slav Defence

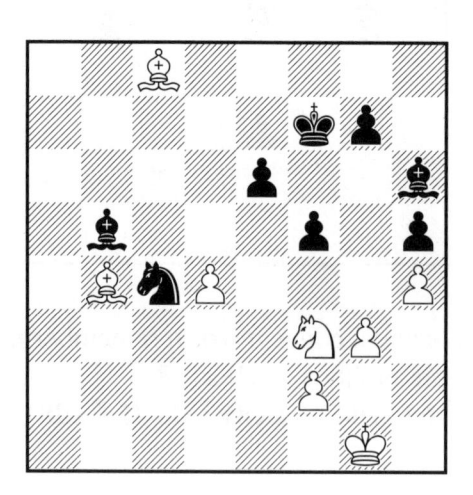

1 d4 d5 2 c4 c6 3 ♘c3 ♘f6 4 ♘f3 ♗f5 5 ♕b3 ♕b6 6 ♕xb6 axb6 7 cxd5 ♘xd5
8 ♘xd5 cxd5 9 e3 ♘c6 10 ♗d2 f6 11 ♗b5 ♗d7 12 ♔e2 e6 13 a3 ♗d6 14 ♖ac1 ♔e7
15 ♖c3 ♘a5 16 ♗d3 b5 17 ♖hc1 ♗c6 18 ♗b1 b4 19 axb4 ♘c4 20 ♔e1 ♘xb2
21 ♖b3 ♘c4 22 b5 ♗d7 23 ♗d3 ♖a4 24 ♗c3 ♔f7 25 h4 h5 26 e4 ♗f4 27 ♖cb1 ♘a3
28 ♖1b2 ♘c4 29 ♖e2 ♖c8 30 g3 ♗h6 31 ♔f1 ♖a3 32 ♖xa3 ♘xa3 33 ♗b4 dxe4
34 ♗xe4 ♖c1+ 35 ♔g2 ♗xb5 36 ♖a2 ♘c4 37 ♖a8 f5 38 ♗xb7 ♖c2 39 ♖c8 ♘e3+
40 ♔g1 ♖xc8 41 ♗xc8 ♘c4

Often in chess all you can do is look for ways to improve your position and hope that you can create problems for your opponent, even though you know that the position should really be a draw. My next move improves my pawn structure while damaging Black's.

42 d5 exd5 43 ♘d4 ♗a4 44 ♘xf5 ♗d2 45 ♗c5 ♗c3 46 ♘d4 ♗xd4 47 ♗xd4

While it is still drawn, of course, at least now I have two theoretical advantages: the two bishops and the better structure. The only way to try and win is to mobilise my kingside pawn majority.

47...♘d6 48 ♗h3 ♗b5 49 f3 g6 50 g4 hxg4 51 fxg4 ♗d3 52 ♔f2 ♘b5 53 ♗e5 d4 54 ♔f3 ♔g8?

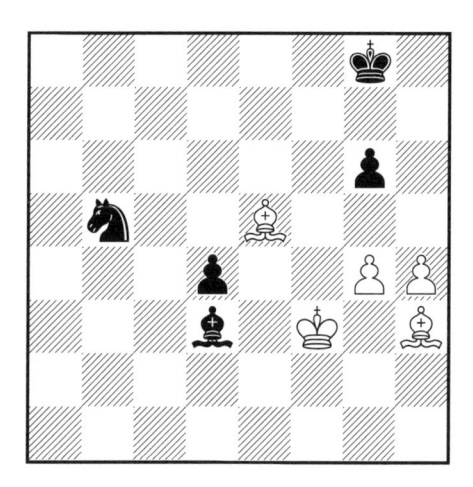

A bad idea. He should have just sat tight with his king on f7, when I would have found progress more difficult.

55 ♔f4 ♔h7 56 ♗g2 ♘c3 57 ♗c6

After 57 ♗xd4 ♘e2+ 58 ♔e5 ♘xd4 59 ♔xd4 there are no winning chances at all.

57...♘e2+ 58 ♔g5 ♗b1 59 ♗e8 ♗e4 60 ♔f6

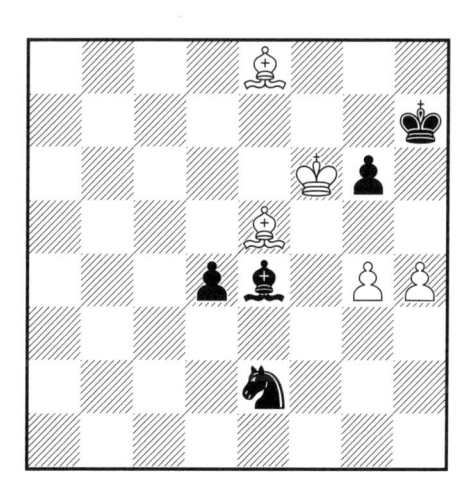

By adding a dominant king to the power of the bishops and the better structure,

I am now able to finish the game with a mating attack. When your opponent has felt confident of holding the position before gradually encountering unexpected difficulties, his resolution often tends to weaken. However, even if there is a defence here, it is very difficult to find.

60...d3 61 h5 gxh5 62 g5 d2 63 g6+ ♗xg6 64 ♗xg6+

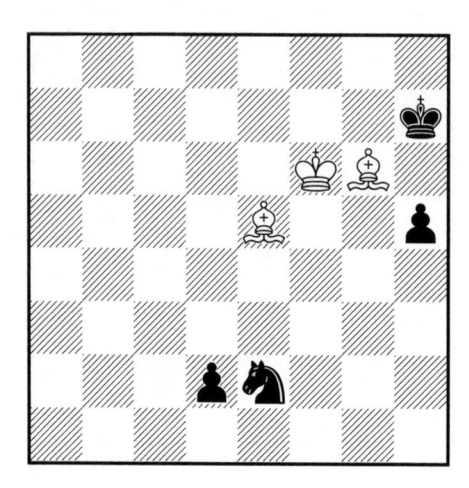

In the ending of two bishops versus knight, the defending side can normally hope to claim a draw after 50 moves because many of the winning variations take longer than that to execute, and in any case are impossible for mere humans to calculate. Here the situation is quite different: even the promotion of his d-pawn will not save Black's king.

64...♔g8 65 ♗f7+ ♔h7 66 ♗b3 h4 67 ♔f7 h3 68 ♗g7 ♘d4 69 ♗d5 ♘f5 70 ♗e4 1-0

9. Arkell-Milliet

It seemed difficult to exploit Black's doubled isolated d-pawns in the following bishop and knight endgame, but I found a way to create some problems by expanding on the kingside.

> **Keith Arkell - Sophie Milliet**
> London Chess Classic Open 2015
> *Ragozin Defence*

1 d4 ♘f6 2 ♘f3 d5 3 c4 e6 4 cxd5 exd5 5 ♘c3 ♗b4 6 ♕a4+ ♘c6 7 ♗g5 h6 8 ♗xf6 ♕xf6 9 e3 0-0 10 ♗e2 ♗e6 11 a3 ♗d6 12 ♘b5 a6 13 ♘xd6 cxd6 14 0-0

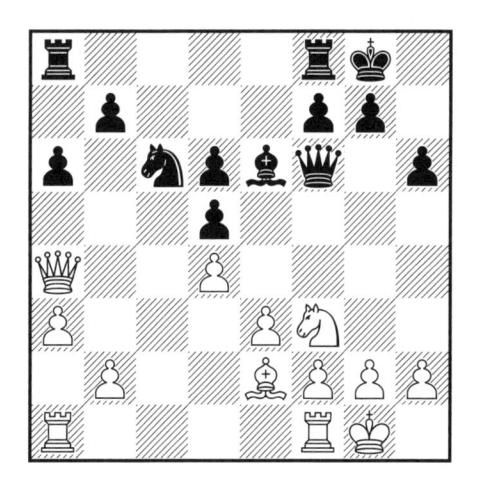

Visually White seems to have a lasting advantage, but how to go about exploiting the doubled d-pawns? Quite frankly I had no idea, since I couldn't recall ever having had such a position. I even wondered whether it might really only be equal. After all, I've lost access to e5 and c5, whereas Black may be able to make use of c4 or e4. All I could do for the time being was to play sensibly and try to get a feel for what was going on.
14...♖fc8 15 ♖fc1 ♕d8 16 ♘e1

It felt natural to bring my knight round to bear on d5.
16...♘e7 17 ♘d3 ♖xc1+ 18 ♖xc1 ♖c8 19 ♕d1 ♖xc1 20 ♕xc1 ♕c8 21 ♕xc8+ ♗xc8 22 ♗f3

These exchanges were all rather sudden and I didn't really have much choice.

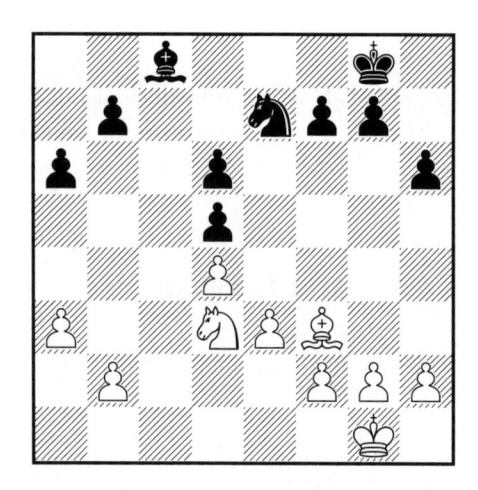

To say that I now formulated a plan is a bit strong, but I felt it would be a good idea to fight for space on the kingside by pushing my pawns and trying to follow with the king. First, however, I transferred my knight to a better square.

22...g5 23 ♘b4 ♗e6 24 ♘a2 ♔f8 25 ♘c3 ♔e8 26 g4 ♔d7 27 ♗d1 ♔c7 28 ♔g2 b5 29 ♔g3 ♔b6

I was a little suspicious of Sophie's plan of wandering over to the queenside with her king. It seemed to me that she should simply have waited with it somewhere in the centre.

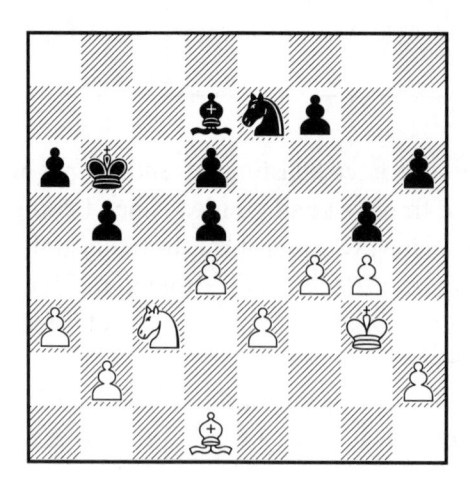

30 f4 ♗d7

As the game progressed, I gradually began to appreciate the benefits to me of

Black's rigid structure. For example, ...gxf4; exf4 will always give me a majority on the kingside for free, and 30...f6 31 h4 followed by a well timed e3-e4, or manoeuvring the knight round to f3, are pleasant options. Now, though, I have the opportunity either to make serious inroads with my king or obtain a dangerous passed h-pawn.

31 fxg5 hxg5 32 h4 gxh4+

Allowing me to play h4-h5 would be tantamount to resignation.

33 ♔xh4 ♔c7 34 ♔g5 ♗e6 35 b4 ♔d8 36 ♔f6 ♘g8+

I expected 36...♔e8 when I intended to increase the pressure by 37 ♗f3 followed by ♘e2-f4.

37 ♔g7 ♘e7 38 ♗f3 ♔d7 39 ♗e2

I could have stayed with the aforementioned regrouping, but playing for a3-a4 is also very strong.

39...♔d8 40 a4

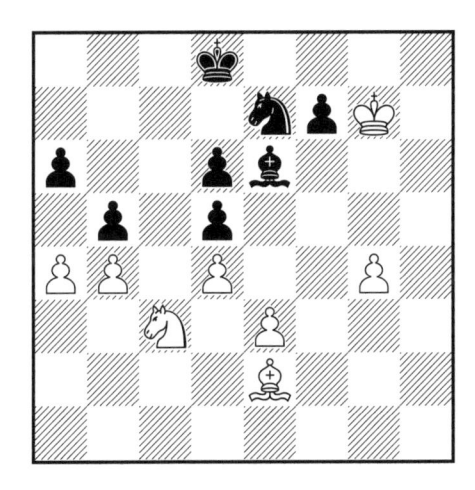

40...♘c6

After the perhaps more tenacious 40...bxa4 41 ♘xa4 ♘c6 42 ♔f6 ♘xb4 43 g5 ♔e8 44 g6 ♔f8 45 ♘b6 Black would have had an extremely difficult time trying to escape from the straight-jacket. The idea is g7+ ♔g8; ♗h5 followed by ♘c8-e7+ when the knight is taboo because of ♗xf7+, while the natural looking 45...♘c2 loses after 46 ♗h5 ♘xe3 (or 46...fxg6 47 ♗xg6 and both black pieces are attacked) 47 ♘d7+! ♗xd7 48 g7+ and the g-pawn queens.

41 axb5 axb5 42 ♘a2

I must still be winning, but it wasn't necessary to change plans here. As in the previous note, 42 ♔f6 and the advance of the g-pawn should win without too much difficulty.

42...♘e7

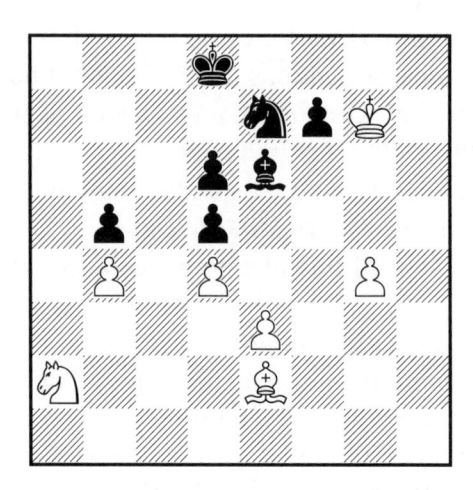

If she defends passively with 42...♘a7 then, again, 43 ♔f6 – the black knight can't be everywhere at once.

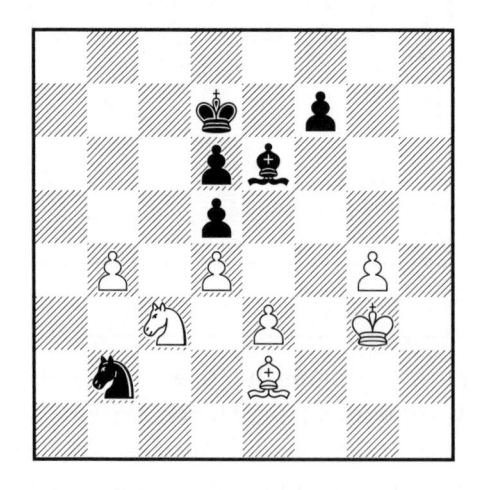

43 ♔f6 ♘g8+ 44 ♔g5 ♔e7 45 ♗xb5 ♘f6 46 ♗e2 ♘e4+ 47 ♔f4 ♔d7 48 ♗f3 ♘f2 49 ♔g3 ♘d3 50 ♗e2 ♘b2 51 ♘c3

Immobilising the knight and guaranteeing a completely winning knight versus bishop ending sooner or later.

51...♔c6 52 ♔f4 f6 53 g5 fxg5+ 54 ♔xg5 ♘c4 55 ♗xc4 dxc4 56 e4 ♗h3 57 ♔f6 ♔d7 58 d5 ♗g2 59 b5 ♔c7 60 ♔e7 ♗h3 61 ♘a4 ♗g4 62 b6+ ♔b7 63 ♔xd6 ♗d1 64 ♘c3 ♗f3 65 ♔c5 ♗g4 66 e5 ♗d7 67 e6 ♗c8 68 ♘e4 ♗a6 69 e7 ♗d7 70 ♔xc4 ♔xb6 71 ♘f6 ♗b5+ 72 ♔d4 1-0

10. Kulaots-Arkell

When I saw that long-term Estonian no.1 Kaido Kulaots had won the super-strong Aeroflot Open last year, I had a feeling we'd played each other somewhere down the road, and after a search I managed to dig up this game. As it was played 25 years ago I have only the faintest recollection of my thoughts during the game, so instead I'll do my best to comment as if it had been played yesterday.

Kaido Kulaots - Keith Arkell
Gelsenkirchen International 1995
French Defence

1 e4 e6 2 d4 d5 3 ♘c3 dxe4 4 ♘xe4 ♗d7 5 ♘f3 ♗c6 6 ♗d3 ♘d7 7 c4 ♗xe4 8 ♗xe4 ♗b4+ 9 ♗d2 ♗xd2+ 10 ♕xd2 c6 11 0-0 ♘gf6 12 ♗c2 0-0 13 ♖ad1 ♕c7 14 ♕e3 c5 15 dxc5 ♕xc5 16 ♕xc5 ♘xc5

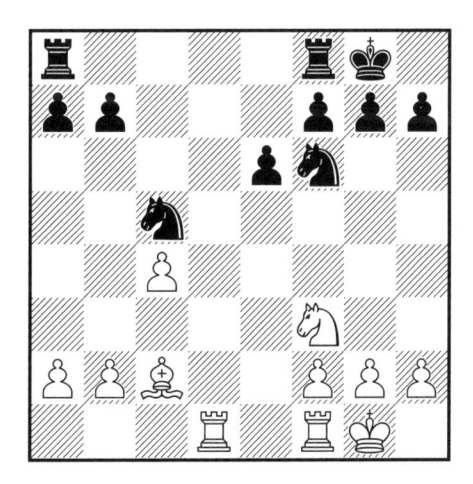

Objectively White is a little better here, but I've had plenty of experience of this type of position in which play typically revolves around the fight for the initiative on the queenside. If White can comfortably advance his majority it could become quite threatening, but in the interim Black will try to break up those same pawns and create targets.
17 ♖d4

17 b4 looks critical, but I should be OK after 17...♘ce4 18 ♗xe4 ♘xe4 19 ♖d7 a5 when there is enough counterplay.

17...♖fd8 18 ♖fd1 ♖xd4 19 ♖xd4 a5 20 ♔f1 ♔f8 21 ♔e2 ♔e7 22 b3 h6 23 ♘e5 ♖c8 24 ♔d2 g5

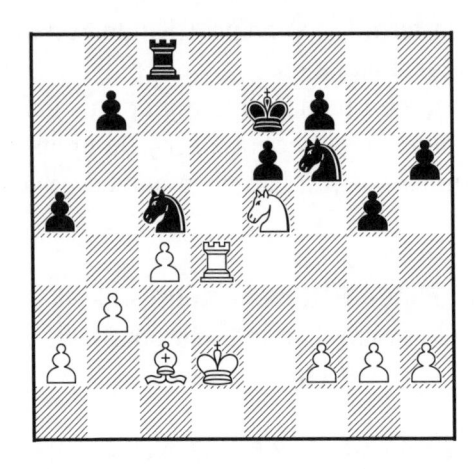

I must have had this exact kingside structure many hundreds of times with both colours. I like to advance my majority with the h- and g-pawns first, and reserve the final push with the e- and f-pawns until later.

25 a3 b6 26 b4 axb4 27 axb4 ♘cd7 28 ♘xd7 ♘xd7 29 ♔c3

I would assess the position as roughly equal, but the knight can make a real nuisance of itself.

29...♖a8 30 ♖d1 g4

If Black can get away with such a move tactically, it should always be played. In one fell swoop all three white kingside pawns are restricted, and any exchange will leave weaknesses.

31 ♖e1 h5 32 ♔b3 f6

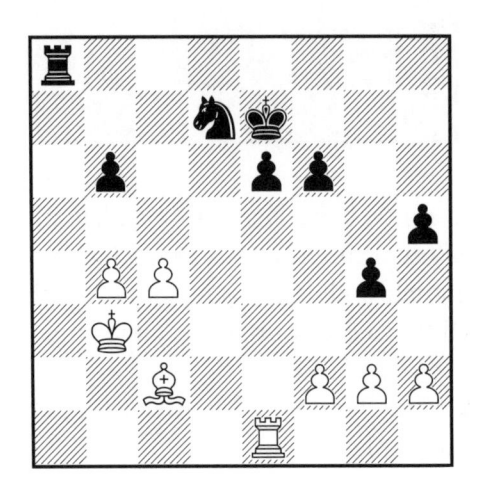

I have secured a very handy square on e5 for my knight.
33 ♗e4 ♖c8 34 f4
A perfectly good move, but at the same time what I was hoping for because my centre pawns will gain in strength.
34...gxf3 35 ♗xf3 ♘e5 36 ♗xh5
Had he covered c4 with 36 ♗e2, I would have continued with 36...h4.
36...♘xc4 37 ♗g4 ♘e5
It's hard to give concrete lines, but I feel I'm now getting slightly on top. Somehow I have the more compact position, and my knight can menace his b-pawn, his king, and even his bishop.
38 ♗e2 ♘c6 39 ♔c4 ♔d6 40 ♗f3
Even the simplified position after 40 ♔b5 ♘d4+ 41 ♔xb6 ♖b8+ 42 ♔a5 ♘c6+ 43 ♔a4 ♖xb4+ offers me some hope because of his uncomfortable king position and my centralised and well coordinated pieces.
40...♘a7+ 41 ♔d3 ♘b5 42 h4

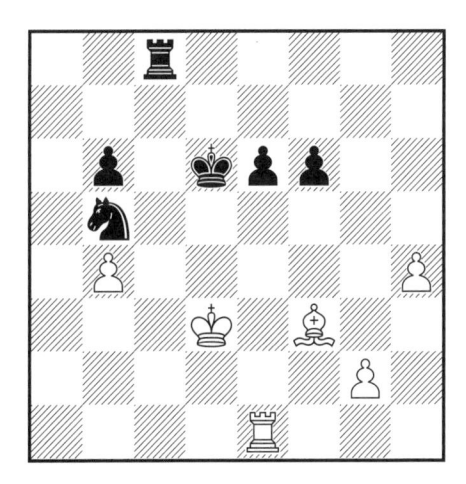

My opponent decides to unleash his trump card...
42...♖c3+
...and I go all in. I could have played the more restrained 42...f5, but decided to chase his b-pawn and trust my judgement that I would be able to deal with his counterplay.
43 ♔d2 ♖b3 44 h5
This is the obvious try, but the game would probably have ended in a draw after 44 ♖e4. One line runs 44...f5 45 ♖c4 ♘a3 46 ♖c6+ ♔e5 47 ♖xb6 ♘c4+ 48 ♔c2 ♖xf3 49 ♖xe6+ ♔xe6 50 gxf3 ♘e5 51 h5 ♘xf3 52 ♔d3 and the more you look at this position, the more you realise that White's outside pawns are good enough to hold the balance.

44...♖xb4 45 ♖h1 ♔e7 46 h6 ♖d4+ 47 ♔e3 ♖d8

I quite fancied my chances now. White should still be able to draw, but it isn't so easy to calculate a precise way of doing so. Meanwhile I plan to concentrate my forces against his h-pawn.

48 ♖a1 e5 49 h7 ♔f7 50 ♖a6 ♔g7 51 ♖xb6 ♘d6 52 ♖c6 ♔xh7

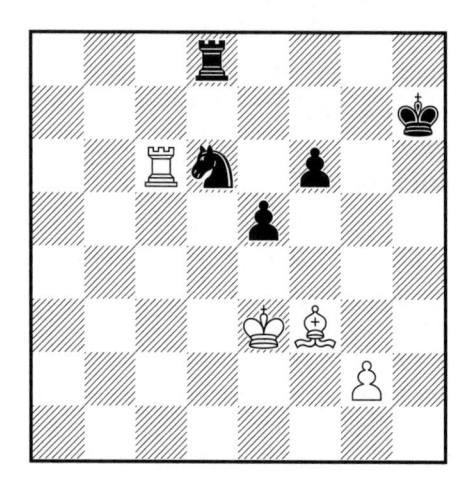

This is about the best I could have hoped for. If White is now to escape, his road will be long and painful.

53 ♗e4+ ♘xe4 54 ♔xe4 ♔g6 55 ♖c7 ♖d4+ 56 ♔e3 ♔f5 57 ♖f7 ♖a4 58 ♖f8 ♖a3+ 59 ♔f2 ♖a2+ 60 ♔g3 ♖a4 61 ♔f3 ♖f4+ 62 ♔e3 ♖g4 63 ♔f3 ♖f4+ 64 ♔e3 ♖b4 65 ♔f3 ♖b3+ 66 ♔f2 e4 67 ♖f7 ♔e5 68 g4 ♖f3+ 69 ♔e2 ♖a3 70 ♖f8 ♖h3 71 ♖f7 ♖h4 72 ♖g7

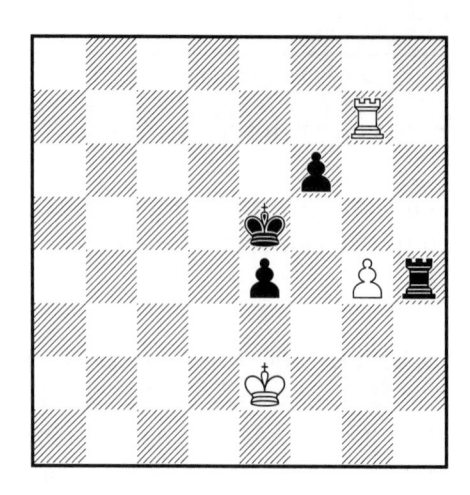

I can't emphasise enough how difficult it is to keep finding forced moves to save such positions, especially as they tend to occur at the end of long gruelling games. Here White was obliged to find the counter-intuitive lifeline 72 ♖e7+ ♔f4 73 ♖e6 ♖h2+ 74 ♔f1 f5 75 ♔g1! (not 75 gxf5 ♔f3 76 ♔g1 ♖g2+ 77 ♔f1 ♖a2 78 ♔g1 ♖a1+ 79 ♔h2 e3 80 f6 ♖a5 81 f7 ♖f5 82 ♔g1 e2 83 ♖e7 ♖f6 – zugzwang – 84 ♖e8 ♖xf7 85 ♖e6 ♖f4 86 ♖e8 ♖g4+ 87 ♔h2 ♖e4 when Black wins) 75...♖a2 76 gxf5 ♔g3 77 ♖g6+ ♔f3 78 f6 ♖a1+ 79 ♔h2 ♖f1 80 f7 ♔e2 81 ♖a6 ♖xf7 82 ♔g3, which is a theoretical draw.

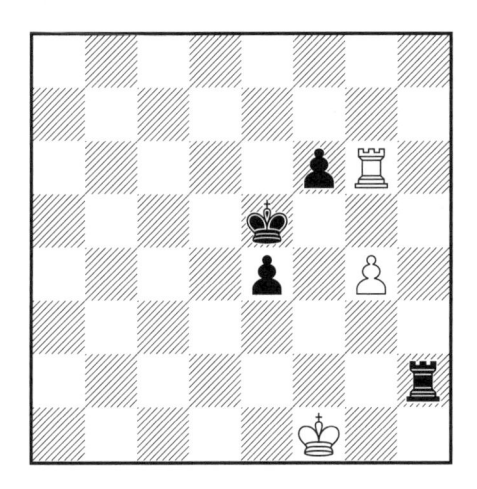

72...♔f4 73 ♖g6 ♖h2+ 74 ♔f1 ♔e5

This is the only way to win.
75 ♖g8 e3?
Now it was my turn to err. I should have played 75...♖a2. In some lines I need to defend my f-pawn temporarily with ...♖a6.
76 ♖e8+?
My opponent returns the favour. Instead, 76 ♖f8 draws.
76...♔f4 77 ♖e6 f5 78 ♔g1 ♖h4 79 gxf5 ♔f3 80 f6 e2 81 f7 ♖g4+ 82 ♔h2 ♖h4+ 83 ♔g1 ♖f4 84 ♖e7 ♖f6 0-1

White is in zugzwang. As mentioned earlier, if 85 ♖e8 ♖xf7 86 ♖e6 ♖f4 87 ♖e8 ♖g4+ 88 ♔h2 ♖e4.

11. Arkell-Holland

My 29th move in this game is well known, but the resulting ending is of some interest in its own right.

Keith Arkell - James Holland
High Wycombe Open 2012
Tarrasch Defence

1 d4 d5 2 c4 e6 3 ♘f3 c5 4 cxd5 exd5 5 ♘c3 ♘c6 6 g3 ♘f6 7 ♗g2 ♗e7 8 0-0 0-0 9 dxc5 ♗xc5 10 ♗g5 d4 11 ♘e4 ♗e7 12 ♗xf6 ♗xf6 13 ♘e1 ♗f5 14 ♘d3 ♗xe4 15 ♗xe4 ♖e8 16 ♗xc6

This is a poor move, unnecessarily weakening my position. The natural 16 ♗f3 would have left me with a comfortable edge.

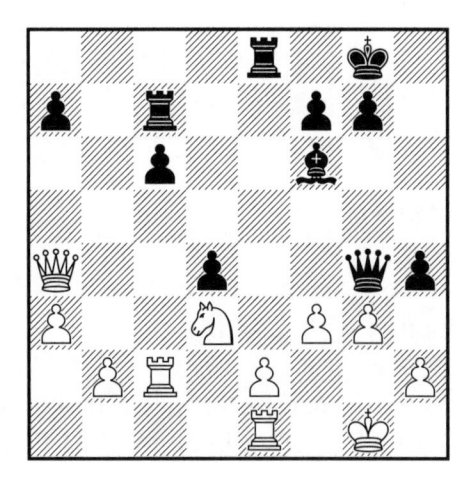

16...bxc6 17 ♖c1 ♕d5 18 a3 ♕e4 19 ♖e1 ♖ac8 20 ♕a4 ♖c7 21 ♘c5 ♕g4 22 ♖c2 h5 23 ♘d3 h4 24 f3

A second dubious move. Had I not been in that 'win at all costs' mentality needed for weekend tournaments, I might have bailed out for a draw with 24 ♖xc6 ♖xc6 25 ♕xc6 ♖xe2 26 ♖xe2 ♕xe2 27 ♕c8+ ♔h7 28 ♕f5+ ♔g8 29 ♕c8+, etc.
24...♕e6 25 g4 h3 26 ♕a5

Objectively speaking I knew I should have been maintaining control of the light squares rather than allowing Black to improve his position further with 26...♕b3, but as I stood worse either way I couldn't resist setting a hidden trap which promised

to swing the evaluation in my favour.
26...♕e3+ 27 ♔f1 ♗h4 28 ♕xc7!

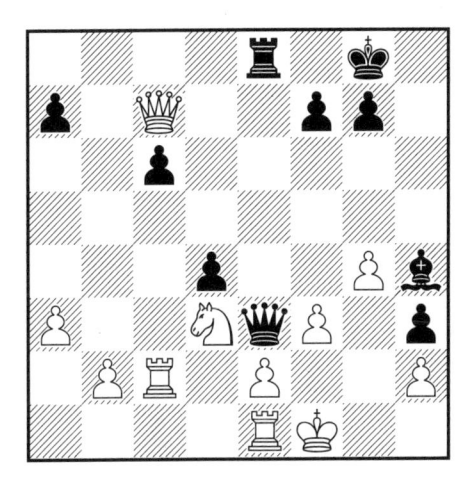

Here is my idea. Holland had automatically assumed that this capture wasn't possible as his reply appears to win on the spot.
28...♕xd3

Threatening 29...♕xc2, 29...♕e3, and 29...♕xf3+, so it appears I must resign.
29 ♕d8!

For my trap to work, the queen must pin Black's rook so preventing 29...♕xf3+, attack the rook with check to avoid 29...♕xc2 followed by ...♗xe1, and threaten the bishop to eliminate 29...♕e3. The best Black can do now is head for an inferior ending. If 29...♕xc2 30 ♕xe8+ ♔h7 31 ♖a1 ♕xb2 32 ♖d1 and I'm well on top.
29...♖xd8 30 exd3 ♗xe1 31 ♔xe1 ♖e8+ 32 ♖e2

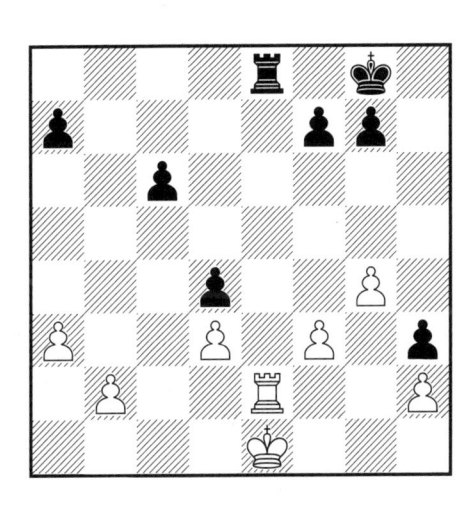

My advantage is only very slim if I allow his rook to come to e3.
32...♖xe2+

A bold, but ultimately incorrect decision. Clearly Black is worse if he moves his rook away, because of the weak h3-pawn. A friend mentioned to me recently that he couldn't beat his engine after it played 32... ♖b8 – either with 33 ♔f2 or 33 b4. However, against my human opponent I would have felt quite confident.
33 ♔xe2 f5

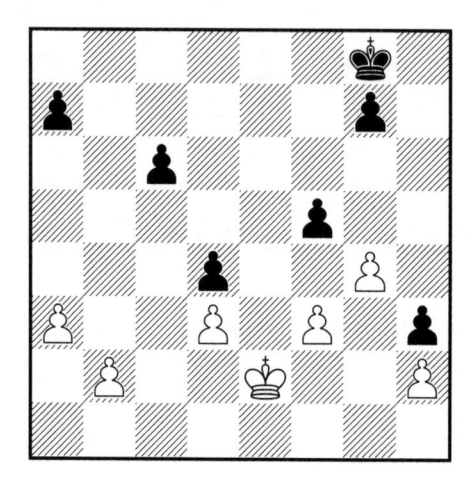

This is a good practical try. There is no point in just letting me come and take his h-pawn.
34 f4

I was incapable of fathoming out the long and complicated variations following 34 gxf5: for instance, 34...♔f7 35 ♔f2 ♔f6 36 ♔g3 ♔xf5 37 f4 g6 when both 38 b4 or 38 f4 might be winning, but I wasn't certain. Neither did I want to let him play 34...f4 himself as I couldn't see a clear-cut win after both kings head for the queenside, and, besides, I couldn't find any defence, either conceptually or analytically, after my chosen move.
34...fxg4 35 ♔f2 c5 36 b3 a5 37 a4

These last two moves were forced, in order to prevent Black creating a passed pawn on the queenside while I was gathering up the g4- and h3-pawns.
37...♔f7 38 ♔g3 ♔e6 39 ♔xg4 ♔d5 40 ♔f3

Of course, I could have taken the pawn immediately, but there is no harm in repeating the position to get to the time control. I'm not risking anything.
40...♔d6 41 ♔g3 ♔d5 42 ♔g4 ♔d6 43 ♔xh3 c4

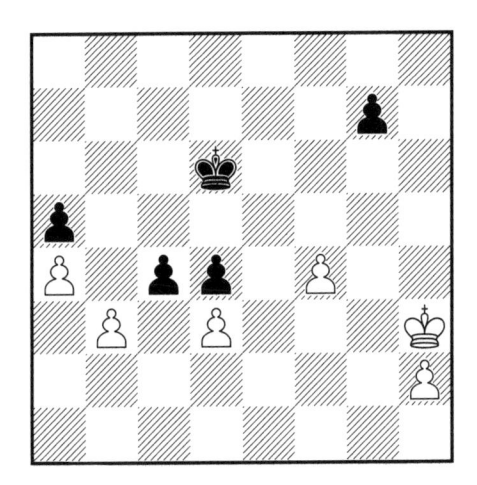

Using the method of conversion I had decided on, this was always going to be the critical moment. I had calculated that I could gain a crucial tempo with my 46th move...

44 bxc4 ♔c5 45 ♔g4 ♔b4 46 c5

...And this was it. Perhaps there were other roads to Rome, but now White wins the race by a tempo.

46...♔xc5 47 f5 ♔b4 48 h4 ♔c3 49 h5 ♔xd3

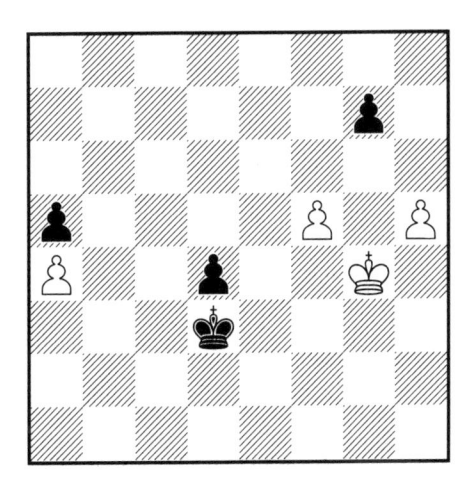

50 h6 gxh6 51 f6 ♔c2 52 f7 d3 53 f8♕ d2 54 ♕c5+ ♔d3 55 ♕d5+ ♔c2 56 ♕c4+ ♔b1 57 ♕d3+ ♔c1 58 ♕c3+ 1-0

12. Houska-Arkell

My opponent in this game was on the road to becoming England's strongest active female player and the perennial British Women's Champion.

Jovanka Houska - Keith Arkell
Mind Sports Olympiad, London 1999
Caro-Kann Defence

1 e4 c6 2 d4 d5 3 f3 e6 4 ♘c3 ♗b4 5 ♘ge2 dxe4 6 fxe4 ♕h4+ 7 ♘g3 ♘f6 8 ♕f3 e5 9 ♗e3 ♗g4 10 ♕f2 ♗e6 11 ♗e2 ♘xe4 12 ♘gxe4 ♕xe4 13 ♗d3 ♕g4 14 dxe5 ♘d7 15 ♕f4

This is rather compliant, whereas the pawn sacrifice 15 0-0 ♘xe5 16 ♗e2 would have kept me on my toes. However, in either case the opening has turned out favourably for Black.

15...♕xf4 16 ♗xf4 ♘c5 17 0-0-0 0-0-0 18 a3 ♘xd3+ 19 ♖xd3 ♖xd3 20 cxd3 ♗e7

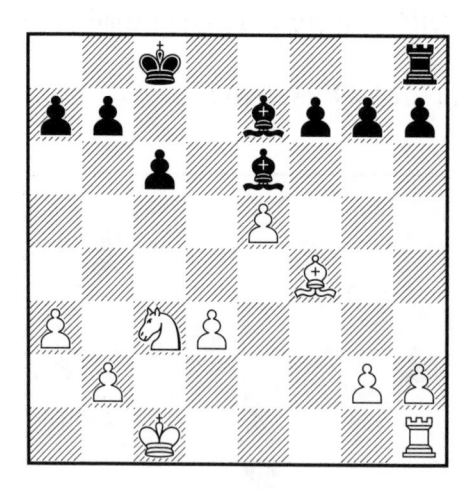

With two bishops and the better pawn structure, I am assured of a lasting advantage. In such situations I often ponder, for example, whether it would be more favourable with or without rooks. I think that here the inclusion of the rooks favours Black simply because of the extra piece with which to probe White's weaknesses. My strategy will now be to advance on both flanks and just see what happens.

21 ♘e4 h6 22 ♔c2 g5 23 ♗e3 b6 24 ♖f1 ♔c7 25 ♔c3 a5 26 ♘d6 c5 27 ♘e4

Today I would be a bit more cautious about playing ...g5, first advancing on the

queenside and activating my rook. Here Jovanka had the opportunity to activate her position with 27 ♘f5 ♗d8 28 d4, and after 28...♔c6 the position looks only about equal.
27...♖d8 28 h4

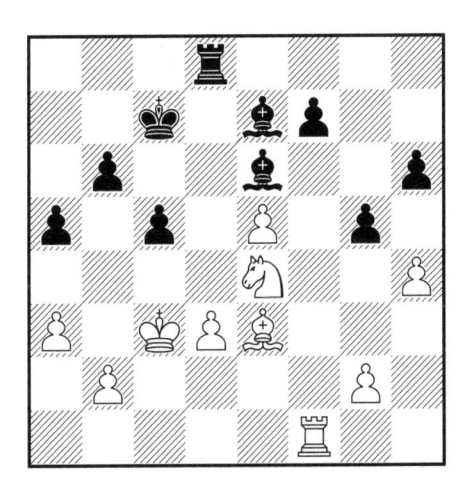

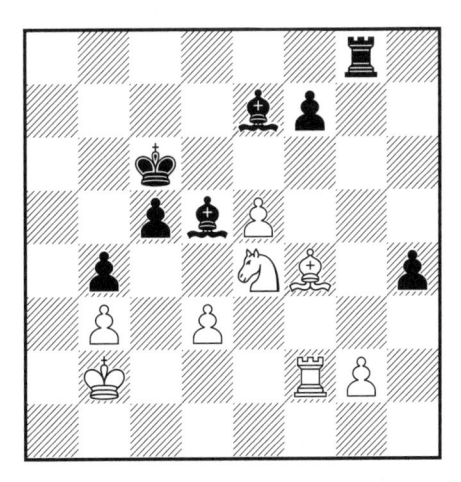

She should just wait, as the opening of the g-file favours Black.
28...gxh4 29 ♗xh6 ♖g8 30 ♖f2 ♔c6 31 ♗f4 b5 32 b3 b4+ 33 axb4 axb4+ 34 ♔b2 ♗d5

All four of White's pawns are now weak or potentially weak, and with her pieces having to take up passive positions to defend them, it isn't surprising that a tactical breakthrough soon follows.
35 ♔c2 ♖g4 36 ♔b2

If 36 ♗c1 I can transfer my king to e6, after which the pawns will start to fall.

36...c4!

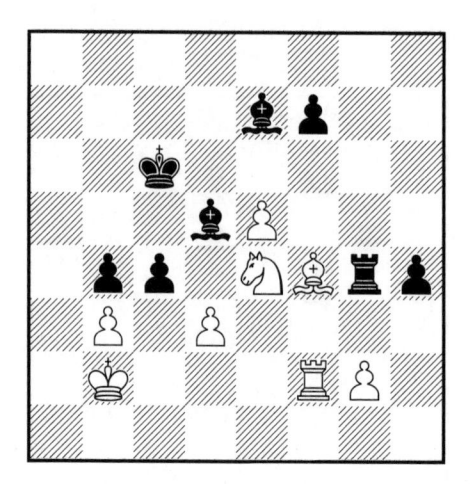

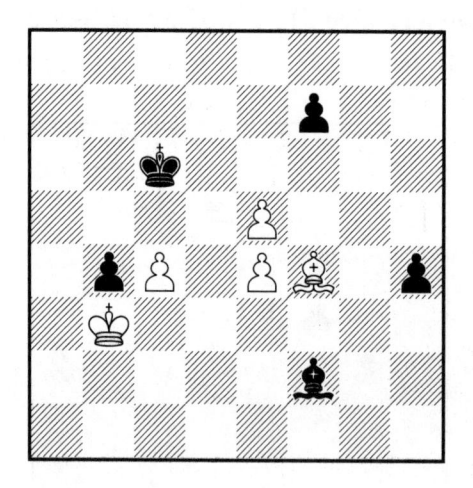

Out of the blue this break wins by force.
37 bxc4 ♗xe4 38 dxe4 ♗c5 39 ♖f3 ♖xg2+ 40 ♔b3 ♖f2 41 ♖xf2 ♗xf2

The h-pawn will cost Black her bishop.
42 ♔xb4 ♗e1+ 43 ♔b3 ♗g3 44 ♗e3 h3 45 ♗g1 h2 46 ♗xh2 ♗xh2 47 ♔b4 ♗xe5 48 c5 ♗d4 49 ♔c4 ♗xc5 50 ♔d3 ♔d6 51 ♔c4 ♔e5 0-1

13. Certek-Arkell

This game has similarities with the previous one in that I was again able to make good use of the two bishops, eventually reaching an endgame with the bishop-pair still intact, and after getting in my favourite advance, ...g5.

Pavel Certek - Keith Arkell
Vienna Open 2016
French Defence

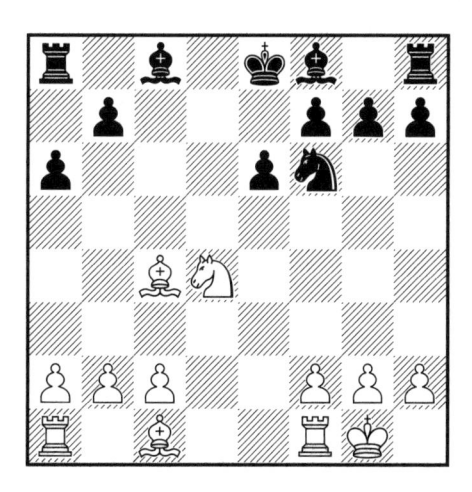

1 d4 e6 2 e4 d5 3 ♘d2 c5 4 exd5 ♕xd5 5 ♘gf3 cxd4 6 ♗c4 ♕d6 7 0-0 ♘f6 8 ♘b3 ♘c6 9 ♘bxd4 ♘xd4 10 ♕xd4 ♕xd4 11 ♘xd4 a6

I've made no secret of the fact that I like both middlegames and endgames in which I have an e-pawn in exchange for my opponent's c-pawn.
12 ♖e1 ♗c5 13 ♘b3 ♗d6 14 ♗e3 ♘g4

I was pleased to see White's last move. Even though I felt there should be some way in which he could give up his h-pawn, I was sure that in practice he would just defend it and part with his best minor piece.
15 g3 ♘xe3 16 ♖xe3 ♔e7

I've learnt by now that to win such positions requires a lot of grinding. Small advantages will have to be accumulated in the hope that at some point White's position will become critical, and then indefensible.

17 ♗f1 ♖d8 18 ♗g2 ♗c7 19 c4 a5

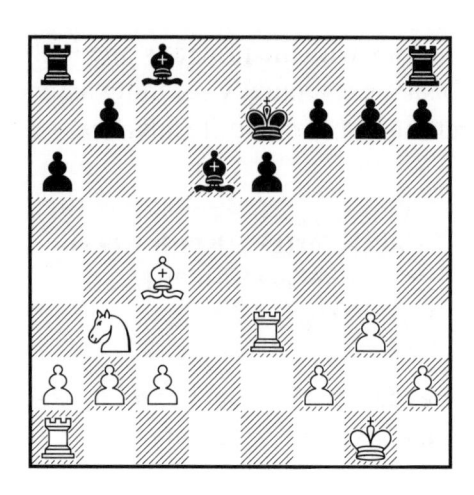

I could have spent any amount of time choosing between this move and the more restrained but equally good 19...♖b8. When there is little to analyse by way of concrete variations, I like to make quick decisions, saving my time and energy for later on.

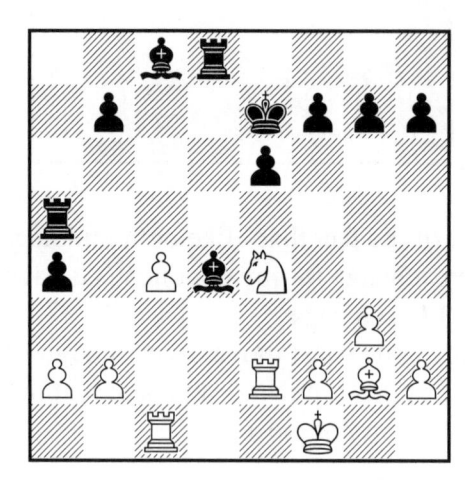

20 ♖e2 a4 21 ♘c5 ♖a7 22 ♖c1 ♗b6 23 ♘e4 ♗d4 24 ♔f1 ♖a5

This is my problem piece and I'm looking for a way to give it more scope, whereas my light-squared bishop can sit happily on c8 for the time being. Since it isn't easy to co-ordinate the rooks it will probably suit me to exchange one of them at some point and then carefully expand on the kingside.

25 ♘c3 ♗c5 26 f4 ♔f8 27 ♔e1 h6 28 ♖d2 ♖xd2 29 ♔xd2 g5

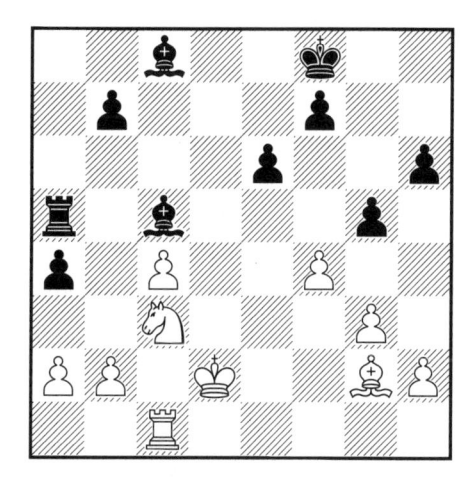

A dual-purpose move. I am trying to create weaknesses in my opponent's structure and at the same time clear the way for the e- and f-pawns.

30 ♖f1 ♗e7 31 ♔d3 a3

Played reluctantly. I would have preferred to leave this pawn on a4, or even better a5, to keep White's queenside pawns in check, but I wanted to free up my rook for active duty.

32 b3 gxf4 33 ♖xf4 ♖h5

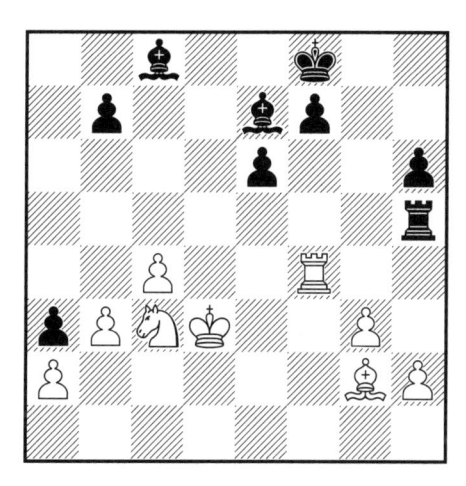

This is perhaps the most important move of the game. If I can induce White to play h2-h4 then not only will his pawns become weaker, but he will lose the option of playing h2-h3 and g3-g4 to try and break up the centre which I later intend to erect.

34 h4 ♖e5 35 ♖e4 ♖f5 36 ♖e3 b6 37 ♖f3 ♖e5 38 ♖e3 ♖f5 39 ♖f3 ♖h5 40 ♖e3 ♗c5 41 ♖e2 ♖f5 42 ♘e4 ♗e7 43 ♔c3 ♖e5 44 ♔d4 f6

You may wonder why I am taking so much time to mobilise my pawns, but it has been known since the days of Steinitz and Tarrasch that to get the most out of the bishop-pair, you should take central squares away from the opposing knight. Hence it would be a gross positional error to move the pawn from e6 and cede the d5-square at this early stage. Eventually the e- and f-pawns will need to get moving, but patience is required.

45 ♘c3 ♗d6 46 ♔d3 ♖xe2

That's enough pottering around. It's now time for my two bishops to flex their muscles.

47 ♘xe2 f5 48 ♔c3 ♗d7

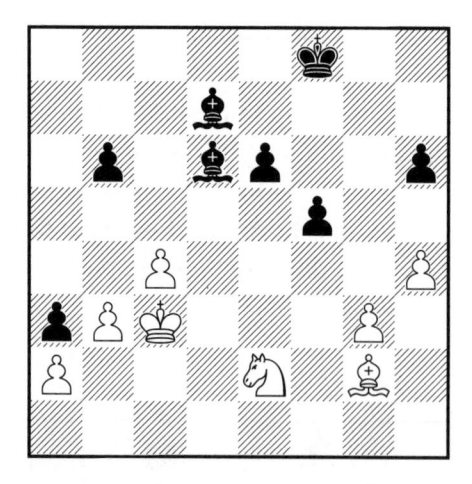

Finally I move this piece – for the first time. Unlike knights, bishops can often do a perfectly good job from the back rank. The intention is to discourage 49 b4 on account of the annoying reply 49...♗a4!, which prevents ♔b3 and threatens ...♗d1.

49 ♗f3 e5 50 ♔d2 ♗b4+ 51 ♔d1 ♔e7

Inch by inch my position has become very nice. I can use my flexible pawns to continue gaining space and pushing him back.

52 ♔c2 ♔d6 53 ♗h5 ♗c6 54 ♘c3 ♔c5 55 g4

As often happens, rather than sit tight and watch his position slowly deteriorate, Certek lashes out, missing a tactic in the process.

55...♗f3 56 ♘a4+

I expected 56 ♘d5, but was sure there would be more than one way to win. Had he played this, I would have had to settle down and, for the first time in the game, do some calculating.

56...♔d4 57 ♘xb6 fxg4

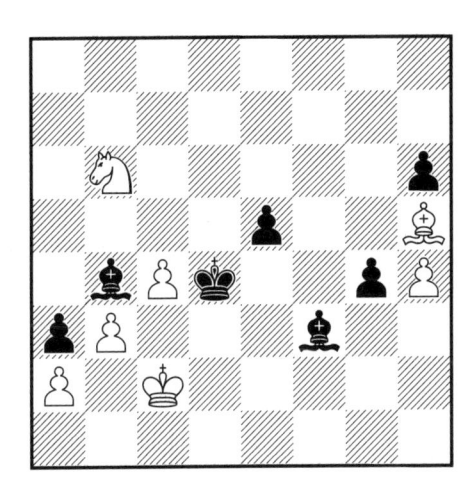

Material is still level, but it was obvious that I will either queen one of my pawns, mate him, or win a piece.

58 ♘d5 ♗e4+ 59 ♔d1 g3 60 ♔e2 g2 61 ♔f2 ♗e1+ 62 ♔g1 ♗xh4 63 ♔e2 ♗e1 64 b4

If he just waits, one way of winning is to play ...♗b1 and ...♗xa2.

64...h5

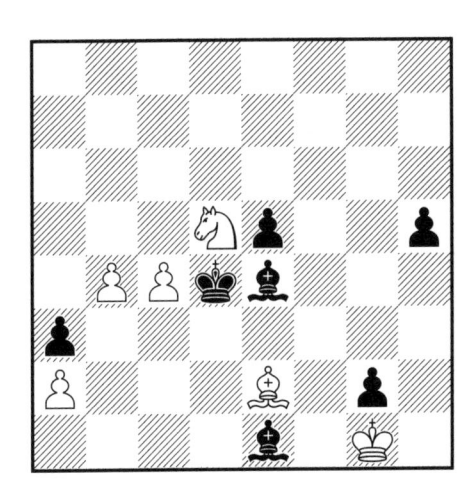

It wasn't difficult to calculate that my pawns are faster.

65 b5 h4 66 b6 h3 67 ♗d3

If 67 b7 ♗g3 and 68...h2#.

67...h2+ 0-1

After 68 ♔xh2 ♗f2 it will soon be mate.

14. Arkell-Wadsworth

Sometimes eking out a win with an extra pawn requires patience, and plenty of manoeuvring. Here, against a young English talent, I inched forward at a pace which would frustrate even a tortoise.

> **Keith Arkell - Matthew Wadsworth**
> Gatwick International 2016
> *Slav Defence*

1 ♘f3 d5 2 c4 c6 3 d4 ♘f6 4 ♕c2 dxc4 5 ♕xc4 ♗g4 6 ♘bd2 ♘bd7 7 g3 e6 8 ♗g2 ♗e7 9 0-0 ♗h5 10 a4 a5 11 ♕b3 ♕b6 12 ♕xb6 ♘xb6 13 b3 ♘fd5 14 ♗b2 0-0 15 ♘c4 ♘xc4

This capture gave me some encouragement as my pawn will gain in stature, and I will have long-term prospects on the b-file.
16 bxc4 ♘b4 17 ♖fd1 ♖fd8 18 c5 ♗f6 19 e3 b6

Against a waiting move I planned ♖ab1 and ♗a3.
20 cxb6 ♖ab8 21 ♖ac1 ♖xb6 22 ♖d2 ♗g6 23 ♗c3 ♗e4

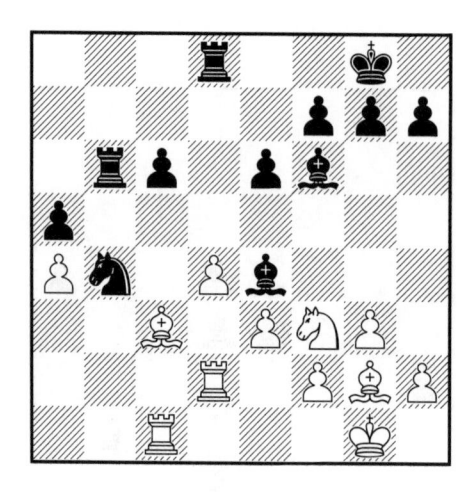

I think this was an oversight and he had missed my 25th move.
24 ♘e5 ♗xg2 25 ♘c4 ♖a6 26 ♔xg2

Now I have the kind of position I like: no weaknesses and a guarantee of permanent pressure against his queenside pawns.
26...♖da8 27 ♘xa5

It was hard to resist playing in this straightforward manner, and besides, if I try increasing the pressure against b4 then 27 ♖b1 runs into 27...c5 and 27 ♖b2 allows 27...♘d3. It will now be a very tough task for Wadsworth to hang on to his backward c-pawn.

27...♘d5 28 ♘b7 ♖xa4 29 ♖dc2 ♖a2 30 ♗e1 g6 31 ♔f3

With e3 defended I'm now threatening to capture his pawn.

31...♖xc2 32 ♖xc2 ♘e7 33 ♗b4 ♖a6 34 ♘c5 ♖a7

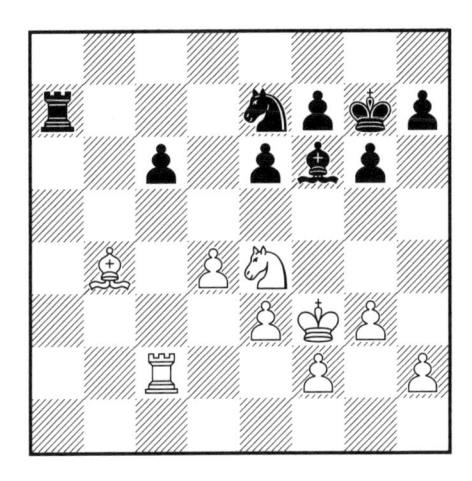

The c-pawn is lost whatever he does: for example, 34...♖b6 35 ♗a5 ♖b5 36 ♗d8 with ♘d3 or ♘e4 to follow.

35 ♘e4 ♔g7

36 ♗xe7

I could have exchanged both minor pieces, but felt that the subsequent ending would be more favourable if I kept the knight, which tends to be more effective than a bishop at close quarters.

36...♗xe7 37 ♖xc6 h5 38 h3

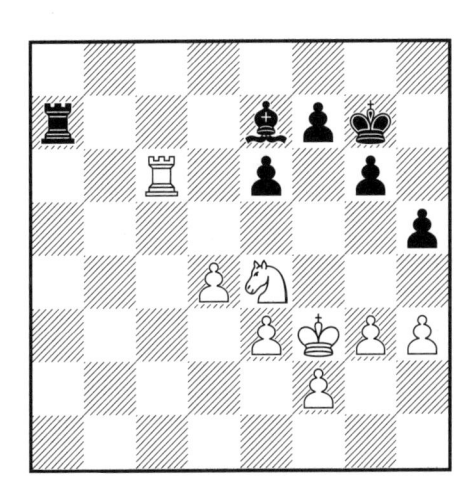

How do you set about winning such a position? Clearly not with the pieces alone, but using pawns will involve exchanges, and you don't want too many swaps as rook, knight and pawn versus rook and bishop is usually a simple draw. The answer is somewhere in-between. Ideally you would like to fix the kingside with g4-g5, and then organise e3-e4 and d4-d5.

38...♖b7 39 g4 hxg4+ 40 hxg4 ♖a7

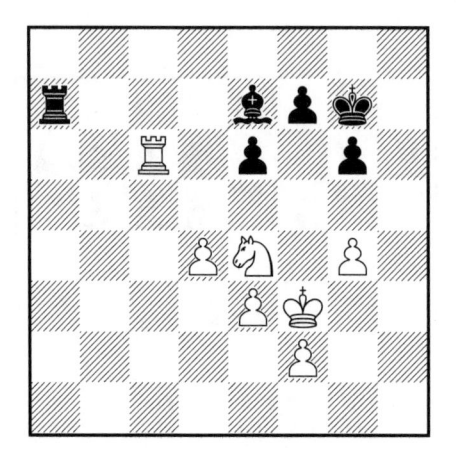

I was pleased to see this and thought he should prefer 40...g5, but I guess he was reluctant to put a pawn on the same colour as his bishop. 40...f5 was also interesting, but I didn't expect him to weaken his pawns in such a cavalier manner.

41 g5

Now I have a free hand to slowly improve my position because ...f6 will always leave Black with too many weaknesses. So many times this is what we strive for in chess – leaving the opponent without any real counterplay is often half the battle.

41...♖a5 42 ♔f4 ♖a7 43 ♖b6 ♗d8 44 ♖b5 ♖d7 45 ♔g4 ♗e7 46 ♖a5 ♗d8 47 ♖a8

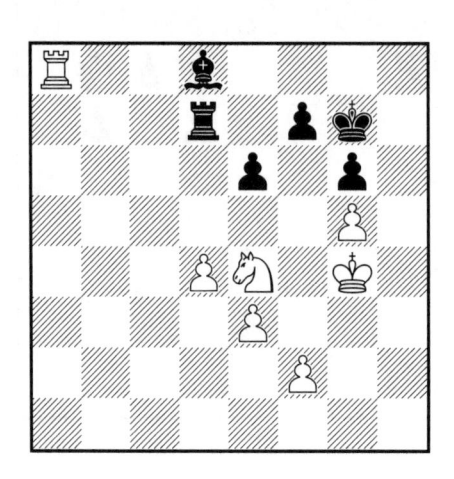

If you study the great endgame players, such as Magnus Carlsen and Anatoly Karpov, you cannot fail to observe their endless patience. Maintaining the tension rather than committing oneself to immediate action tends to have a wearisome effect on the opponent, as well as forcing them to defend accurately to avoid further damage.

47...♗e7 48 ♖c8 ♗b7 49 ♖e8 ♖c7 50 ♖b8 ♖d7 51 f4 ♖c7 52 ♔f3 ♖a7 53 ♘c5 ♖c7 54 ♘d3 ♖a7 55 ♖c8 ♗d6 56 ♔e4 ♖b7 57 ♘f2

From g4 the knight will have a choice of entry points into the heart of Black's position.

57...♗e7 58 ♘g4 ♖a7 59 ♖b8 ♗d6 60 ♖b5 ♗e7 61 ♔e5 ♖a3

Spooked by my intention to make progress with e3-e4 and d4-d5, combined with ♘f6 and ♖b8, Matthew gives some ground.

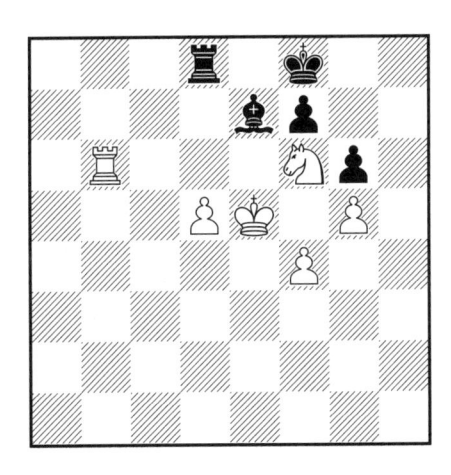

62 ♖b7 ♖a5+ 63 ♔e4 ♔f8 64 ♘f6 ♖a8 65 ♔e5 ♖d8 66 ♘h7+ ♔e8 67 e4 ♖a8 68 ♘f6+ ♔f8 69 d5 exd5 70 exd5 ♖d8 71 ♖b6

Threatening to win on the spot with 72 d6.

71...♗c5 72 ♖c6 ♗a3 73 d6

Inch by inch I've brought about a winning position. The rest is relatively straightforward.

73...♔g7 74 ♔d5 ♗b2 75 ♘g4 ♗a3 76 ♘e5 f6 77 ♖c7+ ♔g8 78 ♘f7 ♗xd6 79 ♘xd6 fxg5 80 fxg5 1-0

15. Arkell-Ledger

I first saw Tony Miles win the ending of rook, knight and four pawns against rook, knight and three pawns, all on the kingside, against Murray Chandler at a Phillips and Drew tournament in 1984. Winning by force or not, the defence is exceedingly difficult.

Keith Arkell - Andrew Ledger
British Championship, Eastbourne 1990
English Opening

1 ♘f3 ♘f6 2 c4 c6 3 b3 g6 4 ♗b2 ♗g7 5 e3 0-0 6 ♗e2 d5 7 0-0 ♖e8 8 ♕c2 a5 9 d3 ♘a6 10 a3 ♗f5 11 ♘bd2 ♖c8 12 ♖fd1 ♕b6 13 ♗d4 ♕c7 14 ♖ac1

I'm a little puzzled why I didn't play the natural 14 ♕b2 here. It makes the difference between being comfortably better and no more than equal.
14...e5 15 ♗a1 e4 16 ♘d4 exd3 17 ♗xd3 ♗xd3 18 ♕xd3 ♘g4 19 g3 ♘e5 20 ♕e2 dxc4 21 ♘xc4 ♘xc4 22 ♕xc4 ♖cd8 23 b4

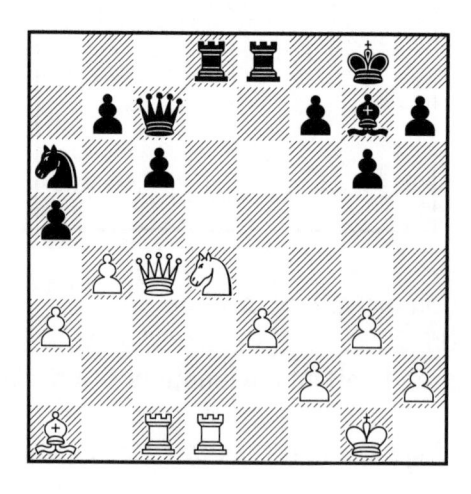

As so often, my plan is to hammer away at Black's queenside pawn structure. If successful I'll emerge a pawn up, with the one I treasure most in chess sitting quietly on e3 holding everything together.
23...axb4 24 axb4 ♕b6 25 ♖b1 ♘c7 26 ♕c5 ♕a6 27 ♕a5 ♕xa5 28 bxa5 ♘a6 29 ♖dc1 ♖d7 30 ♖b6 ♖a8 31 ♔g2 ♖a7 32 ♗b2 ♘c7 33 ♖b3 ♘e8 34 ♗c3 ♘d6 35 ♖a1 ♘e4 36 ♗b2 ♘d2

Andrew has played excellently for 35 moves, but now begins to drift a little. I think he stands a bit better if he sits tight and just improves his position, starting perhaps with 36...♖a6.
37 ♖c3 ♘e4 38 ♖c2 ♖d5

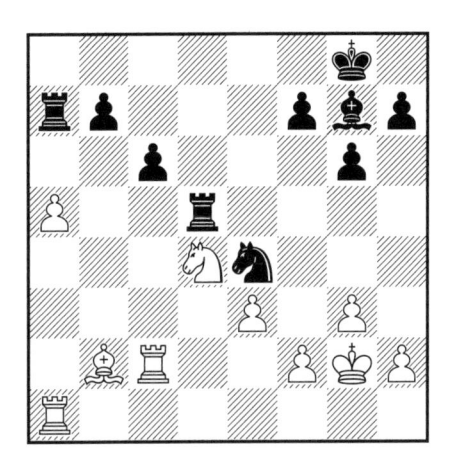

Now at last I have a chance to realise my queenside ambitions.
39 a6 ♖xa6

Short of time, my opponent couldn't find any means of holding on to his pawn.
40 ♖xa6 bxa6 41 ♖xc6 ♖d8

41...a5 42 ♖c8+ ♗f8 43 ♗a3 ♘d6 44 ♖a8 with ♘c6 in the air is not appealing.
42 ♖xa6 ♘c5 43 ♖a7 h5

An important defensive move. If Black lets me play g3-g4 for free there will be many more options for increasing the pressure, such as h2-h4-h5 or h2-h4 and g4-g5.
44 ♘c6 ♖e8 45 ♗xg7 ♔xg7 46 h3

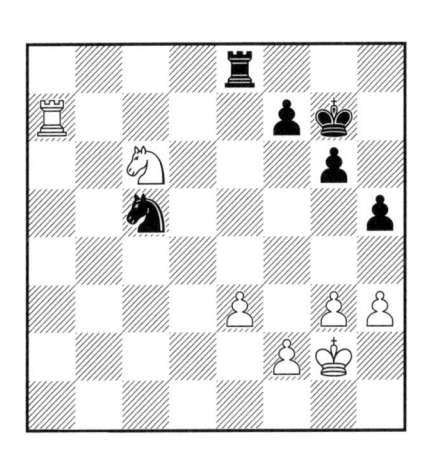

This ending may not be won by force, but it is much more painful for Black with knights on the board. People have often asked me how you are supposed to set about winning such positions, given that pawn advances lead to exchanges and make the draw more likely.

In my experience the best way is first to put the pawn on g5. This fixes the f7 and f6 points. If Black then breaks with ...f6, he will have a weak g-pawn against two flexible pawns, with the white e-pawn eventually becoming dangerous. If Black chooses not to break, the ideal set-up (with the pawn on g5) is knight on g4, pawns on f4 and e3, and king on f3. The white knight is then particularly troublesome, eyeing e5, f6 and h6. White is then also ready to play e3-e4-e5 or e3-e4 and f4-f5 depending on circumstances.

46...♔f6 47 ♖a5 ♘e6 48 f4 ♖c8 49 ♘e5 ♖c7 50 ♔f3 ♖c3 51 ♖a6 ♖c7 52 ♘d3 ♖c3 53 ♘f2 ♔g7 54 ♖a4 ♖c1 55 g4 hxg4+ 56 hxg4 ♖f1 57 ♔e2 ♖g1 58 g5

With stage one accomplished I can make threats against f7, forcing Black's rook on to the defensive.

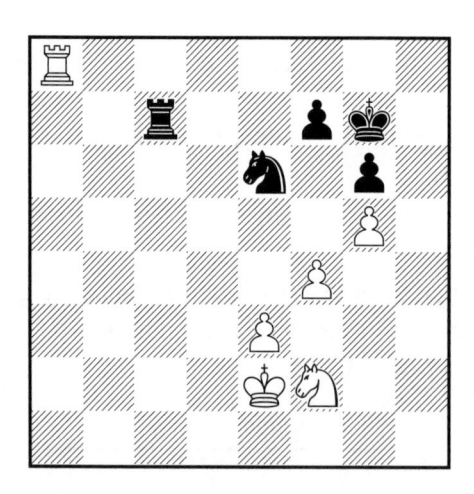

58...♖c1 59 ♖a7 ♖c7 60 ♖a8

I wasn't sure whether the knight ending was winning, but I suspected not, and feared it may even have been quite easy to draw. There is a myth that knight endings are like king and pawn endings, and that therefore an extra pawn usually wins, but this is far from the truth with pawns only on one flank.

If I had this position today I would prefer 60 ♖a6 ♘c5 61 ♖d6 ♘b7 62 ♖b6 followed by ♘g4, not allowing ...f6.

60...f6 61 gxf6+ ♔xf6 62 ♘g4+ ♔g7 63 ♖a6 ♖e7 64 ♔f3 ♘f8 65 ♔g3 ♘e6 66 ♔f3 ♘f8 67 ♘f2 ♘d7 68 ♖d6 ♘f6 69 e4

There are those who squander this precious thrust as early as move one, but I prefer to get myself organised first.

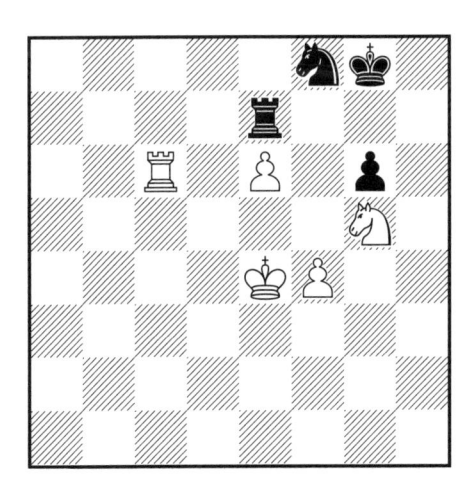

69...♖a7 70 e5 ♘d7 71 ♔g4 ♘f8 72 ♘e4 ♖a1 73 ♘g5 ♖g1+ 74 ♔f3 ♖f1+ 75 ♔g3 ♖g1+ 76 ♔f2 ♖a1 77 ♖c6 ♖a7 78 ♔f3 ♔g8 79 ♔g4 ♖e7 80 ♔f3 ♔g7 81 ♔e4 ♔g8 82 e6

We were still beyond the range of my ability to calculate the win by force, and I could have continued improving my position with, for instance, 82 ♔d5 heading to d6, but it is hard to criticise the text move.

82...♔g7 83 ♔e5 ♖a7 84 ♔d6

This is a bit unnecessary as I can win comfortably with 84 ♖c8 first, i.e. 84...♖a5+ 85 ♔d6 ♖a6+ 86 ♖c6 ♖xc6+ 87 ♔xc6 ♔f6 88 ♔d6 ♘xe6 89 ♘xe6 ♔f5 90 ♔e7.

84...♔f6 85 ♘e4+ ♔f5 86 ♘c5 ♘h7 87 ♘d7 ♖a8 88 e7 g5

After 88...♔xf4 there are many ways to win, but specifically I had it in mind to play 89 ♖c1, then ♖f1+ and ♖f7. Against 88...g5 I was already seeing the final pattern, although not all the details.

89 fxg5 ♔xg5 90 ♘b6 ♖h8 91 ♘d5 ♔g6 92 ♖c1 ♔g7 93 ♖g1+

But by now everything was crystal clear.

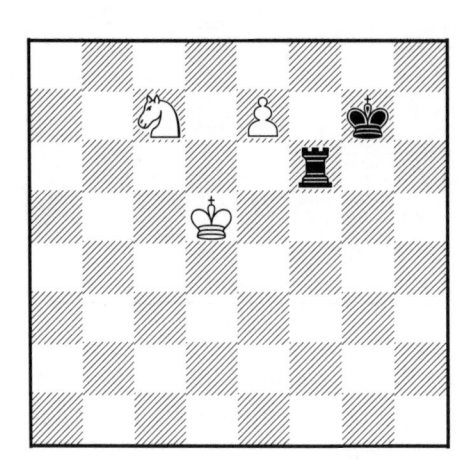

93...♔f7 94 ♖f1+ ♔g7

Or 94...♔e8 95 ♘c7#.

95 ♘c7 ♘f6 96 ♔e6 ♖h6 97 ♖xf6 ♖xf6+ 98 ♔d5

98 ♔e5? ♖f1 wouldn't be too clever.

98...♖f5+ 99 ♔d4 ♖f4+ 100 ♔d3 1-0

The finish would be 100...♖f3+ 101 ♔e2 ♖f8 102 ♘e6+.

16. Ilfeld-Arkell

In the following game my opponent makes a number of exchanges, each one very slightly favouring me. By effecting a series of what GM Jonathan Rowson calls 'micro plans', I am able to create some unease in White's position and prevent the draw which he might otherwise have easily achieved with the white pieces.

Etan Ilfeld-Keith Arkell
London Chess Classic Open 2013
Caro-Kann Defence

1 e4 c6 2 d4 d5 3 ♘d2 dxe4

So here, whenever I play 3...dxe4, and my opponent recaptures with a piece, I already feel that I have made a minute structural gain.

4 ♘xe4 ♘d7 5 ♘f3 ♘gf6 6 ♘xf6+ ♘xf6 7 ♘e5 ♗e6 8 ♗e2 g6 9 0-0 ♗g7 10 c3 0-0 11 ♖e1 ♘d7 12 ♘xd7 ♕xd7 13 ♗f3 ♖fe8 14 ♗f4 h5

Had I instead gone 14...♗d5 to attempt the exchange of my typically rather clumsy Caro bishop, he could have side-stepped with 15 ♗g4, when my bishop would have been vulnerable to a later c3-c4.

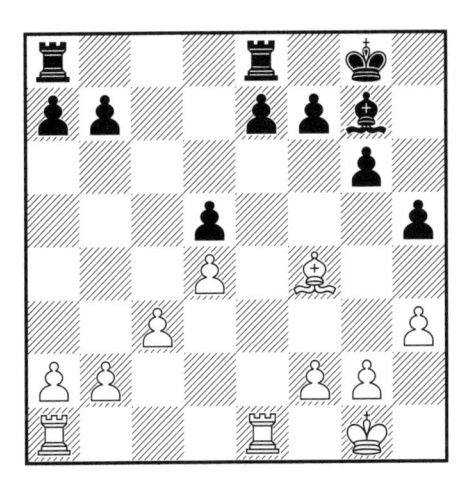

15 ♕e2 ♗g4 16 h3 ♗xf3 17 ♕xf3 ♕d5 18 ♕xd5 cxd5

Notice that this is another gain according to Arkell's Hierarchy of Pawns: my c-pawn has become fractionally more valuable as a d-pawn.

19 ♔f1 b5

If I can achieve ...a5 and ...b4 my opponent will have pawn weaknesses however he responds. Of course, with best play we are still well within the territory of a draw, but bit by bit White is falling back on to the defensive.

20 a3 ♗f6

An important move, or, more precisely, we are dealing with an important principle, i.e. giving the opponent more than one weakness. If all I have is a minority attack on the queenside (firing two pawns at the opponent's three, in order to leave one of them weak), the defence might be quite easy, but with a further weakness on the kingside, White's defence will be that much harder.

21 ♔e2 g5

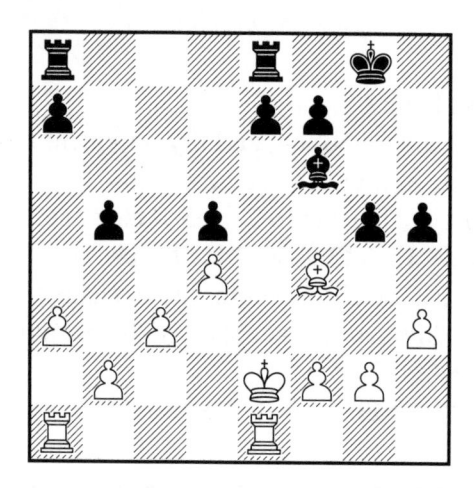

My favourite black move in chess, and a good sign that things are going well.

22 ♗h2 h4 23 ♔d3

Look at the difference between the kings now, and see how this becomes reversed later on, as White strives to deal with threats on both sides of the board.

23...♖ec8 24 ♗e5 ♔g7 25 a4 a6 26 ♖a3 e6 27 ♗xf6+

I think this is another small mistake, and they are adding up. The bishop was doing a good job in restricting my rooks, so he should probably have manoeuvred it to c5 via d6.

27...♗xf6 28 axb5 axb5 29 ♖ea1 ♖ab8 30 b4

An important moment. Had my opponent allowed me to play ...b4 and then lost the game, he would have regretted not fixing my pawn. Already though, despite having played 30 sensible moves with the white pieces, Etan is having to decide how best to stop my progress.

30...♖g8

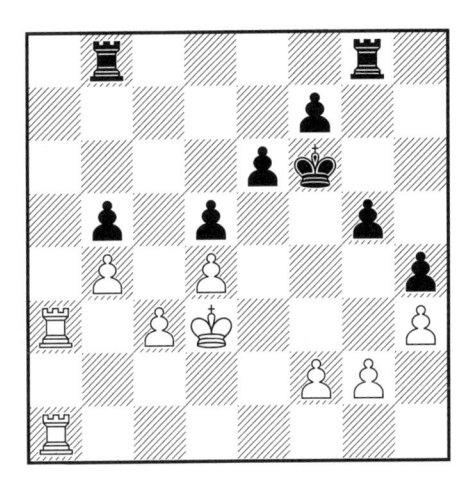

This move, threatening ...g4 in order to create that second weakness, was made possible by my earlier expansion on the kingside with ...g5 and ...h4.

31 f3 ♔f5 32 ♔e3

Because of my favourable pawn structure, my king is beginning to call the shots, whereas its rival is torn between defending the vulnerable spots on c3 and g2. Had White played actively with 32 ♖a7 he might still have been just about OK, but the key point is that I forced him to make a difficult decision. Very quickly now I get seriously on top.

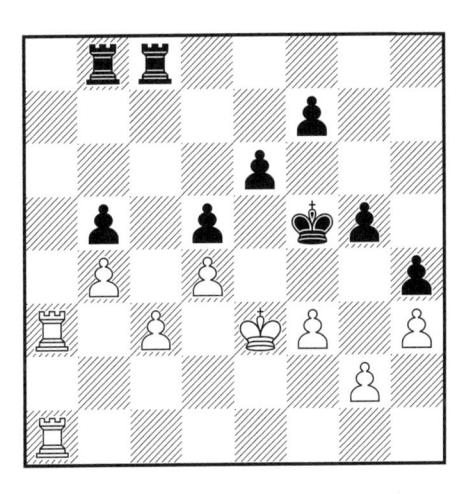

32...♖gc8

33 ♖f1

In my favourite chess book, *Chess For Life*, by Matthew Sadler and Natasha Regan, Matthew suggests that White might just about survive by putting his king back to d3, and meeting 33...♔f4 with 34 ♖a7.

33...♖c7

Here Matthew points out that 33...♖a8 would have been quicker, because of the tactic 34 ♖fa1 ♖xc3+!.

34 f4

Nobody likes to sit by passively and watch his opponent steadily make progress. If Ilfeld just waits, the game might have continued 34 ♖f2 ♖bc8 35 ♖c2 ♖c4, and now there are only two ways to prevent 36...♖xb4: 36 ♔d3 allows further inroads with 36...♔f4, while 36 ♖b3 allows domination of the position by 36...♖a8.

34...g4 35 hxg4+ ♔xg4 36 ♖f3 ♖bb7

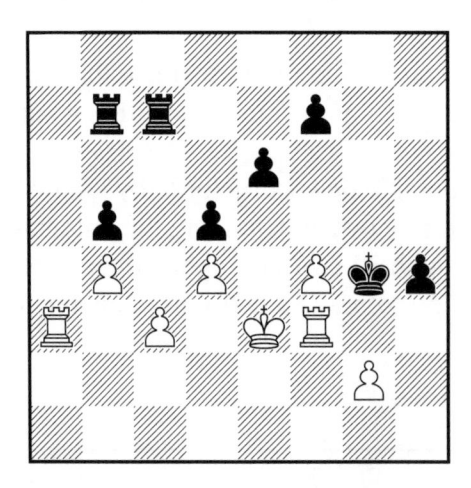

White has been obliged to relinquish the coordination between his rooks allowing me to seize the a-file decisively.

37 ♔f2 ♖a7 38 ♖xa7 ♖xa7 39 f5

It is now far too late for passive defence: 39 ♔g1 ♖a2 40 ♔f1 ♖c2 and White is in zugzwang: 41 ♔g1 ♖e2 followed by ...♖e4 wins.

Until this point my work has been achieved mostly by marginally favourable exchanges and by executing a number of micro plans, but now precise calculation is needed.

39...exf5 40 ♖e3 ♖a2+ 41 ♔f1 f6 42 ♖e6 ♖c2 43 ♖xf6 ♖xc3 44 ♖d6 h3 45 gxh3+ ♔f3

(See diagram overleaf)

Look at the kings now, and all because of the weaknesses in White's pawn structure. I can now combine mating threats with picking off his pawns.

Ilfeld-Arkell

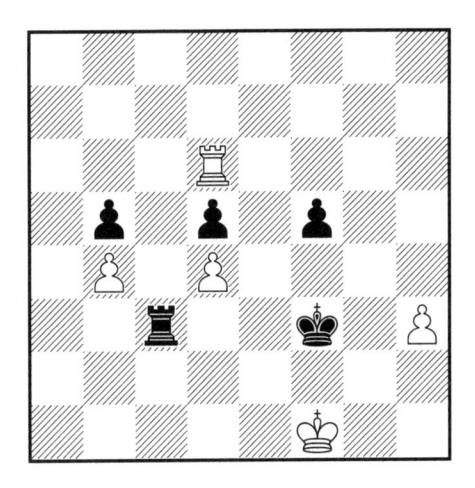

46 ♔g1

If 46 ♔e1 I was ready with 46...♔e3, threatening both mate in one and 46...♔xd4.

46...♖c1+ 47 ♔h2 ♖c2+ 48 ♔g1 ♖g2+

A similar pattern is repeated: 49 ♔f1 ♖d2 threatens both mate and 50...♖xd4.

49 ♔h1 ♖d2

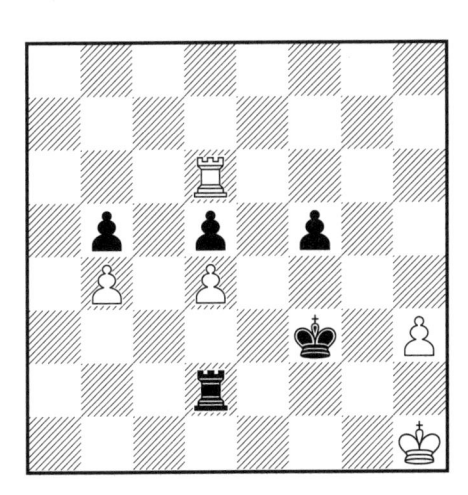

For the third time I use the mate threat to win his d-pawn. 50 ♖xd5 ♔g3 now leads to mate, so finally he is forced to abandon d4, and all his pawns, in fact.

50 ♖f6 ♔g3 51 ♖g6+ ♔xh3 52 ♖h6+ ♔g3 53 ♖g6+ ♔f3 54 ♖b6 ♖xd4 0-1

Because 55 ♖xb5 again allows his king to be ensnared, White resigned.

17. Arkell-Ernst

Here my only advantage was space, but this led to a small structural edge, and, finally, the superiority of bishop over knight when there are passed pawns on both wings. This game also featured a rare early e2-e4 lunge, breaking with my traditional f2 and e3 pawn preference.

Keith Arkell - Sipke Ernst
HZ Open, Vlissingen 2003
Queen's Gambit Accepted

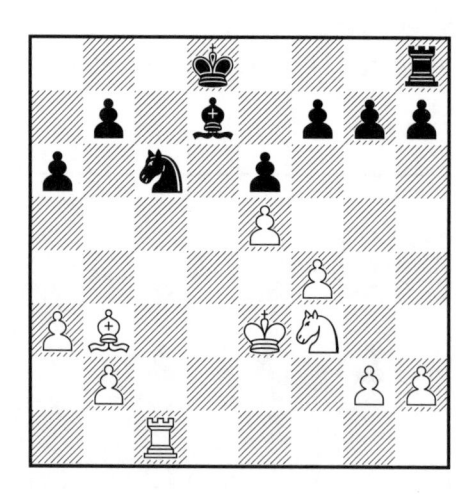

1 d4 d5 2 ♘f3 c5 3 c4 dxc4 4 e4 cxd4 5 ♕xd4 ♕xd4 6 ♘xd4 a6 7 ♘c3 e6 8 ♗xc4 ♗d7 9 ♗e3 ♘c6 10 ♘xc6 ♗xc6 11 f3 ♖c8 12 ♖c1 ♘f6 13 ♔f2 ♗b4 14 ♗b3 ♘d7 15 a3 ♗c5 16 ♘e2 ♗xe3+ 17 ♔xe3 ♘b6 18 ♘d4 ♗d7 19 ♖xc8+ ♘xc8 20 ♖c1 ♔d8 21 e5 ♘e7 22 f4 ♘c6 23 ♘f3

Thus far the play has been very predictable, with White holding a small advantage in the form of more space. I must retain the knights if I'm to have any chance of creating difficulties for him.
23...♔e7 24 ♘g5 f6
Naturally my opponent doesn't want to sit there and watch the knight hop into the holes on his dark squares, but I was pleased to see this loosening of his pawn structure.
25 exf6+ gxf6 26 ♘e4 ♖c8 27 ♖c5 e5
Aimed against my threat of ♖h5.

28 fxe5 ♘xe5 29 ♖xc8 ♗xc8 30 ♔d4 b6 31 ♗g8 h6 32 ♘c3

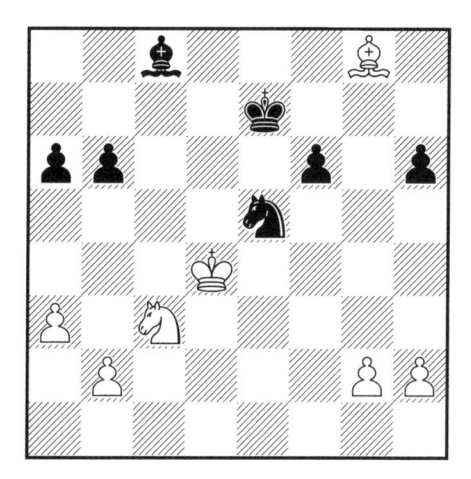

Clearly Black is on the defensive, but I was expecting Sipke to find some accurate moves around here, and that my advantage would fizzle out.
32...♔d6 33 ♘d5 ♘d7 34 g3 b5 35 b4 ♘e5 36 h4 f5 37 ♘f4 ♗b7 38 ♗e6 ♗e4 39 ♗c8 a5 40 bxa5 ♘c6+ 41 ♔c3 ♘xa5 42 ♘e2

42 ♔b4 looks good, but Black has 42...♘c6+ and the b-pawn is taboo.
42...♘c4 43 ♔b4 ♘e3

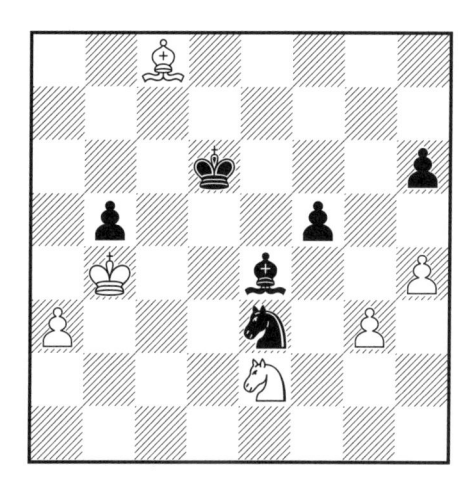

I was quite happy to see this move as I had been bluffing a bit and was well aware that 43...♘b6 44 ♗a6 ♘d5+ 45 ♔a5 (and not 45 ♔xb5? ♘c7+ 46 ♔b6 ♘xa6 47 ♔xa6 ♗d3+) 45...♘c7 46 ♘c3 would have left me with very few winning chances after 46...♘xa6 47 ♔xa6 ♔c5 48 ♘xb5 ♗d3 49 a4 ♔b4 50 ♔b6 ♔xa4.

Arkell's Endings

44 ♘d4

Now I could at least dream that I might be able to do something with my passed a-pawn.

44...♔e5 45 ♘xb5 ♘f1 46 g4 f4 47 ♘c3

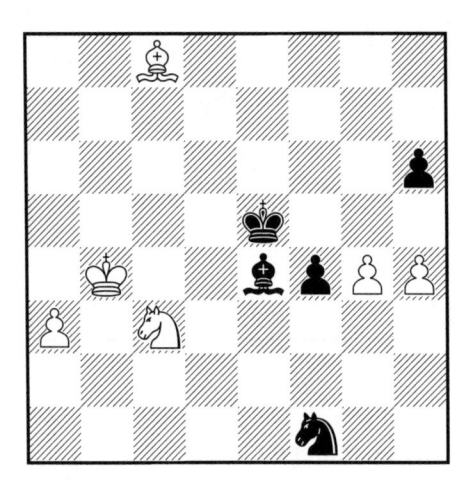

After Black's 43rd move we were pretty much bound to reach this position, and I was growing optimistic about my chances if I could swap knight for bishop. I hadn't done much analysis, but was well aware that a knight can struggle when chasing down a passed a-pawn. On top of that I have the option of g4-g5 to distract his pieces at some point.

47...♘d2

I was sure this was a mistake. If he had preserved his bishop I still expected the game to end in a draw. He can distract me sufficiently with his active king and passed pawn to deal with my remaining two pawns, and can eventually sacrifice a piece for the a-pawn.

48 ♘xe4 ♘xe4 49 a4

I still thought that some exact sequence of moves might hold for Black, but I was equally sure that he had made his situation unnecessarily precarious.

49...f3 50 ♗a6 ♘f6

There isn't time for Black to win a piece: 50...♘d2 51 a5 ♔d6 52 g5 hxg5 53 hxg5 f2 (or 53...♘e4 54 g6 f2 55 g7 ♘f6 56 ♗c4 ♔c7 57 ♔c3, and I can patiently collect his f-pawn before veering towards his knight) 54 g6. I've given concrete variations here, but at the time I knew from experience that these lines should be quite hopeless for Black.

51 g5 hxg5 52 hxg5

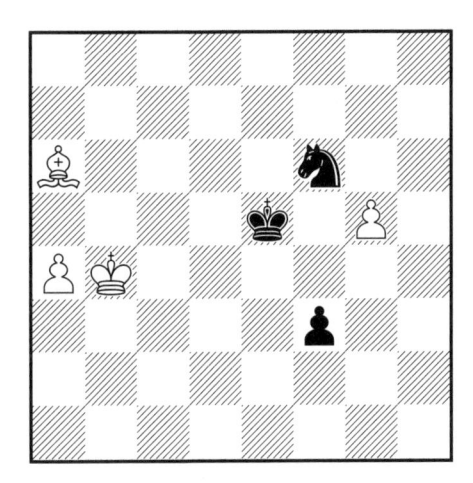

Such positions bear out strongly the advantages of bishop over knight. The knight can only influence a small segment of the board, whereas the bishop has tentacles everywhere.

52...♘d5+ 53 ♔c5 ♘c3 54 a5 ♘e4+ 55 ♔b6 ♘c3 56 ♗f1 ♔d6 57 g6 ♘a4+ 58 ♔b7 ♘c5+ 59 ♔c8 ♔e7 60 ♔c7 1-0

18. Arkell-Spreeuw

A demonstration of why you need not always fear pawn exchanges. With rook and bishop versus the opposite-coloured bishop and knight, no pawns are required because you can go directly for mate with the pieces.

> **Keith Arkell - Jaap Spreeuw**
> British League (4NCL), West Bromwich 2003
> *Slav Defence*

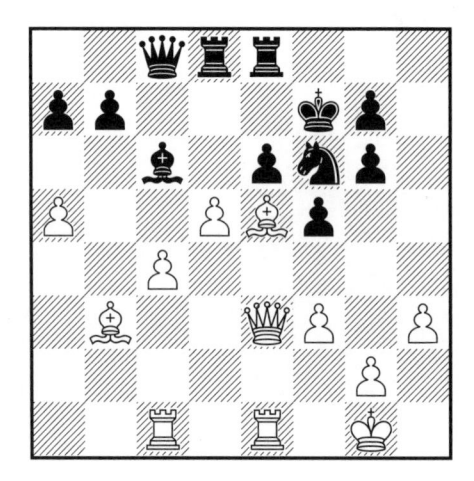

1 d4 d5 2 c4 c6 3 ♘f3 ♘f6 4 ♘c3 dxc4 5 a4 ♗f5 6 ♘h4 ♗c8 7 ♘f3 ♗f5 8 e3 e6 9 ♗xc4 ♗b4 10 0-0 ♘bd7 11 ♗d2 0-0 12 h3 c5 13 ♕b3 ♕b6 14 ♘h4 cxd4 15 exd4 ♗xc3 16 bxc3 ♗e4 17 a5 ♕c7 18 ♗e2 ♖fd8 19 c4 ♘f8 20 ♗e3 ♖d7 21 ♕b4 ♖c8 22 ♖ac1 ♕b8 23 ♖fd1 ♖cd8 24 ♕c3 ♖c8 25 ♗g5 ♘e8 26 ♕e3 ♗c6 27 ♗f4 ♕a8 28 ♗e5 ♘g6 29 ♘xg6 hxg6 30 ♗g4 f5 31 ♗e2 ♔f7 32 ♖e1 ♘f6 33 ♗d1 ♖e8 34 ♗b3 ♖dd8 35 f3 ♕c8 36 d5!

I have had a very good position for much of the game, but it is often difficult to decide whether such a radical move is winning by force. I thought it probably was though.
36...exd5 37 cxd5 ♘xd5 38 ♕xa7 ♕d7 39 a6 ♖a8 40 ♕c5 ♖xa6 41 ♗d6 ♖e6 42 ♖xe6 ♕xe6 43 ♔f2

To this day I have no real idea why I didn't simply settle for 43 ♖d1 when Black can resign. At least this way an interesting endgame arises.
43...♖b6 44 ♕xb6 ♘xb6 45 ♗xe6+ ♔xe6 46 ♗f8 ♔f7 47 ♗c5 ♘d5 48 h4 ♘f4

86

49 ♖d1 ♘e6 50 ♗d6 ♔f6 51 ♖e1 ♔f7 52 ♗e5 ♗d5 53 g4

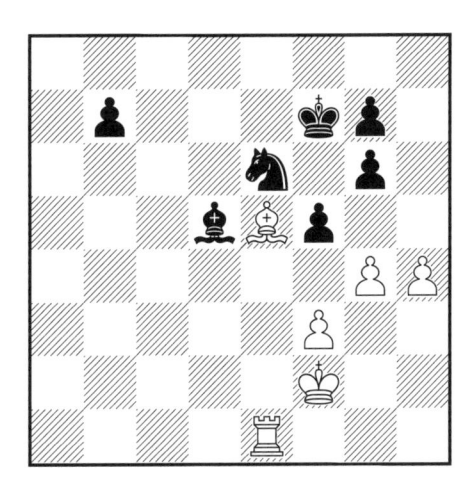

I quickly understood that I would eventually need my king to participate in a mating attack, and the only way seemed to be via the central squares. I couldn't penetrate through the queenside (♔b4-a5-b6-a7-b8-c8), as he could create a fortress with bishop and knight after ...♗c6. However, I didn't fear pawn exchanges, as I was aware of the difficulties of defending rook and bishop versus knight and opposite-coloured bishop.

53...fxg4 54 fxg4 ♗c6 55 ♔g3 ♗d5 56 ♖f1+

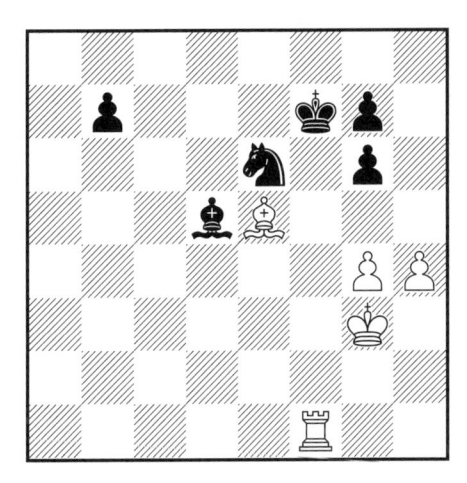

One idea which caught my attention had he now moved to the e-file was firstly to secure my king from knight checks, and then play h5 gxh5; gxh5 followed by ♗xg7 and h5-h6, using the well-known promotion trick which exploits the awkwardness of the defending knight on g7. It is helpful to have a store of these little stratagems which aid your calculations by offering short-cuts. To defend against this idea, he would need to put his bishop on the b1-h7 diagonal.

56...♔g8 57 h5 gxh5 58 gxh5 ♗c6 59 ♔g4 ♗e4 60 ♖e1 ♗c6 61 ♖f1 ♗d5 62 ♗c3

Eventually I will need f5, e5, and d6 for my king to march through.

62...♗c6 63 ♔f5 ♗d7

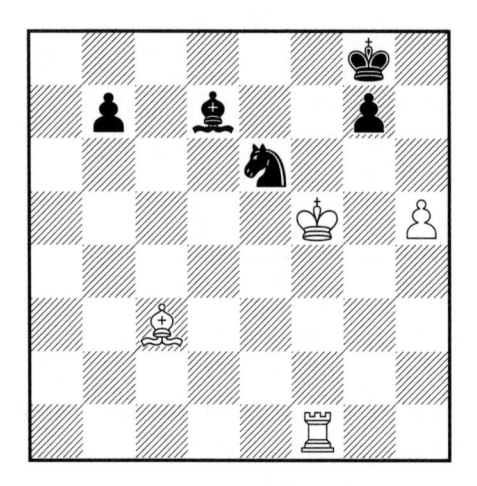

64 ♖d1

I found 64 ♔e5 ♘g5 slightly troublesome, so I shuffled around a bit first. In such cases it rarely does any harm to be patient. In fact these positions highlight rather well why a rook is generally more valuable than a bishop or knight in the endgame, and Black will have to take care in choosing the right squares for his pieces.

64...♘c5+ 65 ♔f4 ♗e8 66 ♖d5 ♘e6+ 67 ♔g4 ♗c6 68 ♖d2 ♔f7 69 ♖f2+ ♔g8 70 ♔f5 ♗d7 71 ♔e5 ♘d8

Compared to the position on my 64th move, I can now meet 71...♘g5 with 72 ♖g2, whereas previously my rook was on f1 and 64 ♔e5 ♘g5 65 ♖g1 would have allowed a fork on f3.

72 ♖g2 ♗e8 73 h6

Obliterating the king's defences and snaring Black in a mating attack.

73...♘f7+ 74 ♔e6 ♘xh6 75 ♔e7 ♗c6 76 ♖xg7+ ♔h8 77 ♔f8 1-0

19. Arkell-Palliser

My records confirm that I have won the endgame rook and bishop versus rook more than twenty times – in fact every time I have reached it and including three wins against IM Lawrence Cooper. I therefore feel bound to include an example or two in this book. However, it is not an easy ending to annotate 'live', so to speak, because essentially you know that it should be a draw, so your only task is to try to lure your opponent into a mistake.

Keith Arkell - Richard Palliser
Monarch Assurance Open, Port Erin 2000
Sicilian Defence

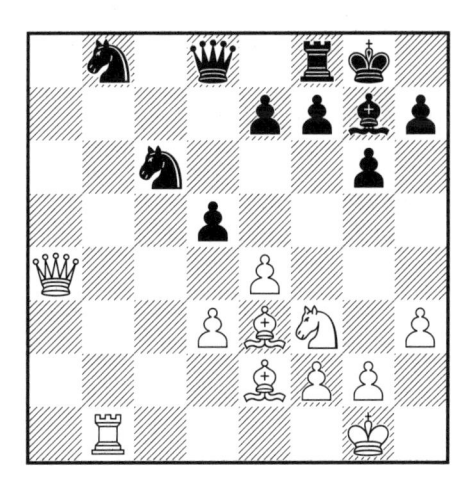

1 e4 c5 2 ♘f3 d6 3 c4 ♗g4 4 ♗e2 ♘c6 5 d3 g6 6 ♘bd2 ♗g7 7 h3 ♗d7 8 ♖b1 a6 9 a3 b5 10 b4 cxb4 11 axb4 a5 12 bxa5 bxc4 13 ♘xc4 ♘xa5 14 ♘b6 ♖b8 15 ♗e3 ♘f6 16 ♘xd7 ♘xd7 17 ♖xb8 ♕xb8 18 ♕a4+ ♘ac6 19 0-0 0-0 20 ♖b1 d5

Clearly I stand better here, but with very little in the way of pawn weaknesses to aim at, and an attack against the king being out of the question, my only prospect is to play against my opponent's passive pieces.

21 ♖b7 ♕d6 22 ♕b5 dxe4 23 dxe4 ♘d7 24 ♕d5 ♘f6

At last a concession, but only a very minor one.

25 ♕xd6 exd6 26 ♘d2 d5 27 ♗b5 ♘d8 28 ♖a7 ♘e6

He had to deal with my threat of 29 ♗c5, but now I can at least unbalance the pawn structure.

29 e5 ♘e4 30 ♘f3 ♖d8 31 ♘d4 ♘xd4

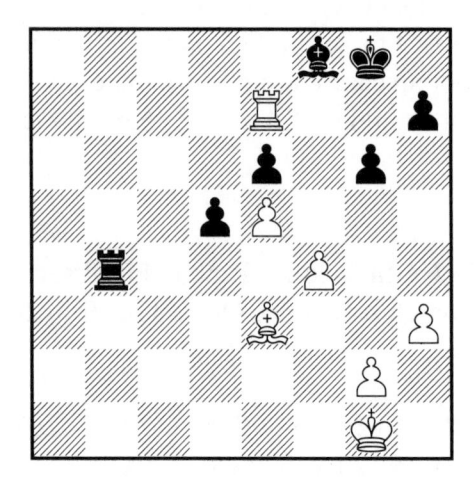

Not 31...♗xe5? 32 ♘c6, winning the exchange.

32 ♗xd4 ♘g5 33 ♗d7 ♖b8 34 f4 ♘e6 35 ♗xe6 fxe6 36 ♖e7 ♖b4 37 ♗e3 ♗f8

This is a very good move, after which Black really shouldn't have any problems at all. Richard has correctly calculated that he will gain far too much counterplay after 38 ♖xe6 d4.

38 ♖d7 ♖b3 39 ♗a7 ♖b4 40 g3 ♖b3 41 ♔g2 h5 42 g4

It was round about here that I decided my only practical chance lay in trying to head for rook and bishop versus rook.

42...hxg4 43 hxg4 ♖c3 44 f5 gxf5 45 gxf5 exf5 46 e6 ♖c6 47 e7 ♗xe7 48 ♖xe7

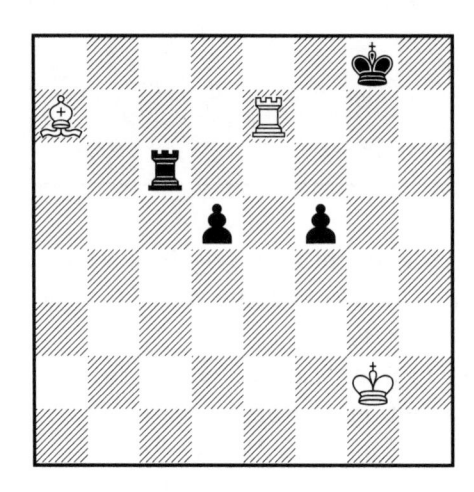

The next stage is to mop up the two pawns. I recall a game I once had with

GM Jacob Murey in which he only had a g-pawn and rook against my rook and bishop, but he defended so well that I wasn't even able to force his pawn off him. This time they fall quite easily, and possibly even by force.

48...♖g6+ 49 ♔f3 ♖g7 50 ♖e8+ ♔f7 51 ♖e5 ♔f6 52 ♗d4 ♖g4 53 ♖xd5+ ♔e6 54 ♖e5+ ♔d6 55 ♗b2 ♖b4 56 ♖e2 ♔d5 57 ♗g7 ♖e4 58 ♖a2 ♔e6 59 ♗h6 ♖b4 60 ♖a6+ ♔d5 61 ♗g5 ♖b1 62 ♗f6 ♖f1+ 63 ♔e3 ♖e1+ 64 ♔f4 ♖f1+ 65 ♔g5 ♖g1+ 66 ♔xf5

I now had 50 moves in which to either deliver checkmate or win Black's rook.

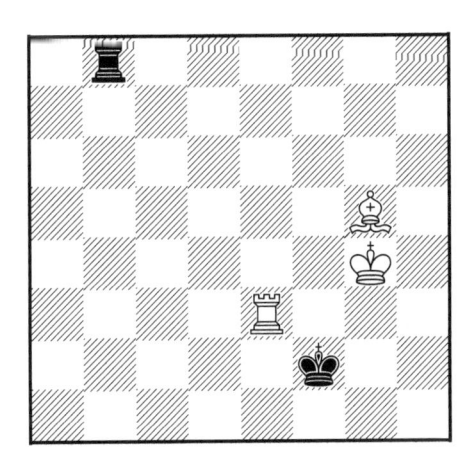

66...♖f1+ 67 ♔g6 ♖g1+ 68 ♔f7 ♖b1 69 ♖a5+ ♔e4 70 ♖e5+ ♔d3 71 ♔e6 ♖b6+ 72 ♔f5 ♖b8 73 ♖d5+ ♔e3 74 ♗g5+ ♔f3 75 ♖d3+ ♔e2 76 ♖e3+ ♔f2 77 ♔g4

And suddenly we have reached the point where Black has to take care.

77...♖g8

Pinning the bishop is a reliable drawing method, preventing the advance of my king towards its opposite number when on its first rank. Another well-known method, the 'second rank defence', is also possible here, utilising stalemate. For example, imagine White with ♔f3, ♗e3 and ♖a8 against ♔f1 and ♖b2, when Black saves the day with 1...♖f2+.

78 ♖e5 ♖g7 79 ♖e8 ♖g6 80 ♖f8+ ♔e2 81 ♖d8 ♖g7 82 ♖d2+ ♔e1 83 ♖g2

This move is more cunning than it looks. It is mostly a psychological trap. I am signalling my intention to bring my king into the attack with ♔f3, when the rook will be defending the bishop. It is natural that Palliser will therefore want to kick my rook away from this square for the pin on the bishop to have any value. Hence his next move, which I was encouraging him to play:

83...♔f1 84 ♖a2 ♖g8?

One careless move at the end of a long game and suddenly it's all over. A reliable drawing method would have been 84...♖d7 85 ♔f3 ♖d3+, when 86 ♗e3 leads nowhere because 86...♔e1 prepares to run after 87 ♖h2 ♔d1, or to block 87 ♖a1+ with 87...♖d1.

85 ♔f3 1-0

And now we can see why I wanted to induce ...♔f1. My bishop is immune from capture because I threaten mate. Had Richard tested me, the finish might have been 85...♖e8 86 ♗f4 ♖e7 87 ♖b2 (I want to use zugzwang to force Black's rook on to its first rank) 87...♖e8 88 ♖h2 ♖g8 (or 88...♔g1 89 ♖h7, threatening 90 ♗e3+, and if 89...♖f8 90 ♖a7) 89 ♗h6 (this is why White wants the black rook on the back rank, so that through zugzwang it can be lured into further trouble on its third rank) 89...♖g6 90 ♗e3 ♖f6+ 91 ♗f4 ♖g6 (or 91...♔g1 92 ♖a2) 92 ♖f2+.

The point of zugzwanging the black rook on to its third rank can be seen in the line 92...♔e1 93 ♖c2, when 93...♖d6 has been ruled out. However, even after 92...♔g1 93 ♖a2 ♔h1 94 ♖a5 (94 ♖a8 ♖g8 is a pest), it will soon be mate. I learnt all this a long time ago, but need to revise it every so often in case I need to play it out quickly.

20. Arkell-Ward

This was a gritty scrap in which my wily grandmaster opponent, by defending resourcefully, kept my advantage to a minimum for much of the time. Finally, I triumphed in a complex rook and pawn endgame.

Keith Arkell - Chris Ward
British Championship, Aberystwyth 2014
Ragozin Defence

1 ♘f3 d5 2 d4 ♘f6 3 c4 e6 4 cxd5 exd5 5 ♘c3 ♗b4 6 ♕a4+ ♘c6 7 ♗g5 0-0 8 a3

It was a bit naive to play this so early since I will now have problems getting castled. Today I am scoring well with 8 e3 h6 9 ♗xf6 ♕xf6 10 ♗e2 to meet 10...♕g6 by 11 0-0 ♗h3 12 ♘e1. My pieces are better than they look here because the knight is only two hops away from the excellent f4-square, and my bishop will be perfectly happy on f3.

8...♗xc3+ 9 bxc3 h6 10 ♗xf6 ♕xf6 11 e3 ♕g6

This is the key move and I now stand worse.

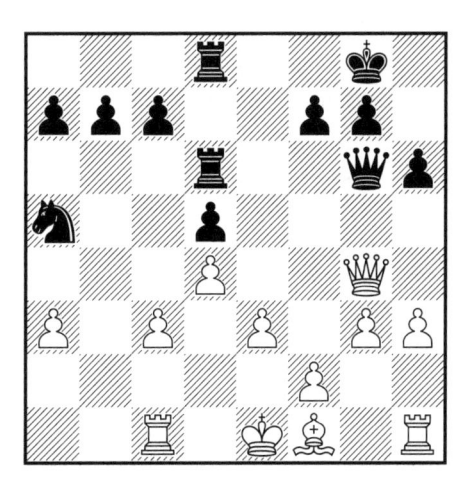

12 ♖c1 ♖d8 13 g3 ♖d6 14 ♕d1 ♗g4 15 h3 ♗xf3 16 ♕xf3 ♘a5 17 ♕g4 ♖ad8

I was very pleased to see this move. If Chris had played 17...♕h7 I would still have had plenty of untangling to do.

18 ♕xg6 ♖xg6 19 ♖b1

Just in time, as I can't let him play ...♖b6 for free.

19...♖b6 20 ♖b4 ♘c6 21 ♖b5 ♖d6 22 ♔d2 ♖xb5 23 ♗xb5 ♘a5 24 ♔c2

I was feeling very confident by now. Almost imperceptibly I'm getting on top. I have a nice-looking bishop, and an extra central pawn with which I can organise future breaks.

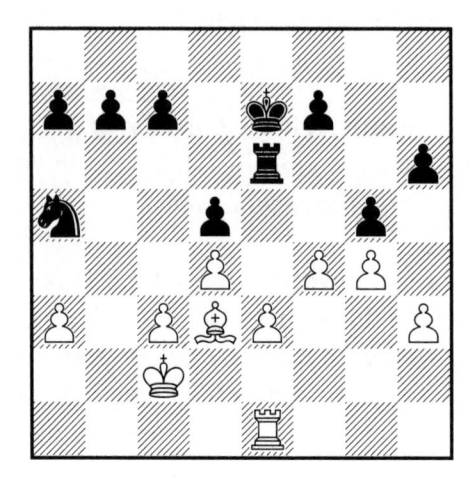

24...♖f6 25 f4 ♖e6 26 ♖e1 ♔f8 27 ♗d3 ♔e7 28 g4 g5

At some point Black has to put the lid on my space gains. If he waits, I will play h3-h4, and then either g4-g5 or h4-h5.

29 f5 ♖b6 30 e4

Not the difficult decision I normally have to make about the best time to play this aggressive thrust...

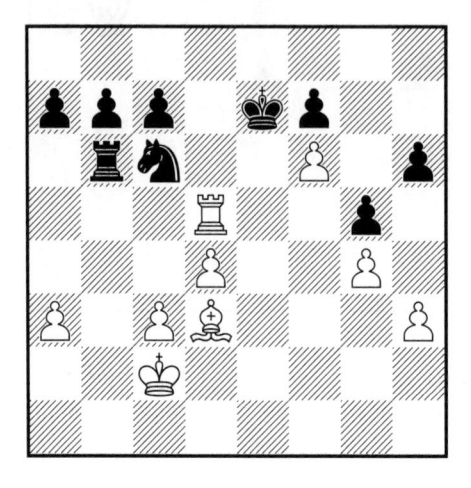

30...dxe4 31 ♖xe4+ ♔d7 32 ♖e5 ♘c6 33 ♖d5+ ♔e7 34 f6+

Whereas this, on the other hand, was quite a tough choice. I had many ways to improve my position, such as 34 a4, or putting the rook back on c5 and then trying something else. I could also have considered 34 ♗e2 to see whether Black is in some kind of zugzwang. 34 f6+ is very committal, as it swaps one type of advantage for another, but by indirectly exchanging pawns I gain even more space for my pieces, and the d-pawn becomes passed.

34...♔xf6 35 ♖d7 ♘e7 36 ♖xc7 ♘d5 37 ♖d7 ♘e3+

This move and his next are forced, to prevent a deadly ♗c4. I was sure a GM and former British Champion wouldn't go down tamely by 37...♘f4 38 ♗c4 ♘e6 39 a4 a5 40 ♗d5, when the b-pawn falls, leaving me with two connected passed pawns.

38 ♔d2 ♔e6 39 ♖c7 ♘d5 40 ♗c4 ♔d6

If instead 40...♖b2+ 41 ♔c1 ♖b6 42 ♔c2 then 42...♔d6 would be forced anyway, because of the threat to win a piece by 43 ♖c5 ♖d6 44 ♔d3 followed by ♖xd5 and ♔e4.

41 ♖xf7 ♖b2+ 42 ♔c1 ♖h2 43 ♗xd5 ♔xd5 44 ♖xb7 ♖xh3 45 ♔c2 ♖g3

Chris has defended extremely well. My advantage persists, but at no point did I think I was winning by force.

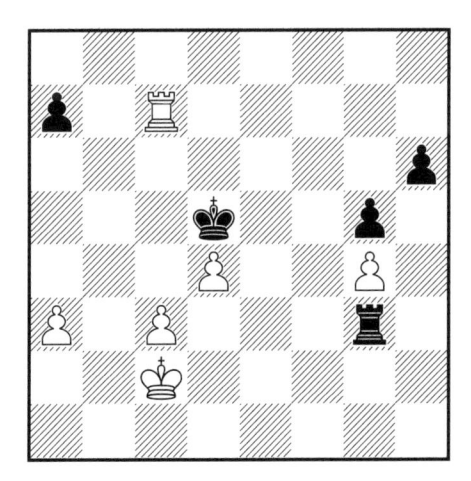

46 ♖d7+ ♔c4 47 ♖c7+ ♔d5

I found this position very difficult to analyse. I didn't want to abandon my g-pawn without gaining his h-pawn in exchange, and I also felt strongly that my passed pawns would have to start moving fairly quickly. The first step was to nudge his king away.

48 ♖c5+ ♔e4

I can't remember whether I was more concerned by this move or 48...♔d6. Against the latter I intended 49 ♖a5 ♖xg4 50 ♖a6+ and 51 ♖xh6.

49 ♖e5+ ♔f4 50 ♖e6 ♖xg4 51 ♖xh6 ♖h4 52 ♖f6+ ♔e4 53 ♖e6+ ♔f5 54 ♖e8 g4 55 ♖g8 ♖h3

He wants to keep my king away from the action, and to ease forward with his g-pawn. There is no point now in 56 d5 as 56...♔e5 is awkward, so I brought my king round to try and support the d-pawn.

56 ♔b3 ♖h6

I thought 56...g3 would be too slow after 57 d5. Black's problem is that his king needs to do two things at once: support the advance of his pawn, and restrain mine. The text move is hoping for 57...♖g6.

57 ♔c4 ♖c6+

Obviously my last move prevented 57...♖g6 as I can exchange when my king stops his g-pawn.

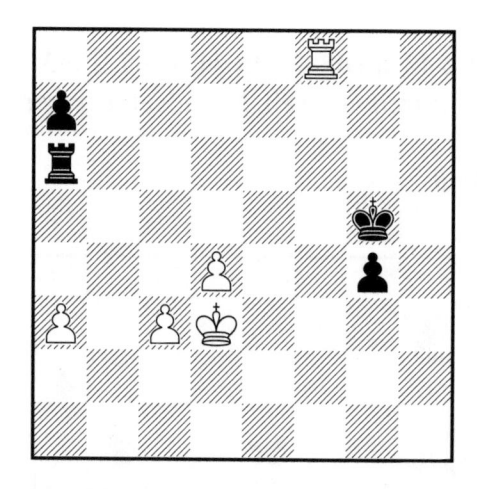

58 ♔d3 ♖a6 59 ♖f8+ ♔g5

At least I'm now able to push my d-pawn, so that whatever the objective assessment might be, Black is bound to have practical problems.

60 d5 ♖xa3

This felt wrong. If Chris was going to save the game I was sure he needed to start with 60...g3.

61 ♔d4 ♖a6 62 ♔e5

Only now was I certain that I would win. After my following move the ...♖g6 resource will be eliminated.

62...g3 63 d6 ♖a5+ 64 ♔e4 ♖a1 65 ♖g8+ ♔h4 66 d7 ♖e1+ 67 ♔f3 1-0

At John Nunn's 60th Birthday Blitz taking on that legend of American chess, Yasser Seirawan. Both flags were on zero when we agreed a draw! Photo: John Saunders

True gentleman and long-time British number one Michael Adams whom I have played countless times over the last 40 years. Photo: Fiona Steil-Antoni

I always enjoy playing on the Isle of Man. Here I'm on the wrong side of a rook ending, but managed to hold against the current women's world champion Ju Wenjun. Photo: John Saunders

Another encounter from the Isle of Man. I'm pictured en route to victory in 2014 over Julio Granda Zuniga (Game 32), who likes theory even less than I do. Photo: Fiona Steil-Antoni

After Simon Williams and Nigel Short battled each other to a standstill in the last round of this year's Bunratty Masters, I was left to grind down Vlastimil Hort in a double rook ending. Photo: Fiona Steil-Antoni

Maxime Vachier-Lagrave was a teenager when he participated in the EU Championship of 2008 in Liverpool, but already rated 2681 when we played (Game 2). Photo: CHESS Magazine Archive

How post-mortems used to be! Mihai Suba (seated centre) analyses with endgame gurus Mark Dvoretsky (right) and Jonathan Speelman (left), as Jon Manley looks on. Photo: CHESS Magazine Archive

Another legendary American player who I enjoyed locking horns with was Robert Byrne. The former candidate suffered with rook against rook and bishop (Game 33). Photo: CHESS Magazine Archive

My long-term rival and very good friend, Mark Hebden, against whom I've played about 150 times, spanning some 41 years. See Game 7.
Photo: CHESS Magazine Archive

What's that opening on the board? No, I didn't start 1 b4, but this is one of my pet lines, the so-called Speckled Egg, an anti-King's Indian.
Photo: Bob Jones

A moment I'll never forget. I'm pictured receiving the gold medal from Garry Kasparov no less at the 2014 European Senior Championships in Porto. Photo: Author's own collection

When we're not in action chess players enjoy the social side of life, and I was delighted when my soulmate Selina stayed with me in Paignton during a return to the UK from Sydney. Photo: Selina Khoo

Sporting a custom-made cowboy hat from Nebraska, and surrounded by (left to right) Simon Williams, Fiona Steil-Antoni, Selina Khoo and Blair Connell. Photo: Author's own collection

It's hard not to smile when you're in Bunratty, not least on a crisp February day. Here I'm out for a stroll with Alex Lopez, Fiona Steil-Antoni, and Anuurai Sainbayar. Photo: Fiona Steil-Antoni

Win or lose, it's always a delight to represent Cheddleton in the 4NCL. Pictured (from left to right): David Howell, Fiona Steil-Antoni, myself, Ezra Kirk, Jonathan Hawkins, David Eggleston and Simon Williams. Photo: Fiona Steil-Antoni

Combining the 'Rocky Horror Picture show' with 'Tales from the Crypt', I'm joined at Ginger GM's innovative fancy dress blitz tournament by Fiona Steil-Antoni, David Howell and Tamas Fodor. Photo: John Saunders

Peripatetic chess players occasionally go on real holidays. Here Lizzy Pähtz and I spent a week at the lovely setting of Muckrach Castle in Scotland. Photo: Author's own collection

A post-tournament toast after sharing first place at Doncaster with brother Nick, who has returned strongly after 30 years away, time spent on his business and family. Photo: Author's own collection

21. Arkell-Bradbury

In this game against an English IM who returned to active chess a few years ago, I applied my tried and tested methods in the Carlsbad structure, which arises after my favourite exchange with cxd5, to grind out a win.

Keith Arkell - Neil Bradbury
EACU Open, Newmarket 2019
Queen's Gambit Declined

1 ♘f3 ♘f6 2 c4 e6 3 ♘c3 d5 4 cxd5 exd5 5 d4 c6 6 ♗g5 ♗f5 7 e3 ♘bd7 8 ♗d3 ♗xd3 9 ♕xd3

Theory dismisses this position as about equal, or at best only very slightly better for White, but my familiarity with the arising structures gives me a good chance to gain the upper hand.

9...♗e7 10 0-0 h6

Normally Black would castle here, but now, by capturing on f6, I would be able to follow up with either 12 ♘e5 or 12 b4.

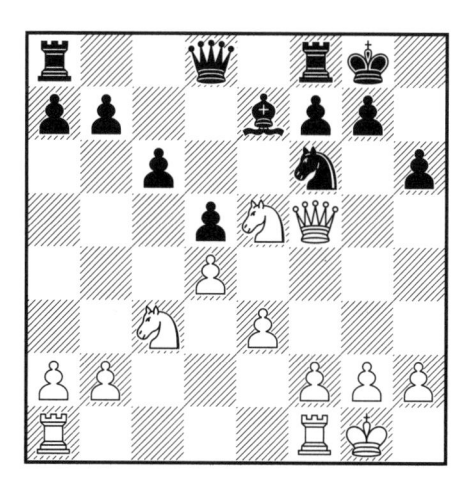

11 ♗xf6 ♘xf6 12 ♘e5 0-0 13 ♕f5

This doesn't look very ambitious, but I am playing for an endgame in which I can probe on the queenside without having to worry about counterplay.

13...♕c8 14 ♕xc8 ♖axc8

My opponent doesn't make any serious mistakes in this game, but this felt like a minor one since the action will most likely take place on the a-, b- and c-files, so the

other recapture was likely preferable.
15 ♖fc1 ♗d6 16 ♘d3 ♖fe8 17 b4

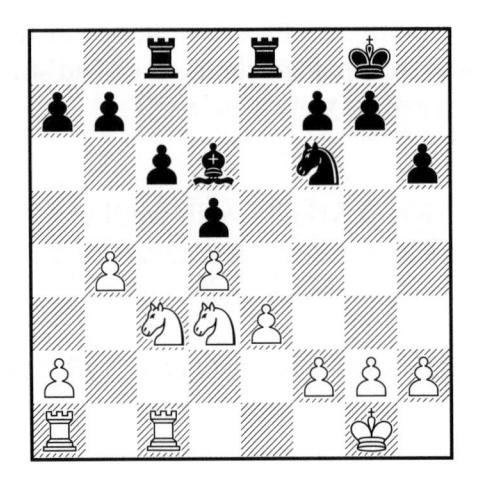

17...♘d7

I had calculated 17...♘e4 18 ♘xe4 dxe4 19 ♘c5 b6 (or 19...♗xc5 20 ♖xc5 when b4-b5 will follow, with overwhelming positional pressure) 20 ♘a6 with the plan of attacking Black's c-pawn.

18 a4

I wasn't sure about the consequences of 18 b5 c5 19 ♘xd5 cxd4 20 exd4 ♖xc1 21 ♖xc1 and then something like 21...♖e2. I'm a pawn up, but it all looks a bit loose, so instead I formulated a plan to fix c6 as a long-term weakness.

18...♘b6 19 a5 ♘c4 20 b5

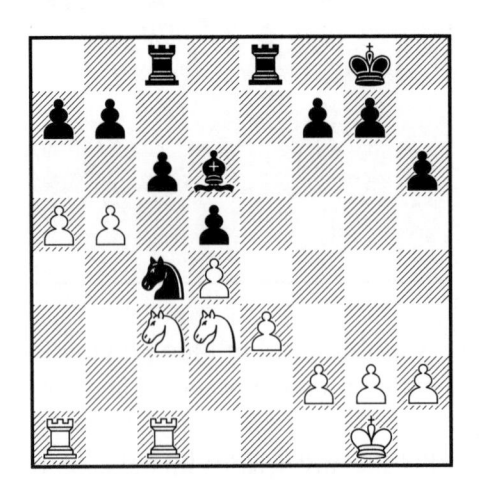

Threatening to undermine Black's whole queenside with a5-a6, so more or less forcing the following sequence.

20...a6 21 bxa6 bxa6 22 ♘a4 ♖b8

22...♘xa5 23 ♘ac5 just plays into my hands.

23 ♘ac5 ♖b5 24 ♘xa6 ♖a8 25 ♘ac5 ♖axa5 26 ♖xa5 ♘xa5

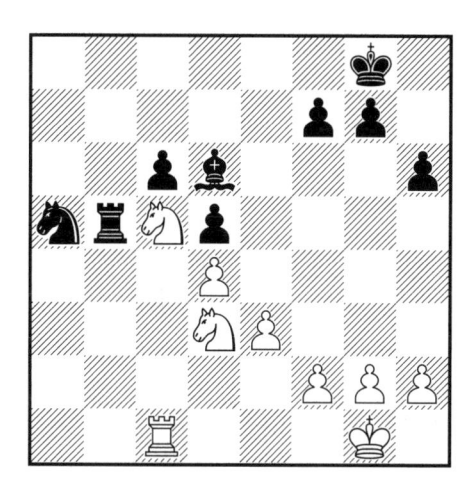

And so we have arrived at base camp – the successful conclusion of the minority attack. I have one pawn island against two; Black has active pieces, so a direct assault against c6 is obviously impossible. The correct procedure therefore is to probe on the kingside in order to inflict a second weakness, or at least to gain some space over there.

27 g4

This is by far the best pawn move. If 27 h4 h5 it will be hard to make progress, as breaks with e3-e4 or g2-g4 will involve ruining my own pawn structure.

27...♘c4 28 ♔g2 ♔f8 29 h4 ♔e7 30 h5

Not only does this move fix a target on g7, but experience of playing these kinds of positions, literally hundreds of times, has taught me that there are certain mating nets Black needs to be wary of.

30...♘b2

I felt this was a little impatient, enabling me to activate my rook. It was better to sit tight and await events.

31 ♖a1 ♘xd3 32 ♖a7+ ♔f6 33 ♘xd3 ♖b3 34 ♘e1 ♖b6

Neil played this quite quickly, but I wasn't sure whether he should be playing 34...c5 instead.

Actually I had a similar game at Harrogate about four months earlier where I managed to win from the structure which would have arisen after ...c5.

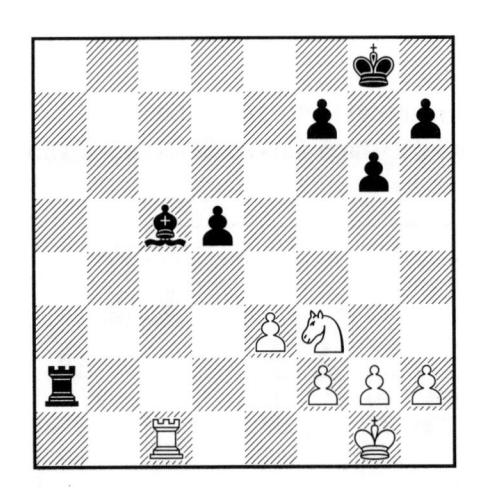

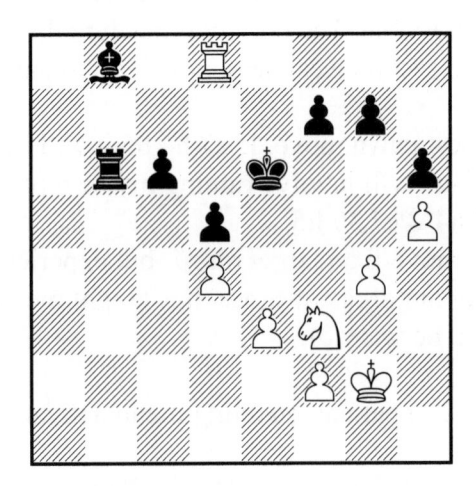

In Arkell-Sumit I was able to exploit my positional trumps as follows: 26 g4 ♖a5 27 ♖d1 ♗e7 28 ♖b1 h6 29 ♔g2 ♗f6 30 ♔g3 ♖a3 31 ♖d1 ♖a5 32 h4 ♗g7 33 ♖b1 ♖a3 34 ♖b8+ ♔h7 35 ♖d8 ♖a5 36 g5 ♖b5 37 ♖d7 ♔g8 38 gxh6 ♗xh6 39 ♘e5 ♖b3 40 ♘xf7 ♗g7 41 ♘g5 ♗e5+ 42 ♔g2 ♖b5 43 f4 ♗c3 44 ♔f3 ♗e1 45 ♘e6 ♗c3 46 ♘c7 ♖b7 47 ♖d8+ ♔f7 48 ♘xd5 ♗f6 49 ♘xf6 ♔xf6 50 ♖d5 ♖h7 51 ♖d6+ 1-0.
35 ♘f3 ♗b8 36 ♖d7 ♔e6 37 ♖d8

My opponent's position has rapidly become critical. I now threaten 38 ♖e8+ ♔f6 39 ♘e5 when he will either be mated or face heavy material losses.
37...♗d6 38 ♖c8

This was a bit lazy. As soon as I had released the rook, I regretted not playing 38 ♖e8+. A few moves earlier I had already calculated such lines as 38...♔f6 39 ♘e5

♖a6 (or 39...♗xe5 40 dxe5+ ♔g5 41 ♔g3 with 42 f4 mate to follow) 40 ♘d7+ ♔g5 41 ♖g8 g6 (41...♔xg4 42 ♖xg7+ ♔xh5 43 ♘f6+ ♔h4 44 ♖g4# won't do) 42 ♖g7, and Black will soon shed too many pawns.

38...♔f6

There was a chance to prolong the game with 38...f5, but I could still keep up the pressure with 39 g5.

39 ♘h4

After this move, heading for f5, I could no longer see any way for Neil to avoid losing material. His c-pawn, g-pawn, bishop, and even his king have come under increasing pressure, all because his pieces were tied down to the defence of the c6-pawn – a product of White's typical minority attack in the Carlsbad structure.

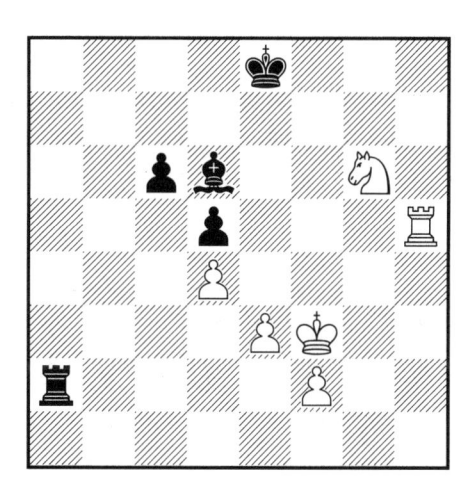

39...g6 40 hxg6 fxg6 41 ♖g8 ♔f7 42 ♖xg6 ♗f8 43 ♔f3 ♖a6 44 g5 hxg5 45 ♖xg5 ♖a2 46 ♖f5+ ♔e8 47 ♘g6 ♗d6 48 ♖h5

I have to be careful to prevent the break ...c5 at a moment when the d-pawn is safe from capture.

48...♔d7 49 ♘h4 ♗b4 50 ♖h7+ ♔e6 51 ♘g6 ♖c2

I was pleased to see this as it enables my knight to reach its ideal post, back on d3. On 51...♗d6 I intended 52 ♖h6 when only an engine might be able to hang on.

52 ♘f4+ ♔d6 53 ♘d3 ♖c4 54 ♖b7 c5 55 ♖b6+ ♔c7 56 dxc5 ♗xc5 57 ♖b5 1-0

Either Black enters a lost king and pawn endgame, or he loses the d-pawn.

22. Arkell-Toma

Here we see the maintenance of a rock-solid f2- and e3-pawn structure, while probing at Black from the wings.

> **Keith Arkell - Katarzyna Toma**
> British Championship, Hull 2018
> *Grünfeld Defence*

1 d4 ♘f6 2 ♘f3 g6 3 c4 ♗g7 4 g3 d5 5 cxd5 ♘xd5 6 ♘c3 ♘b6 7 ♗g2 ♘c6 8 e3

Back in the 1980s I learnt a lot from Jonathan Speelman's handling of these structures. At first I didn't understand why White held back the central pawns, but today I prefer to restrain them while advancing on the queenside to create weaknesses. This is a long-term strategy, which puts a high price on the e- and f-pawns. Even much later in the endgame, when I'm left with four versus three on the kingside, I nearly always go first with my g- and h-pawns, in order to create the most favourable circumstances for the final push with the other two. In this game the strategy succeeds nicely.

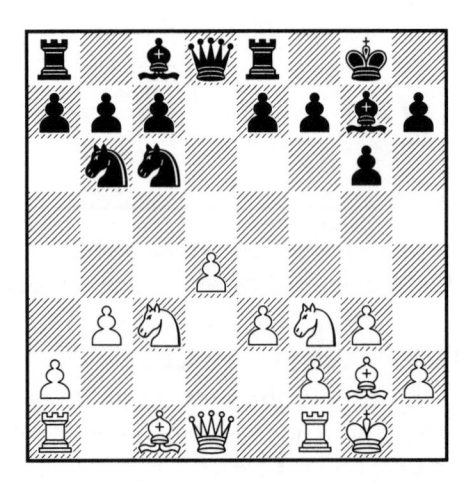

8...0-0 9 0-0 ♖e8 10 b3

In general I tend not to look for an objective advantage out of the opening, but rather to obtain the kind of position which I feel I understand and therefore play well. In this case 10 b3 leads to just such a position.

10...e5 11 ♘xe5 ♘xe5 12 dxe5 ♕xd1

In our game at Hastings 2002/03 Sergey Karjakin preferred to keep the queens

on, but a few moves later he decided that Black's best plan was, after all, to trade them.
13 ♖xd1 ♗xe5 14 ♗b2 c6 15 ♖d2

At this stage I have little interest in doubling rooks on the d-file. This will achieve nothing if Black brings her king to the centre and swaps them all off. Instead, if Katarzyna plays something like 15...a5 or 15...♗e6, the reply is 16 ♘e4, heading for c5.
15...♗f5 16 ♘e2

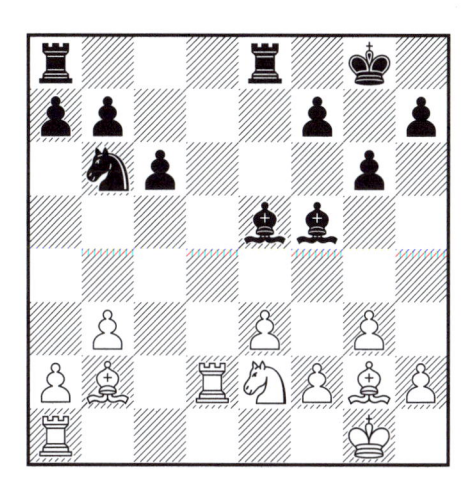

Of course Black has prevented ♘e4, but my more realistic aim is ♘d4, followed by the advance of the b-pawn, aided by the rooks, in order to leave Black with pawn weaknesses. Meanwhile, the structure with pawns on f2 and e3 and the knight on d4 will block any attempt to hurt me on the central files.

16...♗xb2 17 ♖xb2 a5 18 ♘d4 ♗e4 19 f3

This was my first difficult decision. I really dislike making early moves with my e- and f-pawns in this kind of position. In choosing to play 19 f3, I wanted to reduce the bishop's scope.

On another day I might play more simply with 19 ♖c1 ♗xg2 20 ♔xg2, again with the plan of a2-a3, b3-b4, and b4-b5, eventually hunting down Black's remaining isolated pawn. I have a very good score in the resulting endgame of h-, g- and f-pawns each with an extra e-pawn for White. In that scenario I would prefer the knights to remain on the board, if possible, as Black's practical problems will then be greatly magnified.

19...♗d3 20 ♔f2 f5 21 ♖d1 ♗a6 22 f4

To a novice this move is not at all easy to explain since it appears to condemn my e-pawn to exposure on an open file. To understand this advance fully you have to appreciate the potential energy in White's kingside pawn structure. In the long run it will be very hard for my opponent to prevent h2-h3 and g3-g4, leading either to a vulnerable pawn on f5 or, if Black exchanges, the release of the e-pawn which can then ease its way up the board, supported by the f-pawn and the pieces.

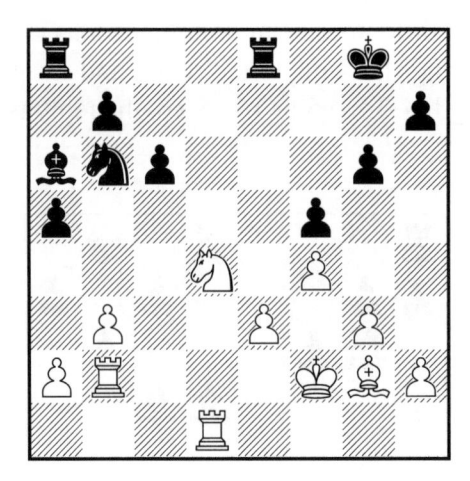

Meanwhile Black can bring very little pressure to bear on the e-file, as my king and one rook will be available for defence. My other rook will then be free to aid the queenside advance. It is also important to add that Black can have no such expansionist plans on the queenside as long as I keep the break ...c5 under lock and key. This is all general thinking, but of course there will still be tactics to deal with.

22...♖ad8 23 ♖bd2

I could have played 23 ♖c2, but didn't want to let her bishop back into the game after 23...♘d5 24 ♗xd5 ♖xd5 25 ♖dc1 ♗d3 26 ♖c5 ♗e4.

23...♖d7

23...♘d5? 24 ♘c2 wins a pawn, whereas 23...c5 allows White control of the board after 24 ♘f3, aiming for e5.

24 ♖c1 ♖ed8

I was pleased that Toma wasn't rushing to play ...♘d5, the move most likely to disrupt my plans.

25 h3 a4 26 g4 axb3 27 axb3 ♘d5 28 ♗xd5+ ♖xd5 29 b4

It was convenient to prevent ...c5 without having to play ♖c2 allowing ...♗d3. Around here I felt I was obtaining a real advantage, as opposed to a position which I simply like playing.

29...fxg4 30 hxg4 h5

I was a little disappointed to see this advance. I expected it though, as Katarzyna Toma is a strong player – a WGM who is hardly going to sit back and let me play on autopilot with g4-g5. In that case all her pieces would have remained restricted, while I would have been free to manoeuvre, and ultimately advance in the centre.

31 ♖g1 ♔f7 32 ♔f3 c5 33 bxc5 ♖xc5 34 gxh5 ♖xh5

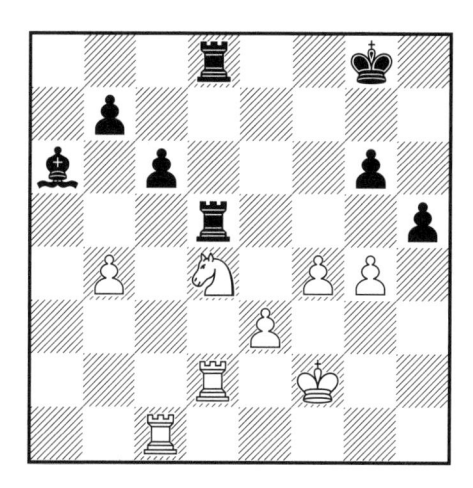

On the one hand, Black has created some activity, but on the other, I still have my monster knight on d4, and two isolated pawns to play against. Overall I was fairly happy here.

35 ♖c2 ♖d7 36 ♖c3 b5

This lunge for freedom is totally understandable as she doesn't just want to wait for me to manoeuvre the knight to e5, or the rook to b6.

37 ♔g3 ♗b7 38 ♖b1 ♗e4

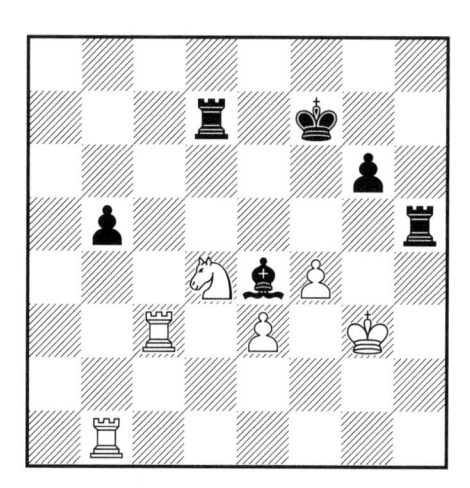

Although I now win the b-pawn, I felt for the first time a little uneasy. My advantage has been slight, but at least there has been plenty of play. Now, however,

there is a real danger that Black can force a simple draw.
39 ♖xb5 ♖xb5 40 ♘xb5 ♖d3 41 ♔g4

My priority is to prevent Black from exchanging her g-pawn.
41...♔f6 42 ♖xd3 ♗xd3 43 ♘d4 ♗e4 44 ♘f3

My next plan is to fix the g-pawn by ♘g5, also supporting e3-e4. I can then activate my king to enable the e-pawn's further advance.
44...♗f5+ 45 ♔g3 ♗c2 46 ♔f2 ♗d3 47 ♘g5 ♗c4 48 e4 ♗b3 49 ♔e3 ♗a2 50 ♔d4 ♗b3 51 ♔c5 ♗c2 52 ♔d5

It would be a trifle silly to allow 52 ♔d6? ♗xe4!.
52...♗d3

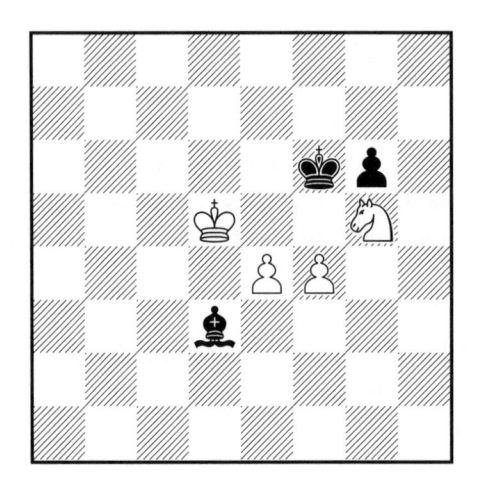

Now that g5 is secured, and I have got my king and e-pawn where I want them, it is time to bring the oscillating knight back to d4, so that after e4-e5 the black king won't have access to f5 and my vulnerable f-pawn. The theme of this book is to try and express my thoughts during the game, as I remember them, rather than to discuss the objective truth. Here I had no idea whether I was winning by force, but I was sure that it would be very awkward for Black in practice, as I continued to improve my position.
53 ♘f3 ♗b1 54 ♘d4 ♔f7

If 54...g5 55 e5+ ♔g6 56 f5+ ♗xf5 57 ♘xf5 ♔xf5 58 e6, and White queens first.
55 e5 ♗a2+ 56 ♔d6

After this I had absolutely no doubt that I was winning since my e-pawn is unstoppable.
56...g5 57 f5 g4 58 ♘e2 ♗b3 59 ♘g3 ♗c2 60 ♔d5 ♔e7 61 ♘e4 ♗b3+ 62 ♔d4

This is the human way to win the position. To avoid complications I simply round up the g-pawn first.
62...♗a4 63 ♔e3 ♗d1 64 ♔f4 ♔f7 65 ♘f2 1-0

23. Bruno-Arkell

The popular website Chess-DB awarded this protracted struggle, against a tough Italian IM, 'Game of the Day' status, perhaps because not much was going on in the chess world on the 2nd of May 2015!

Fabio Bruno - Keith Arkell
European Senior Championship, Eretria 2015
Queen's Indian Defence

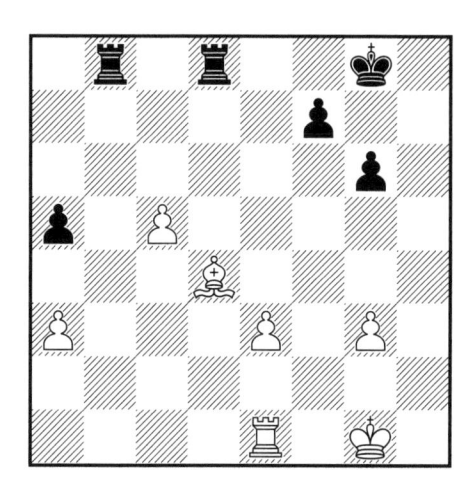

1 d4 ♘f6 2 c4 e6 3 ♘f3 b6 4 g3 ♗a6 5 ♕c2 b5 6 cxb5 ♗xb5 7 ♘c3 ♗a6 8 ♗g2 ♗e7 9 ♘e5 c6 10 0-0 0-0 11 b3 ♕c7 12 ♗b2 d6 13 ♘d3 ♗xd3 14 ♕xd3 d5 15 ♖ac1 ♘bd7 16 ♘a4 ♘b6 17 ♘c5 ♘fd7 18 ♘xd7 ♘xd7 19 ♖c2 ♖fc8 20 ♖fc1 ♕b7 21 e4 g6 22 ♗f1 dxe4 23 ♕xe4 ♘f6 24 ♕f3 ♘d5 25 ♗c4 a5 26 a3 ♗f8 27 h4 ♗h6 28 ♖d1 ♖d8 29 h5 ♕e7 30 hxg6 hxg6 31 ♗d3 ♖ab8 32 ♗c4 ♗g5 33 ♗xd5 cxd5 34 ♖c5 ♖dc8 35 ♕c3 ♕b7 36 ♖d3 ♗f6 37 ♕c2 ♗e7 38 ♖e3 ♗xc5 39 dxc5 d4 40 ♗xd4 ♕d5 41 ♕c3 e5 42 ♖xe5 ♕xb3 43 ♕d2 ♕f3 44 ♖e1 ♖d8 45 ♕e3 ♕xe3 46 fxe3

After playing a risky opening, followed by a middlegame which slowly turned in Black's favour, I entered an ending the exchange for a pawn up. However, because of White's strong point in the centre, anchored by his bishop, I was under no illusions about winning it easily.

46...♖dc8 47 ♔f2 f6 48 ♔f3 ♔f7 49 ♔e4 ♔e6 50 ♖f1 f5+

I would rather have sat tight with 50...♖f8, planning ...♖b3 next, but 51 c6 troubled me too much.

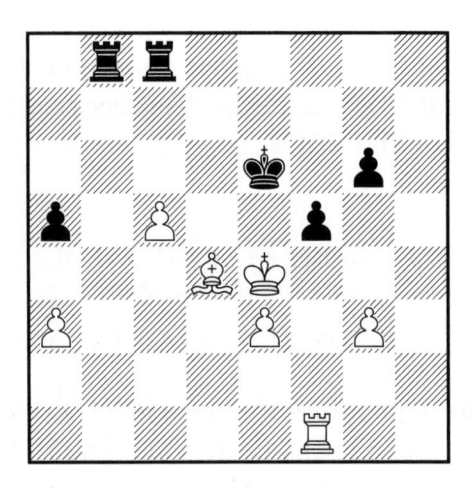

51 ♔f4 ♖b3 52 ♔g5 a4

By playing ...a4 first I wanted to restrict my opponent's activity. I didn't like the look of 52...♖xa3 53 ♖b1, and meanwhile, of course, I am hoping for 53 ♔xg6 ♖g8+ 54 ♔h5 ♖xg3, leaving his king awkwardly placed. Instead, he played the move which worried me most.

53 ♖h1 ♖xa3 54 ♖h6 ♖g8 55 ♖h7 ♖a2 56 ♖a7 ♖g2 57 ♖a6+ ♔d5 58 ♖xa4 ♖xg3+ 59 ♔f4 ♖g4+ 60 ♔f3

So I have picked up a pawn, but winning still proves to be very difficult. He can just leave his central strongpoint intact, and be ready to hassle my f-pawn as soon as I advance my passed pawn.

60...♖h8 61 ♖a6 ♖h3+ 62 ♔e2 ♔c4 63 ♖a4+

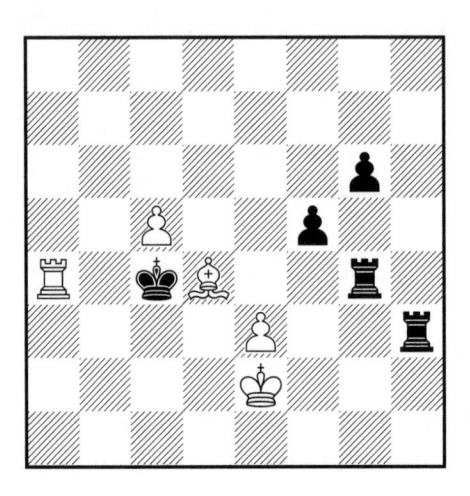

Of course, White isn't going to allow me to force his king to the back rank. From the moment we entered this endgame I felt that the key was to harass his king. First isolate it from the protective block in the centre, and then combine mating threats with plans to push my g-pawn.

63...♔b5 64 ♖a1 ♖h7 65 ♖b1+ ♔c6 66 ♖b6+ ♔d5 67 ♔d3 ♖d7 68 ♖f6 ♖g3 69 ♔c3 ♖d8 70 ♔d3 ♖g2 71 ♔c3 ♔e4 72 ♖e6+ ♔f3 73 ♖f6 ♖g1 74 c6

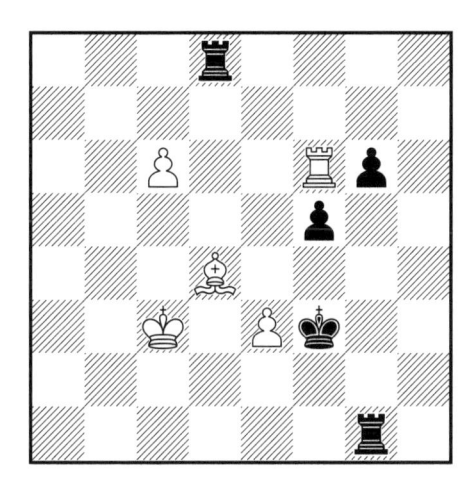

After this a further pair of pawns will be swapped off. I was more concerned about his just sitting tight with 74 ♔d3, when I intended 74...♖c1, hoping for ...♖a8 and ...♖a3+. I found it very difficult to think more than a few moves ahead in this endgame. There were just too many choices for both sides.

74...♔e4 75 c7 ♖c1+ 76 ♔d2 ♖xc7 77 ♖e6+ ♔f3 78 ♖xg6 ♖f7

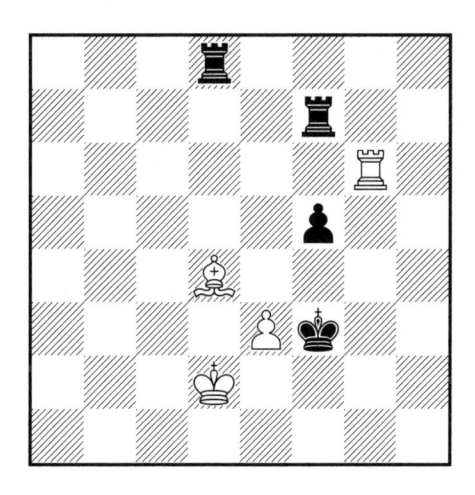

I was now more optimistic about my chances because of the reduced protection around White's king. I still felt that the key was to force him to the edge.
79 ♖a6 ♖b8 80 ♖a3 ♖fb7 81 ♔c3 ♔e4 82 ♖a4 ♖b3+ 83 ♔d2 ♖3b4

As yet there is no alternative plan than mating threats, but I can bully his rook as a swap would surely be fatal.
84 ♖a5 ♖8b5 85 ♖a8 ♔f3 86 ♖f8 ♖a4 87 ♔c3 ♖a6 88 ♔c4 ♖ba5 89 ♗c5 ♔g4 90 ♖g8+ ♔h5 91 ♗d4 ♖g6 92 ♖h8+ ♔g4 93 ♖h1 ♖c6+ 94 ♔b4

This move encouraged me. I was more concerned with 94 ♔d3 ♖a3+ 95 ♔d2 when it isn't very easy to push him back further.
94...♖d5

Now he has to worry about a possible ...f4.
95 ♖g1+ ♔f3 96 ♖f1+ ♔e4 97 ♖f4+ ♔d3

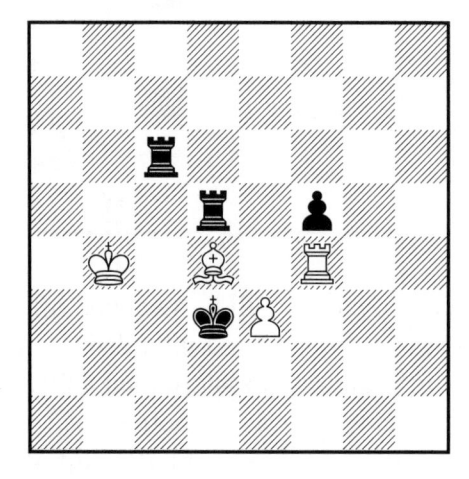

For the first time I was confident of winning. His king will be prised right away from the rest of his forces, and into a mating net.
98 ♗a7 ♖c8 99 ♗d4 ♖c4+ 100 ♔b3 ♖b5+ 101 ♔a3 ♔e2

There are certainly other roads to Rome, but 101...♔e2 places White in zugzwang. He must move his rook away from my f-pawn, freeing up my b5-rook. If instead 101...♖c8, I couldn't see anything clear-cut against 102 ♔a4.
102 ♖h4 ♖c8 103 ♔a4 ♖b7 0-1

With the rook sidetracked, White no longer has the defence ♖xf5, and so there isn't anything to do about the mating attack.

24. Arkell-Zakarian

This is another endgame in which I value centre pawns over queenside pawns. It was possible to play much of the game on instinct, as the motif was the continual improvement of my pieces.

> **Keith Arkell - David Zakarian**
> British League (4NCL), Hinckley 2014
> *Ragozin Defence*

1 d4 ♘f6 2 ♘f3 e6 3 c4 d5 4 cxd5 exd5 5 ♘c3 ♗b4 6 ♕a4+ ♘c6 7 ♗g5 0-0 8 e3 h6 9 ♗xf6 ♕xf6 10 ♗e2 a6 11 a3 ♗xc3+ 12 bxc3 ♗e6 13 ♕c2 ♘a5 14 a4 c5 15 ♕b2 c4 16 ♘d2 ♖fb8 17 ♕b6 ♕d8 18 ♕xd8+ ♖xd8 19 0-0 ♗f5

As it will take time to organise e3-e4, I settled for the other plan: the occupation of the b-file.

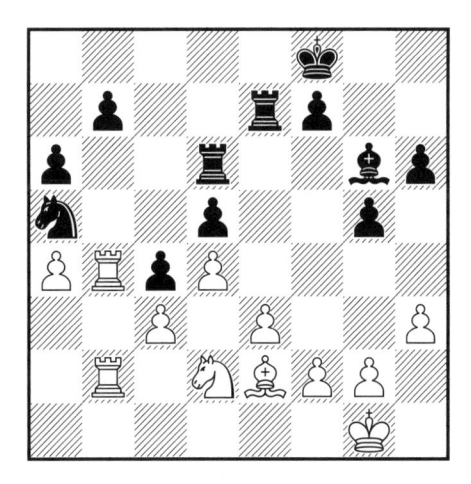

20 ♖a2 ♖d6 21 ♖b2 ♖e8 22 ♖a1 g5 23 h3 ♗g6 24 ♖aa2 ♖e7 25 ♖b4 ♔f8 26 ♖ab2

The plan was a little convoluted because of his bishop on the h7-b1 diagonal, but I have finally got there. What next? Well, I'm not worried about ...f5 just yet, as that gives away the e5-square after ♘f3, but it would be useful to play g2-g4 to gain space, and try to secure f5 for later. I may then be able to bring my knight around to g3, challenge his bishop via c2, and set about playing f2-f3 and e3-e4.

26...♔e8 27 g4 ♔d8 28 ♗d1 ♔c7 29 ♔g2 ♗d3 30 ♘f1 ♖e8 31 ♘g3 ♖b8 32 ♘f5

I decided to preserve the bishop as it does a good job keeping the knight out of

b3, and can also pressure his d5-pawn. And there was another reason for this move. I had in mind a pawn sacrifice which ties down his entire army...
32...♗xf5 33 gxf5 ♖f6 34 ♗f3!
This was it. I was less keen on 34 ♗g4 b6 when I have to start retreating my rooks in order to defend against ...♘c6.
34...♖xf5 35 ♖b6

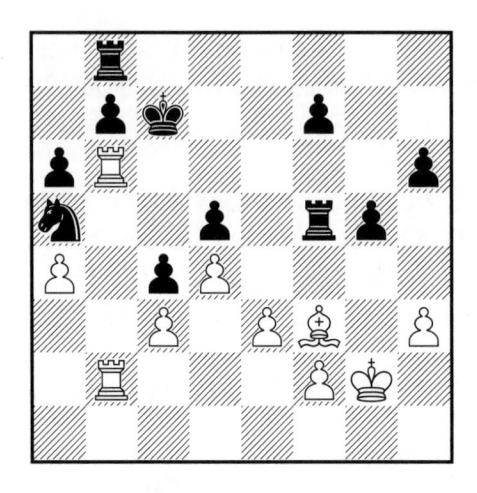

35...♘b3
My idea was to put him in zugzwang with 36 ♖b1 if he had instead defended his h-pawn with 35...♘c6. He can't then move either rook without dropping a vital pawn; he can't play 36...♔c8 or 36...f6 due to 37 ♗g4; 36...h5 is en prise to my bishop; 36 ...a5 37 ♖1b2 just delays matters by one move; and knight moves leave the h6-pawn en prise.
36 ♖xh6
The rest of the game is fairly straightforward as Black has to surrender another pawn to save his rook from the threat of ♗g4.
36...g4 37 hxg4 ♖g5 38 ♖f6 b5
If 38...♖f8 I will soon nudge his rook away from its protection of d5 with 39 ♔g3 and ♔f4.
39 axb5 axb5 40 ♖a2 ♖g7 41 ♖a7+ ♔d8
41...♖b7 drops two more pawns after 42 ♖xb7+ ♔xb7 43 ♖xf7+ ♖xf7 44 ♗xd5+ ♔c7 45 ♗xf7.
42 ♗xd5 ♖xg4+ 43 ♔f3 ♖g7 44 ♗xf7 ♘d2+ 45 ♔f4 b4 46 ♖d6+ 1-0

25. Arkell-Franklin

Another triumph for my centre pawns, this time in a knight ending, and after liquidating all the major pieces in the middlegame.

> **Keith Arkell - Sam Franklin**
> British League (4NCL), Telford 2019
> *King's Indian Defence*

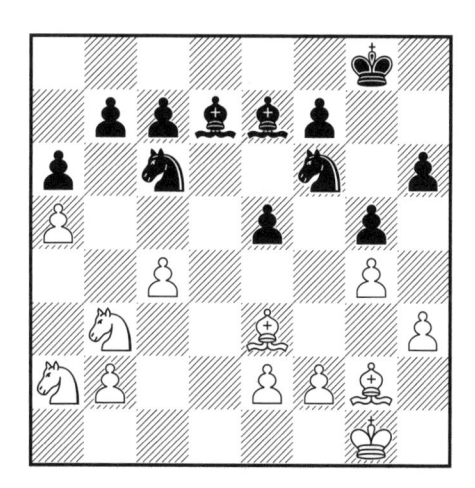

1 ♘f3 ♘f6 2 d4 g6 3 c4 ♗g7 4 ♘c3 0-0 5 g3 d6 6 ♗g2 ♘c6 7 0-0 ♖b8 8 ♗f4 a6 9 a4 h6 10 a5 g5 11 ♗c1 e5 12 dxe5 dxe5 13 ♗e3 ♗e6 14 ♕a4 ♕e7 15 ♖fd1 ♖fd8 16 h3 ♖xd1+ 17 ♖xd1 ♖d8 18 ♖xd8+ ♕xd8 19 ♘d2 ♗d7 20 ♕a1 ♕e7 21 ♘b3 ♕b4 22 ♕a4 ♗f8 23 ♕xb4 ♗xb4 24 ♘a2 ♗e7 25 g4

I felt this position was about equal. Visually White has some advantages – a more flexible kingside pawn structure, and the a5-pawn exercises a cramping effect on the other flank – but these factors shouldn't amount to anything in practice.
25...♔f8 26 ♔f1 ♔e8 27 ♔e1 ♘b4

I didn't really understand this move which forces exchanges favourable to me. If Black had simply waited, I was struggling to find a plan to improve my position.
28 ♘xb4 ♗xb4+ 29 ♗d2 ♗xd2+ 30 ♔xd2 ♗c8 31 ♘c5 c6

Suddenly I have been handed quite a nice position. Black doesn't really want to play 31...c6 because it weakens his dark squares, but 31...b6 32 axb6 cxb6 33 ♘a4 b5 (or 33...♘d7 34 ♗c6) 34 ♘b6 ♔d8 35 cxb5 axb5 36 ♘xc8 ♔xc8 37 ♗c6 leaves his pawns very exposed.

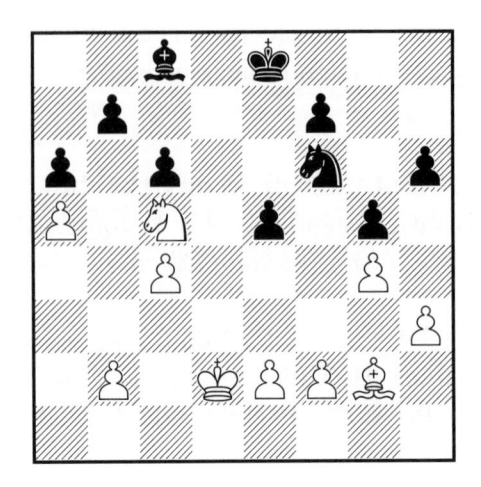

32 ♘d3 ♘d7 33 ♗e4 ♘f6 34 ♗g2

I repeated the position because I wasn't sure how big White's advantage would be after 34 ♔e3 ♘xe4 35 ♔xe4 f6. I was hoping for 34...♘d7 35 ♔e3 ♔e7 and only then 36 ♗e4, after which ♗f5 will leave Black very tied up. Instead, Franklin seizes the opportunity to simplify, and reduce the pressure.

34...h5 35 gxh5 ♘xh5 36 ♘xe5 ♘f4 37 ♗f1 ♗xh3 38 ♗xh3 ♘xh3 39 ♘d3 ♔d7 40 ♘c5+

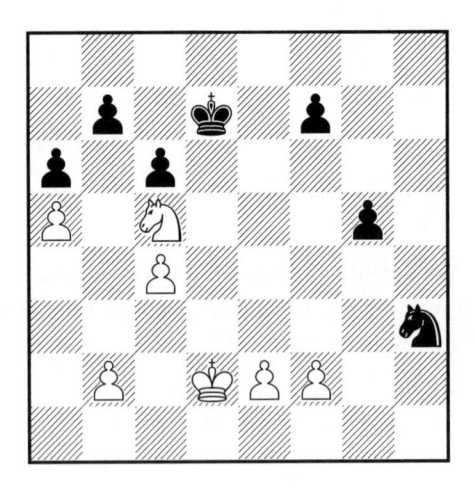

I rushed this move and soon regretted it, wishing I had played 40 e4 instead, when his awkwardly placed knight, fixed queenside, and slightly exposed g5-pawn would have given me good winning chances.

40...♔c7 41 ♔e3 ♘f4

There is no real need to move this knight, but it is understandable that my opponent wanted to recentralise it.

42 ♔f3 f5 43 e3 ♘g6 44 ♘e6+

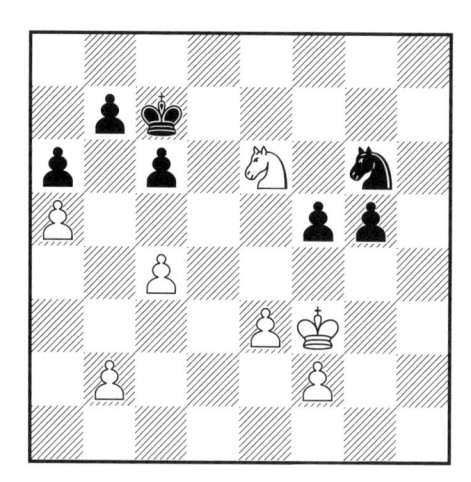

I thought it unlikely that I was winning by force, so decided not to waste time choosing between this and 44 b3.

44...♔d6 45 ♘xg5 ♘e5+

Black can probably also hang on with 45...♔c5, but it seems more sensible to keep his king in the centre and go after my queenside pawns with his knight.

46 ♔f4 ♘xc4 47 ♔xf5 ♘xb2

I was hoping for 47...♘xa5 when he'll have serious problems after 48 ♔f6 followed by hurling my favourite e-pawn up the board.

48 ♘e4+ ♔d5

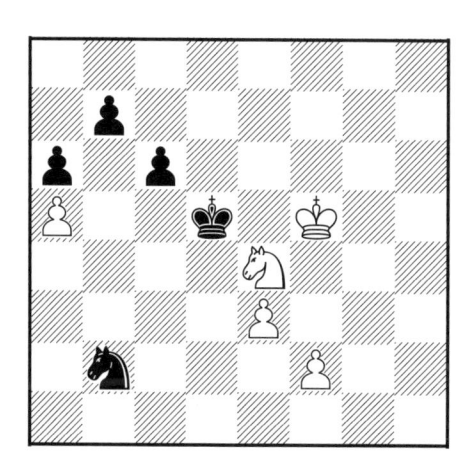

It wasn't very easy to analyse the position over the board, but it seemed to me that both 48...♔e7 and 48...♔c7 were more stubborn.

49 ♘d2 ♔d6 50 e4 ♔e7

One reason for 49 ♘d2 was to meet 50...♘d3 with 51 ♘c4+ ♔c5 52 e5!, and if he takes my knight, the e-pawn will queen. In an ending where there are several candidate moves for each side, often the best you can do is analyse as many mini-variations as possible without any real certainty that you are winning by force.

51 e5 ♘d3 52 f4 ♘c5 53 ♘c4

This was the other reason for 49 ♘d2. While Black's knight scampers back, I can occupy a strategically important square. It is pretty clear that Franklin is on the ropes now, with my e- and f-pawns ready to march while his queenside is temporarily immobilised.

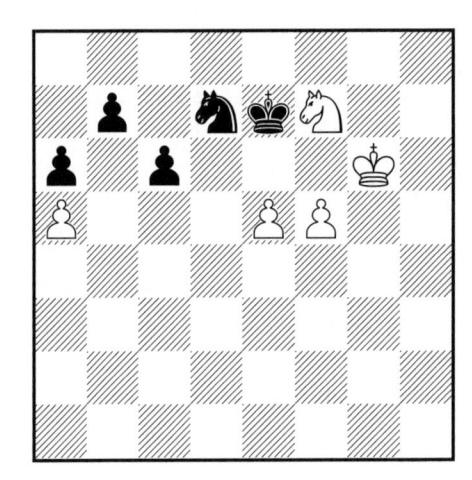

53...♔f7 54 ♘d6+ ♔e7 55 ♔g6 ♔e6 56 ♘f7 ♔e7 57 f5 ♘d7

My next move is obvious by elimination: if 58 f6+? I grind to a halt after 58...♔e6, while 58 e6? won't do after 58...♘f8+ followed by 59...♘xe6.

58 ♔g7! c5 59 e6

Although this move looks obvious in itself, it was only here that I was able to construct the winning sequence.

59...♘f6

I had planned 59...♘f8 60 ♘d8 c4 61 f6+ ♔e8 62 e7 ♘d7 63 ♘xb7 followed by ♘d6+, but later Alexei Shirov pointed out that here 60 ♘g5 is simpler, with the same idea.

60 ♘e5 ♘e8+ 61 ♔g6 ♘c7 62 f6+! ♔xe6 63 ♘d3

And this was my idea. I don't need the e-pawn as I can force the other one through.

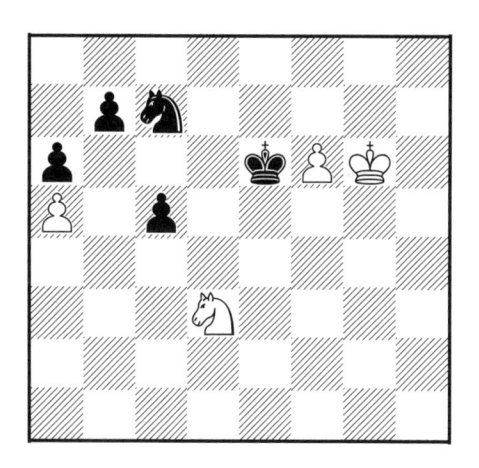

63...c4

Alternatively, if 63...♘e8 64 ♘xc5+ ♔d6 65 f7 ♔e7 66 ♘e6 followed by queening, or 63...♔d6 64 ♘f4 ♘e8 65 f7 ♔e7, and again 66 ♘e6.
64 ♘f4+ ♔d6 65 f7 ♔e7 66 ♘d5+!

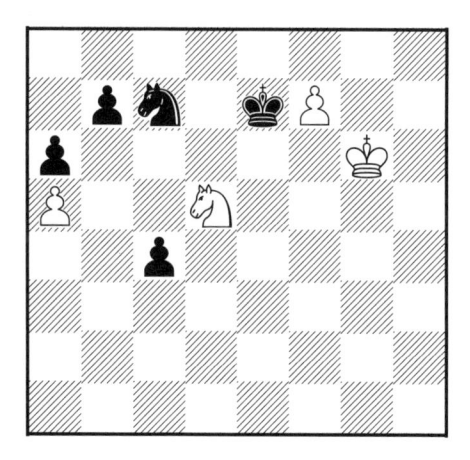

I only discovered later that this was actually the ninth in a series of 11 consecutive 'only winning moves' for White.
66...♘xd5 67 ♔g7 ♔d6 68 f8♕+ ♔c6

Tiredness was by now a factor as hundreds of players battling it out in a vast arena had been reduced to just Sam Franklin and myself, but I managed to stay alert.
69 ♕c8+ ♘c7 70 ♕f5 ♘d5 71 ♔f7 b6 72 axb6 ♘xb6 73 ♕a5 ♘d5 74 ♔e6 ♘c7+ 75 ♔e5 ♘b5 76 ♕b4 c3 77 ♕c4+ ♔b6 78 ♔d5 ♘c7+ 79 ♔d4 ♘b5+ 80 ♔d3 a5 81 ♕a4 ♔a6 82 ♔c4 1-0

26. Arkell-Orr

This endgame was similar to my encounter with Toma, in that I was able to exploit the possession of an extra pawn with my knight against IM Mark Orr's bishop.

> **Keith Arkell - Mark Orr**
> Edinburgh Open 1988
> *Queen's Gambit Declined*

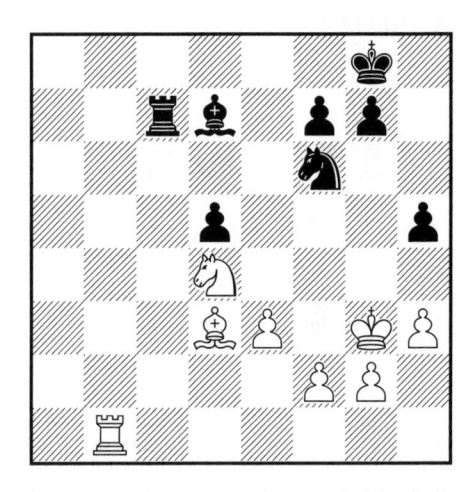

1 d4 ♘f6 2 ♘f3 d5 3 ♗g5 ♘bd7 4 e3 h6 5 ♗h4 e6 6 c4 ♗e7 7 cxd5 exd5 8 ♘c3 0-0 9 ♗d3 ♖e8 10 ♕c2 c6 11 ♗g3 ♘f8 12 0-0 ♗d6 13 ♗xd6 ♕xd6 14 ♖ab1 a5 15 a3 ♗e6 16 b4 axb4 17 axb4 ♘8d7 18 b5 ♖ec8 19 bxc6 bxc6 20 ♘a4 ♖a5 21 ♘b6 ♘xb6 22 ♖xb6 ♕c7 23 ♖fb1 c5 24 ♖b7 ♕d6 25 ♕c3 ♖aa8 26 dxc5 ♕xc5 27 ♕xc5 ♖xc5 28 ♘d4 ♗d7 29 h3 h5 30 ♔h2 ♖ac8 31 ♖a7 ♖8c7 32 ♖xc7 ♖xc7 33 ♔g3

I have a pleasant advantage, and wanted to use my king to obtain a grip on the dark squares.

33...g6 34 ♖b8+ ♔g7 35 ♔f4 ♖c1 36 ♘f3 ♘e4

Perhaps this was a bit impatient and he would have been better off just waiting.

37 ♗xe4 dxe4 38 ♘e5 ♗e6 39 ♔xe4 ♖c2 40 ♔f3 f6 41 ♘d3 g5

I have picked off a pawn, but Black's structure restricts the knight, and makes the ideal placing of my pawns awkward, as I would very much like to play h3-h4.

42 ♖b2 ♖c3 43 ♘b4 h4 44 ♖d2 ♔g6 45 ♖d6 ♔f7 46 ♖d4 ♖c1 47 ♘d3 ♖c2 48 g3

At some point this move will be necessary. I'll also have to exchange another

pawn, and hope to make something of just two pawns against one.
48...hxg3 49 ♔xg3 ♖c4 50 h4 gxh4+ 51 ♔xh4 ♖xd4+ 52 exd4

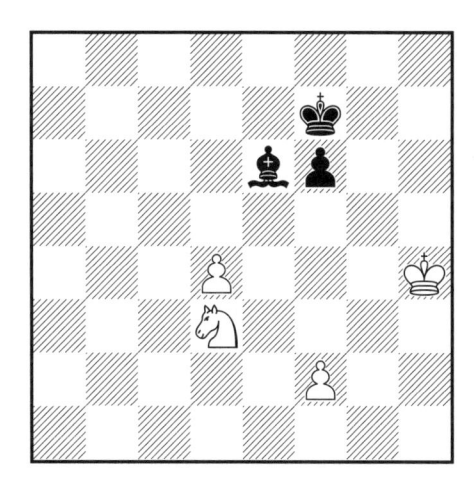

This alteration in the pawn structure suits me. The position is probably a draw with best play, but it won't be easy for Black. I can play around with various ideas for a long time, while he has no prospect of ever exchanging his last pawn.
52...♗f5 53 ♘f4 ♔e7 54 ♔h5 ♔f7 55 ♘d5 ♗e4 56 ♘c3 ♗f5 57 ♔h4 ♔g6

Although it isn't easy to analyse concrete lines, I felt that Black was taking risks moving his king away from my passed pawn.
58 ♔g3 ♔g5 59 d5 ♔g6 60 ♔f4 ♗c2 61 ♔e3 ♔f5

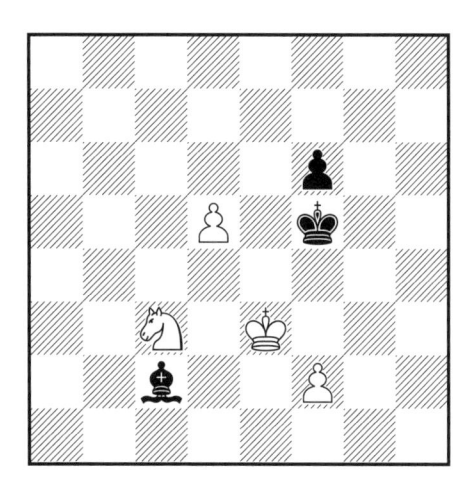

Today it's hard to imagine that in the late 1980s games were still being adjourned, even during international tournaments. Here I was obliged to seal my 62nd

119

move in an envelope.

I dismissed both 62 ♔d4 ♔f4 63 d6 ♗f5, when the bishop contains my d-pawn, while Black's king eyes up the other one, and 62 f4 ♗b3, which seemed to place me in zugzwang: for example, 63 ♔f3 ♗c4 when I can't do anything constructive, or 63 d6 ♔e6 64 ♘e4 ♗c2. That left 62 f3, against which I couldn't see a satisfactory defence.

62 f3! ♗b3

During the adjournment Mark had time to see 62...♔e5 63 f4+ ♔f5 (63...♔d6 64 ♔d4 must be winning) when I'm free to move the knight with decisive effect: 64 ♘b5, or, better still, 64 ♘e2.

63 f4

The point of 62 f3. It is now Black who is in zugzwang. He either has to give ground with his king, or, in continuing to tie my knight to the defence of the d-pawn, place his bishop where it can be attacked.

63...♗c4 64 ♔d4

64...♗b3

Alternatively, if 64...♗a6 65 d6 ♗c8 66 ♘e2 ♔g4 67 ♔e3, followed by ♘d4-b3-c5, winning the bishop. Here Black can also try 65...♔e6, but after 66 ♔c5 ♗c8 (or 66...♔d7 67 ♘d5) 67 ♔c6 ♔f5 68 ♔c7 ♗e6 69 ♘e2 ♔e4 70 d7 ♗xd7 71 ♔xd7 ♔e3 72 ♔e6 White wins.

65 d6 ♗e6

After 65...♔e6 66 ♔c5 ♔d7 67 ♘d5 f5 (or 67...♔e6 68 f5+) 68 ♘e7 ♗e6 69 ♘c6 ♗a2 70 ♘e5+ Black's position is hopeless.

66 ♘e2 ♗c8 67 ♔c5 ♔e6

Or 67...♔e4 68 ♔c6, and again White gets there first.

68 ♔c6 ♗d7+ 69 ♔c7 ♗a4 70 ♘d4+ ♔d5 71 d7 1-0

27. Panzer-Arkell

This game featured a queen endgame in which I did plenty of reasonably accurate calculations at the board. At the time there was much uncertainty about the winning chances in the ending of queen and rook's pawn against queen.

> **Peter Panzer - Keith Arkell**
> Hastings Challengers 1990/91
> *Nimzo-Indian Defence*

1 d4 ♘f6 2 c4 e6 3 ♘c3 ♗b4 4 ♕c2 c5 5 dxc5 0-0 6 a3 ♗xc5 7 ♘f3 ♘c6 8 ♗f4 ♘h5 9 ♗g3 f5 10 e3 g5? 11 0-0-0 g4 12 ♗h4 ♕c7 13 ♘d4 b6 14 ♘b3 ♘e5 15 ♘b5 ♕c6 16 ♘xc5 ♕xc5 17 h3 ♗a6 18 ♘d6 ♘f6 19 b4 ♕c7 20 ♗g3 ♘g6 21 hxg4 ♘xg4 22 ♘xf5 ♕d8 23 ♘h6+ ♘xh6 24 ♖xh6 ♕g5 25 ♖h1 d5 26 ♔b1 ♗xc4 27 ♗d3 ♗xd3 28 ♕xd3 ♖ac8 29 ♖c1 a5 30 ♖xc8 ♖xc8 31 bxa5 bxa5 32 ♖c1 ♖xc1+ 33 ♔xc1 h5 34 ♕b5 h4 35 ♕e8+ ♔g7 36 ♕d7+ ♔h6 37 ♗d6 e5 38 f4 exf4 39 ♗xf4 ♘xf4 40 exf4 ♕xf4+

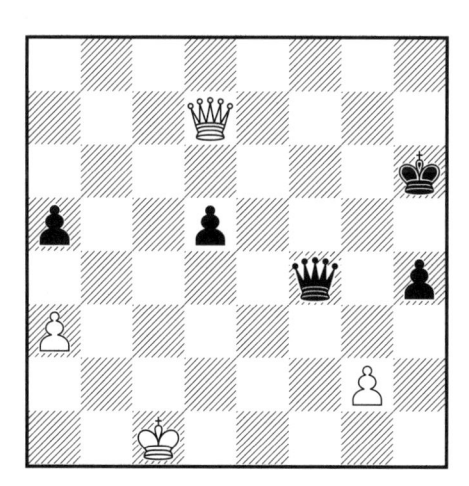

After some pretty shoddy chess I was very happy to arrive in an ending where I obviously have pretty good winning chances.

41 ♔b2 ♕d2+ 42 ♔b3 ♕xg2 43 ♕e6+ ♔h5 44 ♕f5+ ♕g5 45 ♕f3+ ♔g6 46 ♔a4

The position looks almost hopeless for White, but this crafty move utilises stalemate to create an awkward threat of capturing my d-pawn.

46...♕g3 47 ♕f8

He could, of course, have immediately made the capture, but prefers to go after my a-pawn.

47...♕e5 48 ♕g8+ ♔h5?

I must have missed the stalemate trick, or I would never have put my king on such a poor square. After 48...♔h6 I could have met 49 ♕xd5 with 49...♕e8+, and if 50 ♔xa5 ♕h5.

49 ♕xd5! ♕g5 50 ♕f7+ ♔g4 51 ♕d7+ ♕f5

Around here I was only able to calculate lots of mini-sequences, with a view to preventing obvious drawing ideas.

52 ♕g7+ ♔f3 53 ♕c3+ ♔g2 54 ♕g7+ ♔f2 55 ♕d4+ ♔g3 56 ♕g1+ ♔h3 57 ♕h1+ ♔g4 58 ♕g2+ ♔f4 59 ♕d2+ ♔g3 60 ♕e3+ ♔g4 61 ♕e2+ ♔h3 62 ♕e3+ ♔g4 63 ♕e2+ ♕f3 64 ♕e6+ ♔g3 65 ♕e1+ ♔h3 66 ♔xa5

I was pleased to see this as without the a-pawns my queen has more freedom. I had seen that 66 ♕xa5 fails to 66...♕d1+ 67 ♔b4 (or 67 ♔b5 ♕d5+) 67...♕d2+, when I win the race to promote, and also that White is out of checks because 66 ♕e6+ allows the cross-check 66...♕g4+.

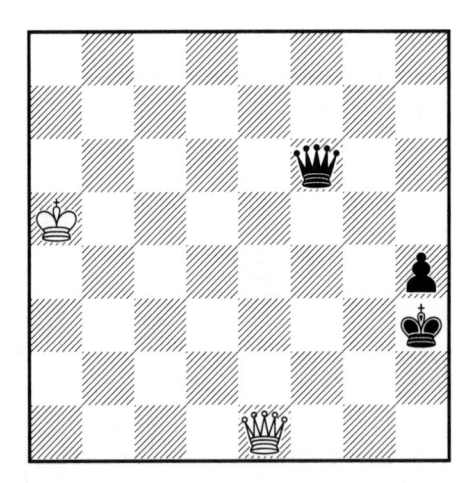

66...♕xa3+ 67 ♔b5 ♕d3+ 68 ♔b6 ♕d4+ 69 ♔a6 ♕f6+ 70 ♔a5

At the start of the 1990s most people had only vague ideas about where White ought best to put his king.

70...♔g4 71 ♕e2+ ♔g5 72 ♕g2+ ♔h5 73 ♕e2+ ♔h6 74 ♕h2

By this stage it is clear that the king is on a bad square, in view of the number of cross-checks which interfere with the defence.

74...♕f5+ 75 ♔a4 h3 76 ♕d6+ ♔h5 77 ♔a3 ♕f3+ 78 ♔b4 ♕e4+ 79 ♔a5 ♕e1+ 80 ♔a6 ♕e2+ 81 ♔a7

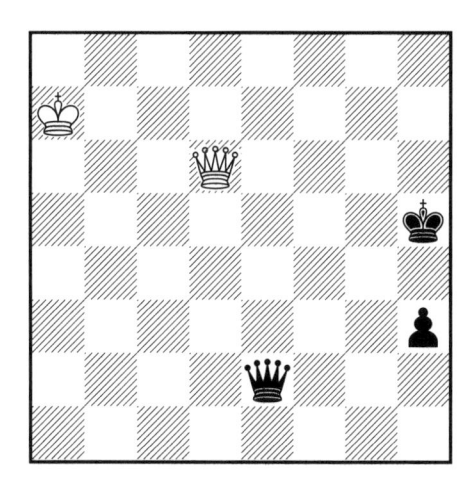

Here the game was adjourned. In 1990 we didn't have engines or tablebases, and endgame books differed in their opinions on queen and rook's pawn against queen. I had with me *Practical Chess Endings* by Paul Keres, which had only this to say: "We shall not examine positions involving Q and RP v Q, which only offer slender winning chances". During the break I didn't do a very good job of analysing or assessing the endgame, but after the resumption I found it possible to calculate some variations quite well at the board.

81...♕f2+ 82 ♔a6 h2 83 ♕e5+ ♔g6 84 ♕e4+ ♔g7 85 ♕b7+

After 85 ♕g4+ ♔f6 White is out of sensible checks, so the end will come more quickly.

85...♕f7 86 ♕h1

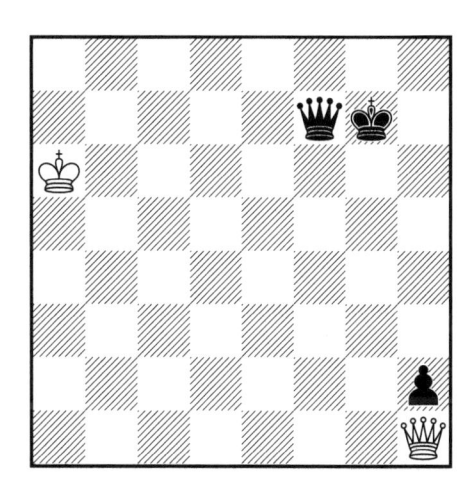

Clearly this is the only way to hang on, and now I was able to calculate an unusually long way ahead – made possible by the small number of side variations.
86...♕g6+ 87 ♔a5

And not 87 ♔b7? ♕g1, winning on the spot.
87...♕g1 88 ♕b7+ ♔h6 89 ♕c6+ ♕g6 90 ♕h1 ♕g5+

The point is to force the king on to the fourth rank, and here is why: against 90...♕g1 White has 91 ♕c6+ ♔g5 92 ♕d5+ ♔h4 93 ♕e4+ ♕g4 94 ♕e1+, and there is no end in sight to the checks.
91 ♔a4

Just as in the note to White's 87th move, if he goes forwards then 91...♕g1 92 ♕c6+ ♕g6 wins immediately.
91...♕g1 92 ♕c6+ ♔g5 93 ♕d5+ ♔h4 94 ♕d8+

Obviously the only sensible check. By forcing the king on to the fourth rank I have vastly reduced his options. Each check up to and including the 101st move is now the only one available.
94...♕g5 95 ♕h8+ ♔g3 96 ♕c3+ ♔g4 97 ♕c8+ ♕f5 98 ♕g8+ ♔f4 99 ♕b8+ ♕e5 100 ♕f8+ ♔e3 101 ♕a3+ ♔e4 102 ♕c1

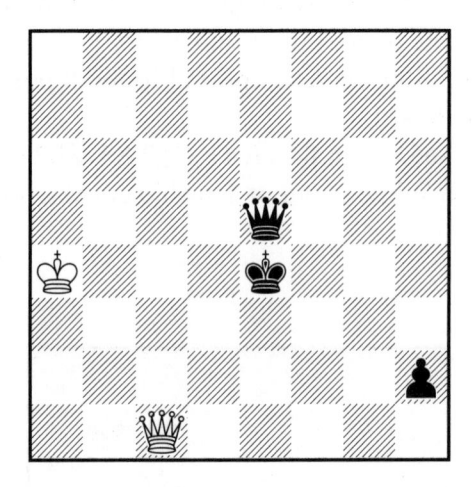

Now that the checks have run out, he is reduced to directly preventing my pawn from queening, and 102 ♕h3 won't do after 102...♕a1+ and 103...h1♕.
102...♕f4 103 ♕h1+

Wherever White goes with his queen, I will soon get my pawn home.
103...♔e3+ 104 ♔a3 ♔f2 0-1

28. Arkell-Groves

The following game, against England International Carey Groves, probably holds the record for the most unwinnable-looking ending from which I've managed to extract the whole point. I'll pass through the first 72 moves without comment as they weren't very interesting, and for a long time the position was a trivial draw.

> **Keith Arkell - Carey Groves**
> Jersey International 1985
> *Pirc Defence*

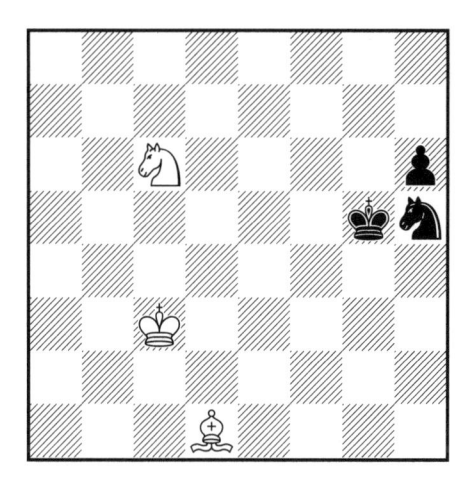

1 e4 d6 2 d4 ♘f6 3 ♘c3 g6 4 ♘f3 ♗g7 5 ♗e2 0-0 6 0-0 a6 7 a4 b6 8 ♗g5 ♗b7 9 e5 dxe5 10 dxe5 ♘g4 11 e6 fxe6 12 ♕xd8 ♖xd8 13 ♗xe7 ♖e8 14 ♗a3 ♘d7 15 ♘g5 ♘ge5 16 ♖ad1 ♘f6 17 ♖fe1 h6 18 ♗f1 ♘d5 19 ♘ge4 ♘xc3 20 ♘xc3 ♖ad8 21 h3 g5 22 ♗e2 ♖xd1 23 ♖xd1 ♗f6 24 f3 ♖d8 25 ♖xd8+ ♗xd8 26 ♔f2 ♔f7 27 ♔e3 ♗e7 28 ♗xe7 ♔xe7 29 ♘e4 ♘g6 30 g3 a5 31 c3 ♗c6 32 ♗d1 ♗d7 33 ♗c2 e5 34 ♘f2 ♗e8 35 ♔e4 ♗d7 36 b3 ♔d6 37 ♔e3 ♘e7 38 ♘e4+ ♔e6 39 ♗d3 ♘d5+ 40 ♔d2 ♔e7 41 ♘f2 ♘f6 42 ♗g6 ♗e6 43 b4 ♗b3 44 ♗c2 ♗d5 45 bxa5 bxa5 46 ♔e3 ♗c6 47 ♘d3 ♘d5+ 48 ♔d2 ♔f6 49 ♘c5 ♘b6 50 ♘a6 ♘xa4 51 ♘xc7 ♘c5 52 ♔e3 ♗e7 53 c4 ♘e6 54 ♘b5 ♘c5 55 f4 gxf4+ 56 gxf4 exf4+ 57 ♔xf4 ♗d7 58 ♗f5 ♗c6 59 ♔e5 ♘b3 60 ♗c2 ♘d2 61 ♔d4 ♗d7 62 ♔c3 ♘f3 63 ♗d1 ♘e5 64 h4 ♗e6 65 c5 ♘c6 66 ♗f3 ♗d7 67 ♘d6 ♔f6 68 ♗d1 ♘e5 69 ♘b7 ♘g6 70 h5 ♘f4 71 ♘xa5 ♔g5 72 c6 ♗xc6 73 ♘xc6 ♘xh5

I suspect a very high percentage of players would shake hands here, or indeed would have done so many moves earlier. When I had the same ending minus the pawn against the Australian IM Alex Wohl in Calicut a few years later, my opponent was visibly irritated that I was playing on. Times were different then, and I was one of the few players who liked to squeeze every drop of blood out of my endgames. Furthermore, it's only by persisting that you learn the level of difficulty for the defence.

At any rate, my only thought here was whether I might possibly be able to separate Black's knight from her king, and then round it up, using a similar technique to some rook versus knight endings.

74 ♔d4 ♘g7 75 ♔e5 ♘f5 76 ♘d8 ♘e3 77 ♘f7+ ♔g6 78 ♗b3 ♘g4+ 79 ♔f4 ♘f6 80 ♘e5+ ♔h7 81 ♔f5

I have made some progress, and was daring to hope that I just might acquire some winning chances. It seemed that we might be beyond the point where the knight can simply dance around willy nilly. This book only concerns itself with my thoughts during live play, but I have accessed the tablebases to see whether Black could possibly go wrong, and it seems that here 81...♘h5 loses in 41 moves, beginning with 82 ♗d1.

81...♔g7 82 ♗c4 ♘e8 83 ♗d3 ♘f6 84 ♘g6 ♔f7 85 ♗c4+ ♔g7 86 ♘f4 ♘e8 87 ♘h5+ ♔h7

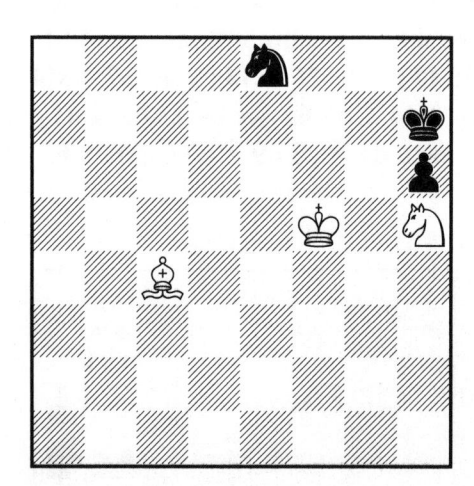

You are rarely looking for a forced win in such a position. It's all about luring your opponent into a mistake. Here I had been hoping for 87...♔h8 88 ♔g6, prising the two pieces apart. After that the objective assessment would be impossible to establish over the board, although for the curious, 88 ♔g6 leads to mate in 34.

What some people might regard as going from the sublime to the ridiculous, but which I happen to find entertaining, is that after 87...♔h8 the weaker 88 ♔e5 only forces mate in 92(!) moves, and, indeed, is based on the same plan of separating king and knight. Here is the sequence, with best play from both sides: 88...♔h7 89 ♗f7 ♘c7 90 ♔f6 ♘b5 91 ♗e6 ♘d6 92 ♔e7 ♘b5 93 ♗f5+ ♔h8 94 ♔f8 ♘d6 95 ♗b1 ♘f7 96 ♘f4 ♘g5 97 ♘g6+ ♔h7 98 ♘h4+ ♔h8 99 ♗a2 h5 100 ♗b1 ♘h7+ 101 ♔f7 ♘g5+ 102 ♔g6 ♘h3 103 ♗a2 ♘f2 104 ♘f3 ♘h3 105 ♗c4 ♘f2 106 ♔h6 ♘g4+ 107 ♔xh5 ♘e3 108 ♗b3 ♘f5 109 ♔g5 ♘d6 110 ♔g6 ♘e4 111 ♘h2 ♘c5 112 ♗d5 ♘d7 113 ♔f7 ♘e5+ 114 ♔e6 ♘d3 115 ♔f6 ♘f2 116 ♘f3 ♘d3 117 ♘d2 ♘c5 118 ♘c4 ♘a4 119 ♘e5 ♘c3 120 ♗c4 ♔h7 121 ♘g4 ♘e4+ 122 ♔e5 ♘g5 123 ♔f5 ♘f3 124 ♗d5 ♘g1 125 ♔f6 ♘e2 126 ♔f7 ♔h8 127 ♗e4 ♘c3 128 ♗d3 ♘a4 129 ♘e5 ♘b2 130 ♗e2 ♘a4 131 ♗d1 ♘c5 132 ♗c2 ♘d7 133 ♘g6+ ♔h7 134 ♔e6 ♘b6 135 ♘e7+ ♔g7 136 ♘f5+ ♔f8 137 ♘d6...

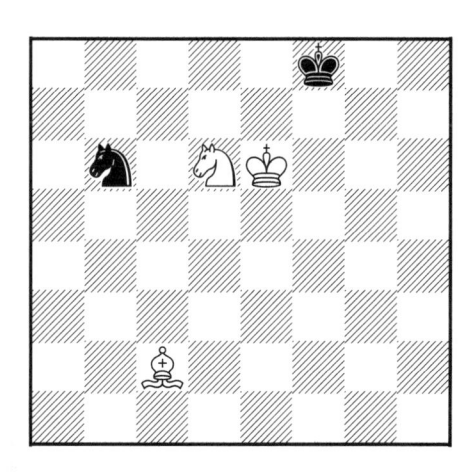

...137...♔g8 138 ♗d1 ♔g7 139 ♗e2 ♘a8 140 ♘e4 ♔f8 141 ♔d6 ♔e8 142 ♘c5 ♔d8 143 ♗g4 ♘b6 144 ♘b7+ ♔e8 145 ♗e6 ♘a8 146 ♘c5 ♘b6 147 ♔c6 ♘a8 148 ♔b7 ♔e7 149 ♗c4 ♔d8 150 ♘e6+ ♔e8 151 ♔xa8 ♔e7 152 ♗b3 ♔d7 153 ♔b7 ♔d6 154 ♔b6 ♔d7 155 ♔c5 ♔e7 156 ♔d5 ♔f7 157 ♘f4 ♔f6 158 ♔e4 ♔g7 159 ♔e5 ♔h7 160 ♔f6 ♔h6 161 ♘g6 ♔h7 162 ♗a2 ♔h6 163 ♗g8 ♔h5 164 ♘e5 ♔h4 165 ♗d5 ♔h5 166 ♗e4 ♔h6 167 ♘f7+ ♔h5 168 ♗f3+ ♔h4 169 ♔f5 ♔g3 170 ♘e5 ♔h3 171 ♔f4 ♔h4 172 ♘g6+ ♔h3 173 ♗e4 ♔h2 174 ♔f3 ♔h3 175 ♗d3 ♔h2 176 ♘f4 ♔g1 177 ♔g3 ♔h1 178 ♗e2 ♔g1 179 ♘h3+ ♔h1 180 ♗f3#.

It's worth noting that there was no 50-move violation during that process. Anyway, back to the game:
88 ♗d3 ♔g8 89 ♔g6 ♘d6 90 ♔f6 ♔f8

The fact this is the only defence demonstrates that things are going my way. For example, 90...♘c8 loses in 104 moves, but I will spare the reader this torture.
91 ♘f4 ♔e8 92 ♔e6 ♘b7 93 ♗g6+ ♔f8

This still draws, though of course I was unaware of it at the time. With both players very tired, Carey probably vaguely disliked 93...♔d8 94 ♘d5, but heading

towards the knight would surely be more prudent. I suspect that while my optimism was increasing with every move, she was oblivious to the possibility that she might lose.
94 ♔f6

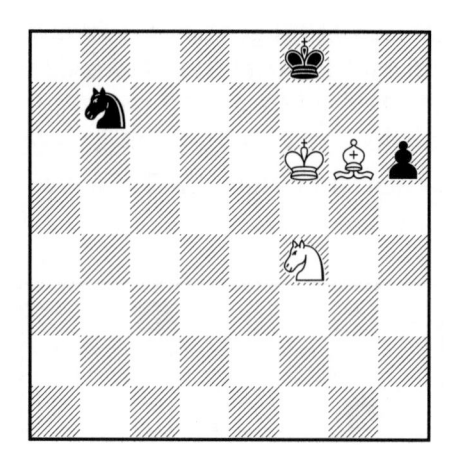

I now threaten mate in two with 95 ♗f7 followed by 96 ♘g6# or 96 ♘e6#, and the tablebases inform me that 94...♘c5 is the only defence.
94...♘d8?

I can't resist showing one more tablebase win, and that is against the apparently reasonable 94...♘d6: 95 ♘e6+ ♔g8 96 ♘c5 h5 97 ♗xh5 ♔h7 98 ♔g5 ♔g8 99 ♘e6 ♘c4 100 ♔f6 ♔h7 101 ♗e2 ♘e3 102 ♘g5+ ♔h6 103 ♘f7+ ♔h7 104 ♗f3 ♘c4 105 ♗d5 ♘e3 106 ♗b3 ♘f1 107 ♗c2+ ♔g8 108 ♘g5 ♘e3 109 ♗b3+ ♔f8 110 ♘e6+ ♔g8 111 ♔g6 ♘f1 112 ♗c4 ♘e3 113 ♗a2 ♘d1 114 ♗b3 ♘c3 115 ♔f6 ♔h7 116 ♘g5+ ♔h8 117 ♗c4 ♘d5+ 118 ♔g6 ♘b6 119 ♗e6 ♘a4 120 ♔f7 ♘c5 121 ♗h3 ♘d7 122 ♘f3 ♘b6 123 ♘e5 ♔h7 124 ♘g4 ♘c4...

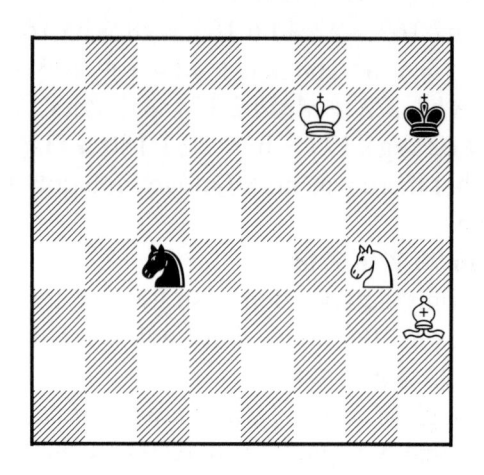

...125 ♗f1 ♘d6+ 126 ♔e6 ♘b7 127 ♗g2 ♘c5+ 128 ♔f7 ♘d3 129 ♗d5 ♔h8 130 ♔f6 ♘f4 131 ♗a2 ♘e2 132 ♗c4 ♘d4 133 ♘h6 ♔h7 134 ♘f7 ♘c6 135 ♗d3+ ♔g8 136 ♘h6+ ♔f8 137 ♘f5 ♘a7 138 ♘g7 ♘c8 139 ♘e6+ ♔g8 140 ♘f4 ♔f8 141 ♗b5 ♘d6 142 ♘g6+ ♔g8 143 ♗c6 ♘c8 144 ♔e6 ♘b6 145 ♘e7+ ♔g7 146 ♘f5+ ♔g6 147 ♘e3 ♔g5 148 ♔e5 ♔h5 149 ♔d6 ♘c8+ 150 ♔d7 ♘a7 151 ♗a4 ♔g5 152 ♘c2 ♔f5 153 ♔c7 ♔e5 154 ♔b7 ♔d5 155 ♔xa7 ♔c5 156 ♗e8 ♔d5 157 ♔b6 ♔e5 158 ♗c6 ♔f5 159 ♔c5 ♔e5 160 ♘d4 ♔f4 161 ♗d5 ♔e3 162 ♗a4 ♔d3 163 ♗c2+ ♔c3 164 ♔c5 ♔b2 165 ♔c4 ♔a2 166 ♔c3 ♔a1 167 ♘b3+ ♔a2 168 ♔d3 ♔a3 169 ♗b1 ♔a4 170 ♘d4 ♔a5 171 ♗e4 ♔a4 172 ♗d5 ♔a3 173 ♘c2+ ♔a4 174 ♗c6+ ♔a5 175 ♔c4 ♔b6 176 ♘d4 ♔a6 177 ♔c5 ♔a5 178 ♘f5 ♔a6 179 ♘d6 ♔a5 180 ♗d7 ♔a6 181 ♗b5+ ♔a7 182 ♔c6 ♔b8 183 ♔b6 ♔a8 184 ♔c7 ♔a7 185 ♘c8+ ♔a8 186 ♗c6#.
95 ♗h5

This is by far the most efficient, but it appears that 95 ♗d3 and 95 ♗c2 also get there in the end.
95...♔g8 96 ♗e2

Unfortunately it's now too late to protect the knight as 96...♔f8? 97 ♘g6+ ♔e8 98 ♗b5+ is curtains.
96...♔h7 97 ♗f3 h5 98 ♘xh5

There's no need to rush with 98 ♔e7 as the knight isn't going anywhere.
98...♔h6 99 ♘g3 ♔h7 100 ♗e4+ ♔g8 101 ♔e7 ♔g7 102 ♔xd8 ♔f6 103 ♘e2 ♔e5 104 ♗d3 ♔d6 105 ♔e8 ♔e6 106 ♗c2 ♔d6 107 ♔f7 ♔e5 108 ♗d3 ♔d5 109 ♔f6 ♔d6 110 ♘d4 ♔d5 111 ♘b3 ♔d6 112 ♗e4 ♔c7 113 ♔e6 ♔b6 114 ♗d3 ♔c6 115 ♗c4 ♔c7 116 ♗b5 ♔b6 117 ♗a4 ♔c7 118 ♔e7 ♔c8 119 ♔d6 ♔b7 120 ♘d2 ♔b6 121 ♘c4+ ♔b7 122 ♗c6+ ♔a6 123 ♔c7 ♔a7 124 ♗b5 ♔a8 125 ♘b6+ ♔a7 126 ♘c8+ 1-0

29. Webb-Arkell

I could fill an entire book with double-rook endgames alone. Here my three pawns were just that little bit more compact than my opponent's.

Laurence Webb - Keith Arkell
Hastings Masters 2009/10
Sicilian Defence

1 e4 c5 2 ♘f3 d6

I've reached this position with Black two or three times at most. Fortunately my opponent didn't now play very critically.

3 ♗b5+ ♗d7 4 ♗xd7+ ♕xd7 5 c4 ♘c6 6 d4 cxd4 7 ♘xd4 g6 8 ♘c3 ♗g7 9 ♗e3 ♘f6 10 f3 0-0 11 0-0 ♖fc8 12 b3 ♕d8 13 ♕d2 a6 14 ♖fd1 ♕a5 15 a4 ♘d7

By playing sensible chess I've accidentally followed what little theory there is in this line. Perhaps the most testing move is 16 ♖ab1, but instead Laurence swaps off into an equal endgame.

16 ♘d5 ♕xd2 17 ♖xd2 ♔f8 18 ♖b1 ♘xd4 19 ♗xd4 ♗xd4+ 20 ♖xd4 b5

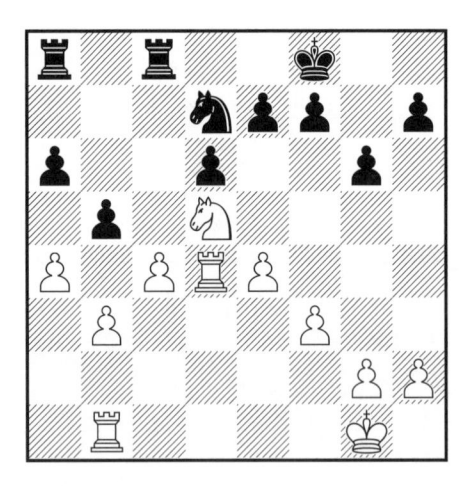

I knew this shouldn't be good, but if I could get away with it then positionally it would be excellent because it breaks up White's pawn structure.

21 cxb5 axb5 22 axb5 ♖a5 23 ♖c4 ♖d8 24 ♘c3 ♖a7 25 ♖a4 ♖c7 26 ♖c4 ♖b7

Of course, I should take a draw here, if White really is willing to continue the repetition, but I played riskily because I was looking for imbalance in the hope that he

130

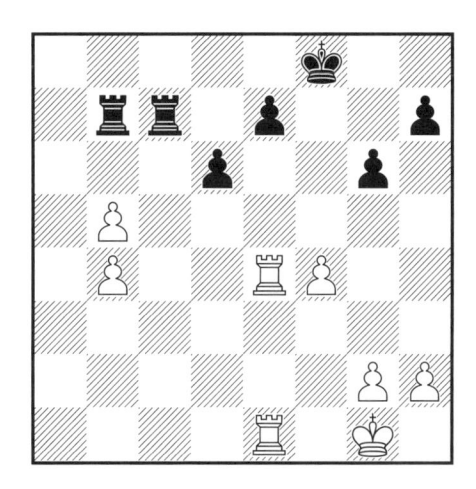

would go wrong.
27 ♖a1 ♘c5 28 b4 ♘d3 29 ♖d4 ♘e5 30 f4 ♘d7 31 ♖c4 f5

I also considered 31...g5, hoping for 32 fxg5 ♘e5 33 ♖d4 ♖c8 with excellent counterplay, but White simply replies 32 g3.

32 ♖e1 fxe4 33 ♖cxe4 ♘f6 34 ♖d4

At last, after reacting excellently to my provocation for many moves, my opponent errs, and allows me sufficient counterplay. It would have been more difficult after 34 ♖c4.

34...♖c8 35 ♘e4

35 ♖e3 ♖bc7 36 ♖dd3 ♖c4 is beginning to look promising for Black.

35...♘xe4 36 ♖dxe4 ♖cc7

The ending is now marginally better for Black because my pawns are nice and compact, and more so than White's. With best play the game should, of course, end in a draw, but I have the kind of position I was hoping for with 20...b5. I can probe against the b-pawn while trying to activate my rooks, and White has the additional worry of needing to react to ...g5 without allowing me two connected passed pawns.

37 g3 ♖xb5 38 ♖1e2 g5 39 ♖b2 gxf4 40 gxf4

With three isolated pawns to harass, I now have some practical chances to squeeze something out of the position.

40...♔f7 41 ♔f2 ♔f6 42 ♖be2 ♖cb7 43 ♖e6+ ♔f7 44 ♖h6 ♔g7 45 ♖he6 ♔f8 46 ♔g3

Laurence could also have continued 46 ♖h6 to meet 46...♖xb4 with 47 ♔g3 ♔g7 48 ♖he6. Then the number of pawns would reduce to two apiece, leaving me with very few winning chances. I would therefore have met 46 ♖h6 with 46...♖f5 47 ♔g3 ♖f7, as per the game.

46...♖f5 47 ♔g4 ♖f7 48 ♖6e4 ♖b5 49 ♖a2 ♖g7+ 50 ♔f3 ♖h5 51 ♔e3 ♖g1 52 ♖e2

♖a1 53 ♔f3 ♖a7 54 ♔g4 ♖b5 55 f5

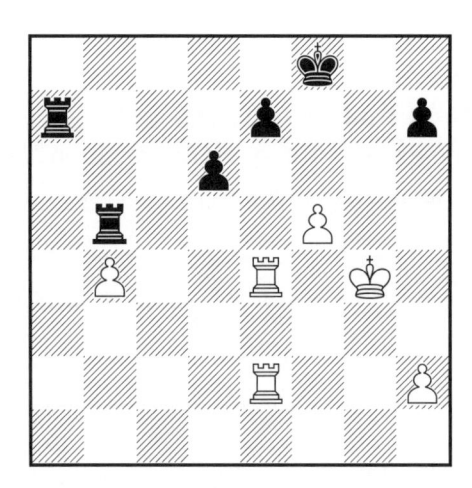

Very committal, but the defence is awkward. I was threatening to improve my position slowly with 55...♖ab7 56 ♖b2 ♔f7 followed by ...♔f6, and then moves like ...h5 and/or ...e6 followed by ...d5. When you are on the defensive it is notoriously difficult to decide when to do nothing, and when to seek counterplay.

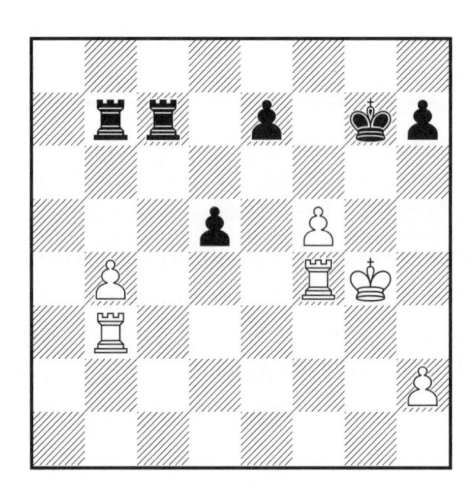

55...♖ab7 56 ♖b2 ♔f7 57 ♖b3 ♖c7 58 ♖h3 ♔g7 59 ♖he3 ♖bb7 60 ♖b3 d5 61 ♖f4

I would prefer to defend with the more active 61 ♖e6.

61...♔f6 62 b5 ♖c2 63 h4 ♖b6 64 ♖a4 h5+

Even if the position is still tenable with perfect play, this move leaves my opponent with insurmountable practical problems, which is all that matters.

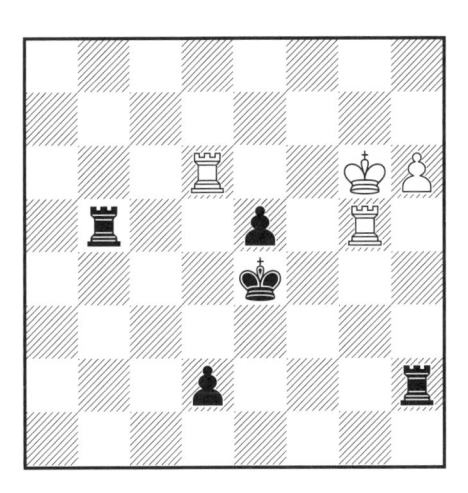

65 ♔xh5 ♔xf5 66 ♖f3+ ♔e5 67 ♖e3+ ♔d6 68 ♖a7 e6 69 ♔g6 d4 70 ♖g3 e5 71 h5 ♔d5+ 72 ♔g7 ♖h2 73 ♖g5 ♔e4 74 ♖a6 ♖xb5 75 h6 d3 76 ♖d6 d2 77 ♔g6

77...♖b6

77...♖b1 would have been more straightforward.

78 ♖xb6 d1♕ 79 ♖e6

Suddenly I have to be very careful. I cannot, for example, defend the pawn with my queen as he would take it anyway, and either check me forever or draw with his h-pawn against my rook.

79...♕c2 80 ♖gxe5+ ♔f4+ 81 ♖e4+ ♔f3 82 ♔g7 ♕c7+ 83 ♖e7 ♖g2+ 84 ♔f6 ♕d6+ 85 ♖7e6 ♕f8+ 86 ♔e5 ♖g5+ 87 ♔d4 ♕c5+ 0-1

30. Sugden-Arkell

Again a rook and pawn ending with the better pawn structure. This one has similarities to Ilfeld-Arkell in that mating themes are involved.

> **John Sugden - Keith Arkell**
> British Championship, Canterbury 2010
> *Caro-Kann Defence*

1 e4 c6 2 ♘c3 d5

Already setting up a favourable exchange according to Arkell's hierarchy of pawns.

3 ♘f3 ♗g4 4 h3 ♗xf3 5 ♕xf3 dxe4

I think there are better moves here, but I've chosen this game as it highlights the way I play these types of positions. However there are methods by which White can exploit his space advantage and two bishops: for example, with a plan involving queenside castling.

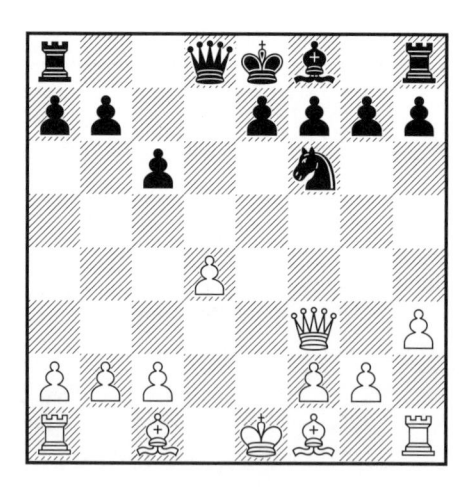

6 ♘xe4 ♘d7 7 d4 ♘df6 8 ♘xf6+ ♘xf6

I want to demonstrate what can happen when Black succeeds in executing a lot of micro-plans. Here there is a small gain for Black in swapping off a pair of knights. The reason for this is quite subtle. There is the obvious principle that exchanges favour the player with less space, but also a second knight will just get in the way of Black achieving harmony amongst his pieces.

Where would you keep this knight? On d7 it interferes with the ideal placement of heavy pieces on the d-file, and on g6 it is a sitting duck to that typical White plan of advancing his h-pawn. Furthermore, a knight on g6 prevents me from putting my bishop on the ideal square, g7.

9 c3 e6 10 ♗d3 ♗e7 11 ♗f4 0-0 12 0-0

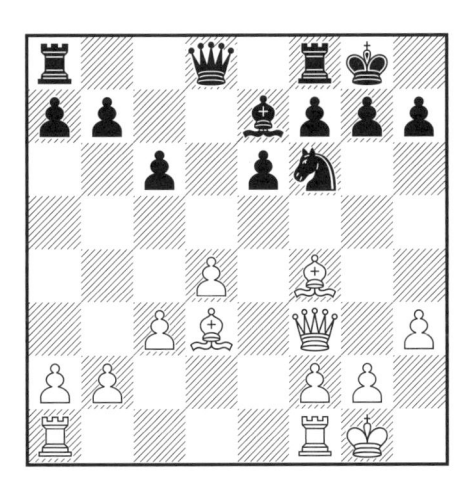

I think the majority of players would see the two bishops and extra space, and suppose that White has a comfortable edge with very little risk of losing. White does indeed have a slight pull here, but to make something of this requires a deep understanding and a very high level of play.

That there are ways in which Black can get on top by applying the mini-plans available to him is probably less well appreciated. Essentially these are:

i. Swap off the dark-squared bishops. On the surface this seems obvious because in doing so the opponent's kingside attacking potential is reduced, and he will no longer have the two bishops. The deeper reason is that the only useful role Black's bishop can play is to oppose its opposite number. Otherwise, just like the superfluous second knight, it gets in the way of the ideal piece set-up.

ii. Swap queens. As with the bishop, the queen has little to do other than try to neutralise her counterpart.

iii. Double rooks on the d-file, and keep the threat to break with...c5 hanging over White's head.

iv. Usually with a pawn on g6 and the king on g7, the remaining white bishop is a somewhat clumsy piece and can even be a target. By this stage Black's pawn structure is wonderfully flexible, whereas White's is slightly more rigid and the knight will be free to dance around the board, and gently probe.

Of course, you can't religiously set out to win the game using the four steps listed above, but if you can appreciate the finer points, then you see before you a position full of potential, rather than just one in which you stand slightly worse, and with few prospects of winning.

12...♕d5 13 ♕xd5?

This is too compliant. 13 ♕e2 would be more appropriate.

13...♘xd5

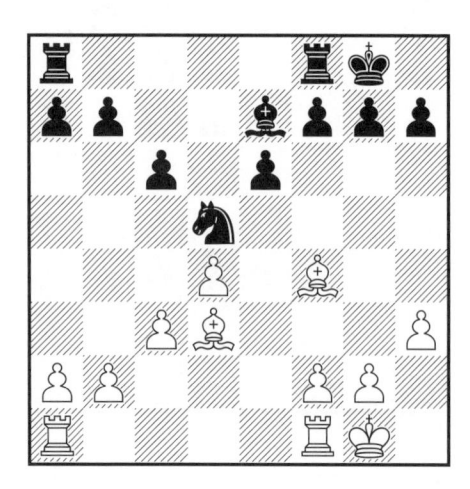

25 years ago I would probably have automatically recaptured with the c-pawn, intending the long-term advance of the b-pawn, and a minority attack. Against reasonably competent play, however, I now understand that this is a forlorn hope.

14 ♗e5 ♖fd8 15 ♖ad1 ♗d6 16 ♗xd6 ♖xd6

I have now achieved many of the mini-plans, and would always take the black side in such a position, even if the engines say it is about equal. A few inaccuracies from White, and you quickly see just how brittle his position can be.

17 g3 ♖ad8 18 ♗c2 g5!

I always feel that if I can play...g5 in such positions, it is a sign that I am getting on top, if only ever so slightly. Apart from stealing a bit of space, it nips in the bud one of White's strategic aims: to play f2-f4, g3-g4, and f4-f5. White would also feel a little more comfortable were he able to place his pawn on h4.

19 ♔g2 ♔g7 20 ♔f3 f5

This is quite a bold choice, and one which on another occasion I might not play. I am putting all my eggs in the basket of kingside expansion, and am ruling out any long-term plan of a queenside minority attack. Why? Because if White captures a piece on d5, and I recapture with the c-pawn, all I would achieve with a minority attack (...b5, ...a5, and ...b4 versus pawns on c3 and a3), would be white pawns on c3 and d4 against Black pawns on e6 and d5, and the weakness of e6 would balance out that of c3.

These are all very refined details about a position which would almost certainly

lead to a draw with best play, but much of chess – especially modern chess – is like this, with players simply looking for ways to apply a little pressure. Hence 20...f5 is a positional concession in one way, but on the bright side, after the break ...c5, and White's capture dxc5, Black, with his king on f6, will be ready to roll with his e-pawn.
21 ♗b3 ♔f6 22 ♖fe1 h5 23 ♗xd5 ♖xd5 24 ♖e5 ♖h8 25 ♖xd5 cxd5

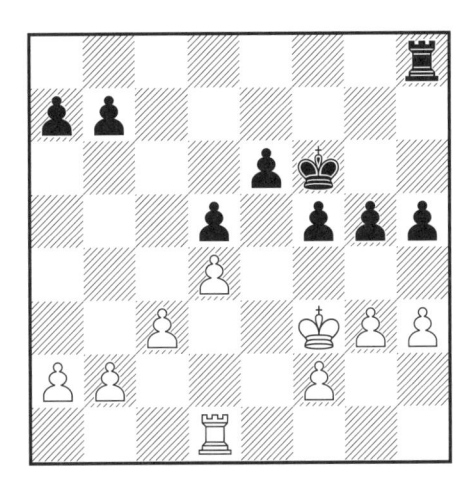

So finally I did recapture with my c-pawn, but I was thinking more about expanding on the kingside than hurling my b-pawn at him. And what would the aim of that expansion be? This is very hard to express in a concrete way, but decades of experience have taught me that as the black forces advance on the king's flank, possibilities for my rook may appear on the queenside. Ideally White will then be overstretched as he tries to cope with threats on both wings.

26 ♖g1 g4+ 27 hxg4 hxg4+ 28 ♔e3 ♔g5

My brother Nick, having returned to chess in recent years after a successful life away from the game for three decades, made the pertinent observation that a computer assessment of equal is not always very helpful, because there are some kinds of 'equality' which are only such if the defender plays a whole series of accurate moves. This is one such position. I am clearly in the driving seat, and there are many ways in which White can get in trouble by playing routinely. Black, on the other hand, has a wide margin of error. Computer engines simply do not understand these very human considerations.

29 b3

Finally, a real, if very small, mistake. My opponent faced the defender's typical dilemma: to sit back and do nothing, or to try for active counterplay. Such decisions are often very difficult even for the very strongest players.

29...b5 30 ♖e1 ♖h2 31 a4

Here the engine catches up, realising that White stands worse, and needs to take some action.

31...bxa4 32 bxa4 f4+ 33 gxf4+ ♔f5

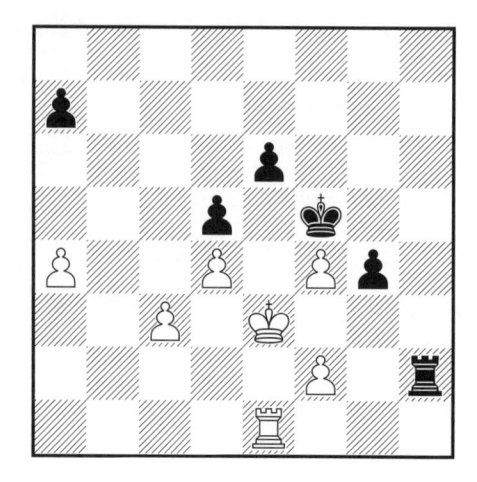

Now the finer points of positional play take a back seat, and concrete calculation takes over. Through the accumulation of very small gains, Black has created serious winning chances from a seemingly dry opening in which White was mostly intent on not losing. Whether this should suffice to win against best defence is a moot point.

34 ♖b1

In time-trouble my opponent may have calculated the critical line 34 ♖g1 ♖h3+ 35 ♖g3 a5 (zugzwang) 36 ♖xh3 gxh3 37 ♔f3 h2 38 ♔g2 ♔e4 39 ♔xh2 ♔d3 40 ♔g3 ♔xc3 41 f5 exf5 42 ♔f4 ♔xd4 43 ♔xf5 ♔c3, and realised that he was losing, or perhaps he dismissed the idea because it looked lost. I don't know. Instead, he made the typical human choice to seize the open file. I think his last chance to stay in the game was 34 ♖f1, when it might be a draw with best play, but before that I can continue to probe, and give him awkward decisions to make.

34...♖h3+ 35 ♔d2 ♖f3 36 ♖b7 ♖xf2+ 37 ♔e1 ♖a2

I can win by sheltering behind his f-pawn instead of capturing it, in order to escort the g-pawn home while preventing checks.

38 ♖xa7 ♔e4 39 ♖e7 g3 40 ♖xe6+ ♔f3 0-1

31. Arkell-McDonald

In this game, from my favourite Carlsbad pawn structure, I won a pawn, but still had to work hard to haul in the point against gritty defence.

> **Keith Arkell - Neil McDonald**
> Southend GM 2009
> *Queen's Gambit Declined*

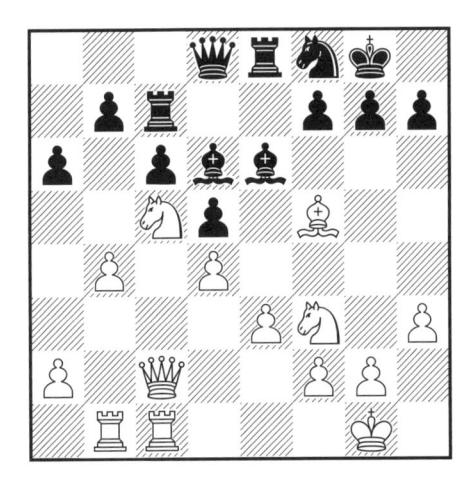

1 d4 d5 2 ♘f3 ♘f6 3 c4 e6 4 cxd5 exd5 5 ♘c3 ♗e7 6 ♗g5 0-0 7 e3 ♘bd7 8 ♗d3 ♖e8 9 0-0 c6 10 ♕c2 ♘f8 11 h3 ♗e6 12 ♗xf6 ♗xf6 13 b4 ♖c8 14 ♖ab1 ♗e7 15 ♖fc1 a6 16 ♘a4 ♗d6 17 ♘c5 ♖c7 18 ♗f5

Black's light-squared bishop is more useful here than its opposite number. It can be used for both attack and defence, whereas the one on d3 just gets in the way of my knights. It would be invaluable were I attacking on the kingside, but I don't have the right set-up for that. Because Black is a little cramped however, I did feel that maybe I was letting him off the hook a bit, and that the simple continuation of the minority attack by 18 a4 might have been better.

18...g6 19 ♗xe6 ♘xe6 20 a4 ♘g5 21 ♘xg5 ♕xg5 22 ♘d3 f5 23 b5

If my e3-pawn were better defended, the positionally powerful 23 f4 followed by ♘e5 would be playable, but here it drops a pawn to 23...♕g3.

23...cxb5 24 ♕b3 ♖xc1+ 25 ♖xc1 f4 26 exf4 ♗xf4 27 ♖a1 bxa4 28 ♕xb7 a5 29 ♕b5 ♖f8 30 ♕xa5 ♗d2 31 ♕xa4

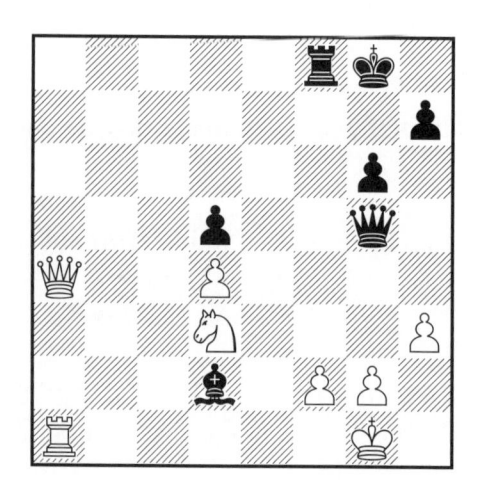

The game has gone smoothly so far, with the minority attack resulting in the win of a pawn for very little compensation, but the conversion of this to a full point is still very problematic. For example, if the d-pawns came off there would be a high likelihood of a draw.

31...♕f5 32 ♕c2 ♗h6 33 ♘e1

Neil's active queen dispels any real hopes of making progress, so this wasn't a difficult decision.

33...♕xc2 34 ♘xc2 ♗g7 35 ♖d1

My knight is unstable on c2, so I prepare to manoeuvre it to the more robust f3-square.

35...♖b8 36 ♘e1 ♖b4 37 ♘f3 ♗f6 38 g4

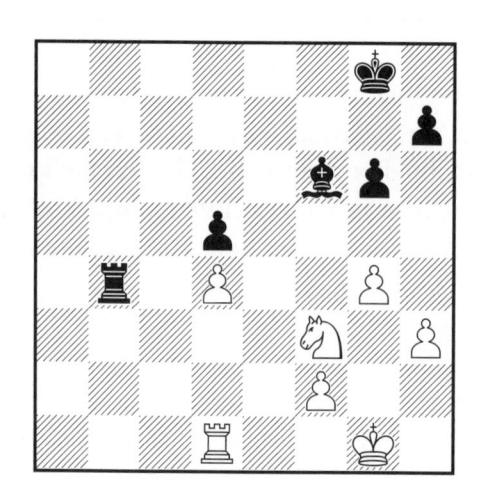

My instinct was to gain space on the kingside before Black played ...h5.

38...♔f7 39 ♔f1 ♔e6 40 ♔e2 ♖a4 41 ♔e3

By overprotecting d4 I have given myself more options: for example, the possibility of playing ♖d3, ♖b3, and ♖b6+ followed by ♖b7+.

41...♖a3+ 42 ♖d3 ♖a1

It's very hard to say for sure, but intuitively we both felt that I would have more options of making progress without the rooks.

43 ♔f4 ♖a2 44 ♘g5+

Here was one of those moments we chessplayers constantly face. I had to weigh up which of two sequences offered me the best winning chances. The alternative was something like 44 ♖e3+ ♔d6 45 ♖b3 ♖xf2 46 ♖b6+ ♔e7 47 ♔g3 ♖a2 48 ♖b7+ ♔e6 49 ♖xh7. In this line I may get a chance to play a strong ♘g5+ at some point, but I feared Black might have some easy way to hold on. The text move seemed to create a very difficult rook and pawn endgame for him.

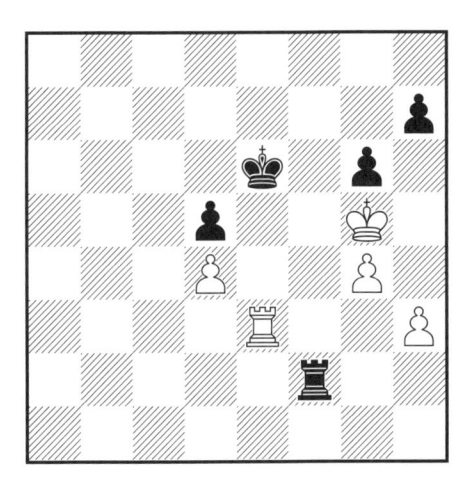

44...♗xg5+ 45 ♔xg5 ♖xf2 46 ♖e3+

One advantage of my choice is that Neil now has a very difficult decision to make. Should he put his king on f7 or d6? Possibly f7 was the better choice, but it's hard to abandon the d-pawn so readily after 46...♔f7 47 ♖e5.

46...♔d6 47 ♔h6 ♖f7 48 ♖b3

Because I can now force my rook to the back rank and round to h8, I thought, for the first time, that I had a winning position.

48...♔c6 49 ♖c3+ ♔d6 50 ♖b3 ♔c6 51 g5 ♖e7 52 ♖b8 ♖e4 53 ♔xh7 ♖xd4 54 ♔xg6 ♖h4 55 ♖b3 d4 56 ♔f5 ♔d5 57 g6 ♖h8 58 g7 ♖a8 59 ♖g3 1-0

32. Arkell-Granda Zuniga

In this game I was able to exploit the advantages of bishop over knight, and the slightly better pawn structure, in quite a straightforward manner against a very strong grandmaster.

> **Keith Arkell - Julio Granda Zuniga**
> Isle of Man Open, Douglas 2014
> *Owen's Defence*

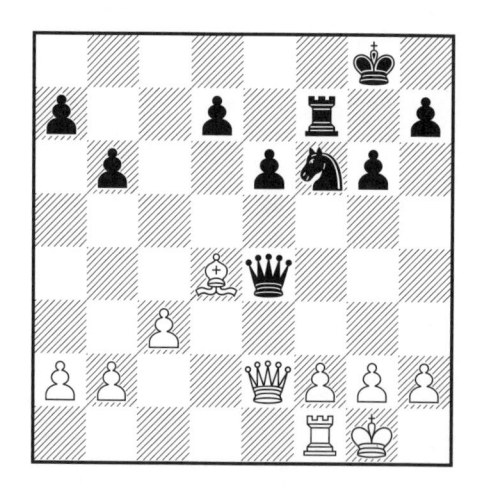

1 d4 b6 2 e4 ♗b7 3 ♗d3 e6 4 ♘f3 c5 5 c3 ♘f6 6 ♕e2 ♗e7 7 0-0 0-0 8 e5 ♘d5 9 ♕e4 g6 10 ♕g4 cxd4 11 ♘xd4 ♘c6 12 ♘xc6 ♗xc6 13 ♗h6 f5 14 exf6 ♘xf6 15 ♕e2 ♖f7 16 ♘d2 ♘h5 17 ♗e4 ♖c8 18 ♗xc6 ♖xc6 19 ♘f3 ♗d6 20 ♘e5 ♗xe5 21 ♕xe5 ♖c5 22 ♕e2 ♕h4 23 ♖ad1 ♘f6 24 ♗e3 ♖d5 25 ♖d4 ♖xd4 26 ♗xd4 ♕e4

I didn't really handle my opponent's unusual opening particularly well, but now I've managed to obtain a small endgame advantage in the form of bishop versus knight in an open position, and two pawn islands against three. The inflexibility of Black's pawn structure is what counts here, since any exchange will leave its neighbour isolated.

27 ♕xe4 ♘xe4 28 ♖d1 d5 29 ♖e1

I wanted to crystallise Black's pawn structure by playing c4 and cxd5, and my thinly-veiled threat against his e6-pawn gains time for this.

29...♖e7 30 c4

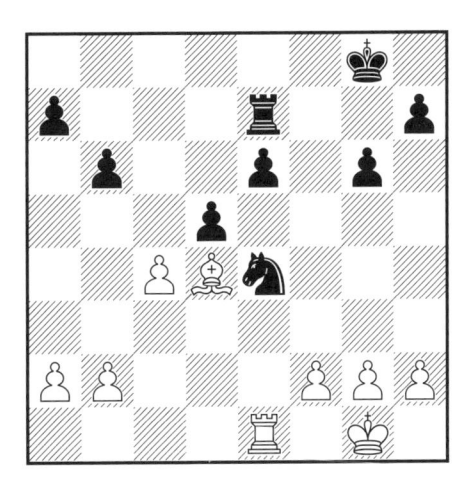

I clearly remember calculating that if Granda Zuniga had now played 30...e5 the game would most likely have finished in a draw, but as I was searching for some possible advantage in the subsequent rook ending, he played a different move. I had looked at 31 cxd5 exd4, and quickly seen that 32 f3? ♘c3! even loses after 33 ♖xe7 d3! – all strong players seem to have a built-in alarm system which alerts them to such moves. My intended reply was 32 d6 ♖d7 33 ♖xe4 ♖xd6 34 ♔f1 d3 35 ♔e1, but he has only to find some move like 35...♖c6 to be completely fine.

30...♖d7 31 cxd5 exd5 32 ♔f1

I now felt that I stood slightly better, but still expected him to find some sequence which would thwart my winning attempts.

32...♔f7 33 ♔e2 ♘c5 34 ♔d2 ♘e6 35 ♗e5 d4

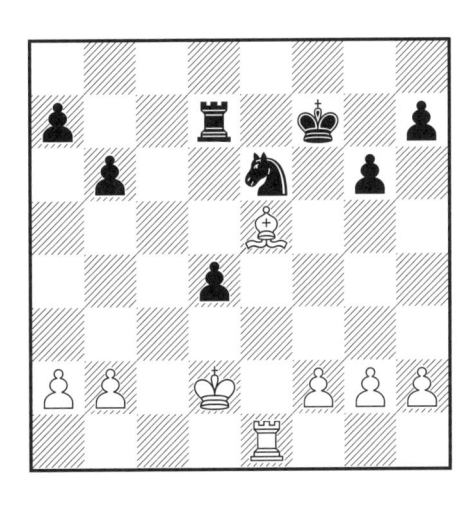

This move encouraged me. Maybe Black is still OK, but I felt that he was unnecessarily weakening his pawn.

36 b4 a5 37 bxa5 bxa5 38 ♔d3 ♖d5 39 ♔e4 ♖b5 40 ♖e2 ♖b4 41 ♖d2 ♔e7 42 f4 ♖a4 43 ♔d5 d3 44 g3 h5?

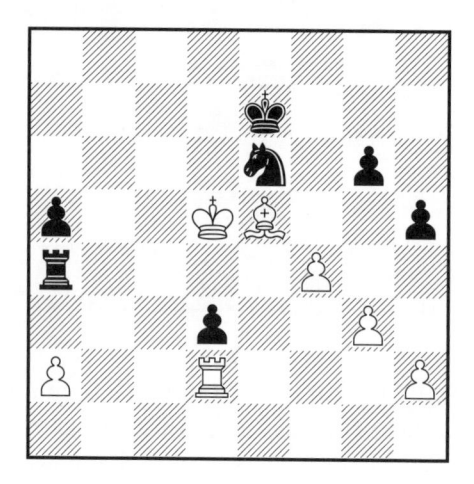

This is simply a tactical oversight, but clearly White is well on top in any case.

45 a3! 1-0

My a-pawn is immune because of ♗d6+, so I will be able to continue 46 ♖xd3 with an overwhelming position, as well as an extra pawn.

33. Arkell-Byrne

My opponent in this game was a world championship candidate, eliminated by former champion Boris Spassky in 1974. His less strong, younger brother was well known for losing brilliantly to a 13-year-old Bobby Fischer in 'The Game of the Century' in 1956.

> **Keith Arkell - Robert Byrne**
> Watson, Farley & Williams, London 1991
> *King's Indian Defence*

1 d4 ♘f6 2 ♘f3 g6 3 g3 ♗g7 4 ♗g2 0-0 5 0-0 d6 6 c4 ♘c6 7 ♘c3 a6 8 h3 ♖b8 9 e4 b5 10 cxb5 axb5 11 e5 dxe5 12 dxe5 ♕xd1 13 ♖xd1 ♘d7 14 e6 fxe6 15 ♗f4 ♘de5 16 ♘xe5 ♘xe5 17 ♖ac1 c5 18 ♖c2 c4 19 ♖e2

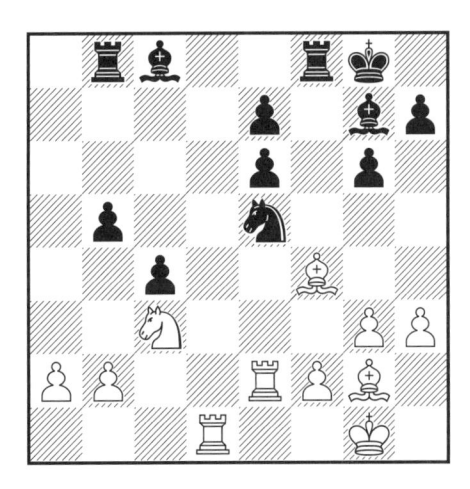

I remember feeling a little uncomfortable about the way the game had gone up to now, and so decided at least to force my opponent to surrender material.
19...♖xf4! 20 gxf4 ♘d3

The exchange sacrifice is, of course, good for Black, and my main concern was to avoid losing by force.
21 ♗e4 b4 22 ♘a4 ♘xf4

Had Byrne inserted the moves 22...♗d7 23 b3 I would have had more to worry about.
23 ♖d8+ ♔f7 24 ♖e3 ♗e5 25 ♗c6 c3

I was very pleased to see this move as I can now return the exchange and tie up

most of his pieces.
26 bxc3 bxc3 27 ♖xe5! c2 28 ♖c5 c1♕+ 29 ♖xc1 ♘e2+ 30 ♔h2 ♘xc1 31 ♘c3

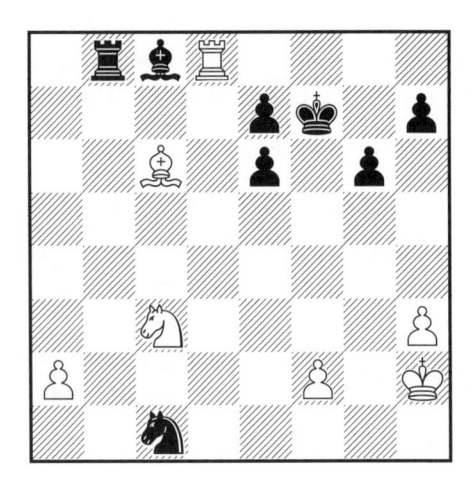

Suddenly his rook, bishop, and knight are all completely stuck.
31...♖b2

Black has to try this, or I will simply come and collect his knight with my king.
32 ♖xc8 ♖xf2+ 33 ♔g3 ♖c2 34 ♘e4 ♘e2+ 35 ♔h4 ♖xa2 36 ♘g5+ ♔g7 37 ♖c7

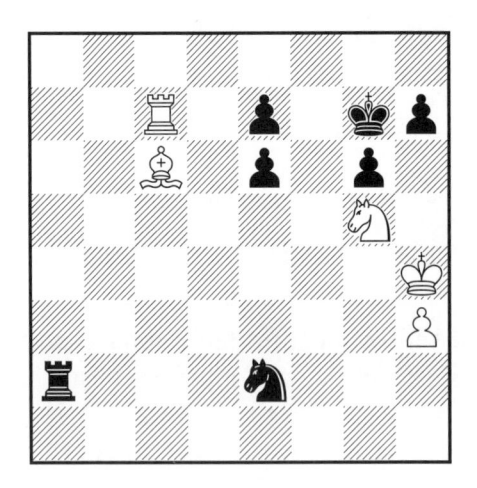

For most of my chess life I seem to have made a habit of grinding away for many moves in search of an endgame win which is by no means assured. Here is a case in point. The position is difficult to calculate, especially when a little short of time, but this was bad judgement, and I ought to have played 37 ♘xe6+. However, in neither case can I be certain that White is winning.

37...♘d4
   37...h6 38 ♖xe7+ ♔f6 39 ♖f7+ ♔e5 40 ♘f3+ ♔d6 would have left my pieces a little awkward, and my own king in a spot of bother.
38 ♖xe7+ ♔f6 39 ♖f7+ ♔e5 40 ♘f3+ ♘xf3+ 41 ♖xf3 ♖c2 42 ♗e8 ♖g2 43 ♗f7

   Byrne could have forced the ending of rook and bishop against rook here, with the sequence 43...g5+ 44 ♔h5 g4 45 hxg4 ♖h2+ 46 ♔g5 h6+ 47 ♔g6 ♖g2. When I mentioned this after the game he confessed to overlooking the line, but claimed he would have drawn easily, and that he was the inventor of the well-known 'Second Rank Defence'.
43...h5 44 ♖f1 ♔d6 45 ♖e1 ♔e7
   Giving up his e-pawn in order to set up a fortress.
46 ♗xe6 ♔f6 47 ♗d5 ♖d2 48 ♗f3 ♖d3 49 ♖f1 ♔g7 50 ♔g5 ♖a3

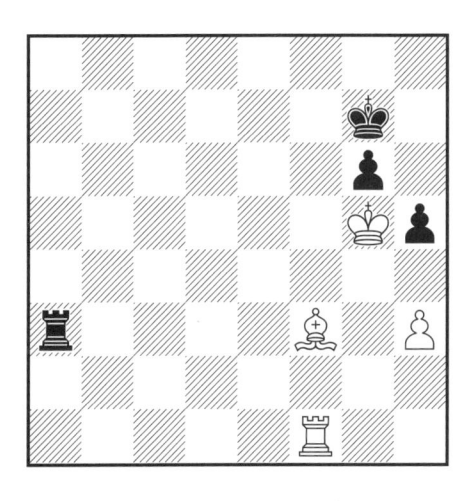

I had no idea whether or not this ending was winning, and even today I'm still not sure, but suspect that it should be drawn.

51 ♔f4 ♚h6 52 h4

Necessary sooner or later if I wish to use my bishop.

52...♜a6 53 ♖g1 ♜f6+ 54 ♔e3 ♜a6 55 ♗e4 ♜b6 56 ♔d4 ♜a6 57 ♔e5 ♚g7 58 ♗d3 ♜f6 59 ♖g2 ♜c6 60 ♗e4 ♜a6 61 ♖b2 ♜a5+ 62 ♔f4 ♜a1 63 ♖b6 ♜g1 64 ♗f3 ♜f1 65 ♖b7+ ♚f6 66 ♖b5 ♜e1 67 ♖g5 ♜f1 68 ♔e3 ♚f7 69 ♗e4 ♜f6 70 ♖c5 ♚g7 71 ♗d5 ♜f8 72 ♗c4 ♜e8+ 73 ♔f4 ♜f8+ 74 ♔g3 ♜f5 75 ♖c7+ ♚f8

After 75...♚h6 I would probably have had to force rook and bishop versus rook with ♗g8 at some stage soon.

76 ♗d3 ♜f6 77 ♗e4 ♚g8 78 ♗f3 ♚f8 79 ♗d5 ♜f5 80 ♗e4 ♜f6 81 ♖a7 ♚g8 82 ♗f3 ♚f8 83 ♖a4 ♚g7 84 ♔f2 ♜f7 85 ♔e3 ♜e7+ 86 ♗e4 ♜f7 87 ♖a1 ♜f6 88 ♗d5 ♜f5 89 ♖a7+ ♚f8

89...♚h6 was more reliable. Now I have the opportunity to penetrate Black's position with a combination of king and bishop.

90 ♔e4 ♜f1 91 ♔e5 ♜f5+ 92 ♔e6 ♜f4 93 ♗b3 ♜f2 94 ♖c7 ♚g8

Finally my opponent goes irredeemably wrong. Even at this late stage he can still escape into a theoretically drawn rook and bishop against rook position with 94...♜f4: for example, 95 ♗d5 ♜xh4 96 ♔f6 (96 ♖f7+ ♚e8 97 ♗c6+ ♚d8 98 ♔d6 ♜d4+ 99 ♗d5 ♚e8 holds) 96...♜f4+ 97 ♔xg6 ♚e8.

95 ♗c2 ♜g2 96 ♔f6 1-0

96...♜g4 97 ♗xg6 ♜f4+ 98 ♗f5 wins.

Afterword
Simon Williams pays homage to Keith Arkell's talent

It feels like I have known Keith my entire life, as we've faced each other across the chessboard at tournaments for the entirety of my chess career. As well as being on-and-off rivals, we have more often been great friends; sharing many a story and social drink in the nearest bar to whichever venue we're playing at.

Keith, along with Mark Hebden, is the stalwart of the classic English weekender; both should be celebrated for their dedication to tirelessly traversing the country from end to end to make a living, nay a lifelong career. Plenty of the numerous congresses and many international tournaments won by Keith and Mark have provided invaluable experience and sometimes even norms for future IMs and GMs.

My first recollection of Keith was when I faced him over-the-board in a tournament in Paignton, the annual late-summer open that Keith has to date won a record 25 times. Our inaugural clash began with an English Opening, leading to a lengthy game in which Keith would go on to defeat me in a display of his relative adept mastery.

As I am sure you're by now well aware, Keith is an renowned endgame expert. His typical opening and middlegame play is solid and positional, leading him into endgames where he is comfortable and can demonstrate his prevailing knowledge and prowess of fundamental chess principles.

However, like with any self-respecting grandmaster, there is another side to Keith: a tactical, deadly side. Given the chance, he can destroy his opponent with some beautiful combinations and attacking play. To give balance to this book, I thought that it would be a good idea to show a little of that subtle-yet-combative side, by examining some very impressive games of Keith's that you might not be aware of, until now.

I had the pleasure of sitting next to the following game whilst it was played. I say pleasure, but at the time it felt a guilty one, as I found it extremely hard to concentrate on my own game with such excitement going on next to me. Julian Hodgson has historically been know for his sparkling attacking play, but in this game he gets a taste of his own medicine.

Julian Hodgson - Keith Arkell
Surrey Easter Open, Sutton 1996
French Defence

1 d4 e6

You can normally expect a French or a Caro-Kann from Keith, as both of these openings often lead to one of his favourite pawn structures. After the exchange of Black's d-pawn for White's e-pawn, Black will be left with four pawns on the kingside versus White's three pawns, a structure that Keith tends to favour. This pawn majority has given Keith many chances to play his favourite move ...g5, as we will see later on.
2 e4 d5 3 e5

Stopping any trade on e4 and not allowing the 4 vs 3 pawn structure, which Keith's favourite Fort Knox variation would have brought about: 3 ♘c3 (or 3 ♘d2) 3...dxe4 4 ♘xe4 ♗d7.
3...c5 4 c3 ♘c6 5 ♘f3 ♕b6

5...♗d7 is a way that I sometimes play this position, with the idea of playing ...♕c7, ...f6, and ...0-0-0, but 5...♕b6 is, of course, the main line.
6 a3 c4!?

A sensible idea, depending on what kind of game you are looking for (retaining the tension with 6...♗d7 is the other main approach). With this move, Black locks down the queenside and attempts to steer the game into quieter waters. I have favoured this approach myself, using the plan that Keith plays next. Possibly I even learnt the idea from watching this game live.
7 ♘bd2 ♘a5!

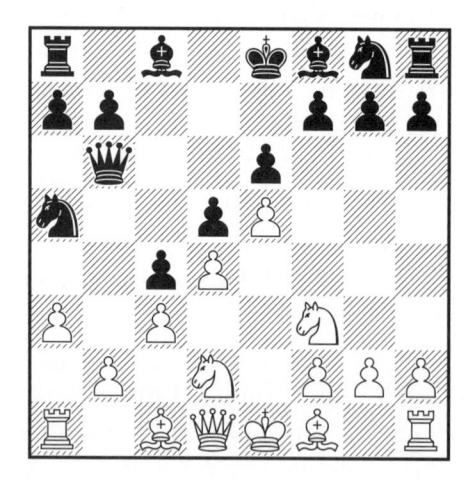

Aiming to use the b3-square and also preparing ...♗d7, ideally followed by ...♗a4 and ...♗c2, from where the bishop shows its face.
8 h4

The standard approach for White. He wants to develop his bishop on h3, from where it works to stop ...f6 and to support f4-f5.
8...♗d7 9 h5?!

I am not entirely sure that this is a wise idea. Now Black will always be able to

break open the kingside with ...g6.
9...0-0-0 10 g3 f5

A natural move, aiming to keep the position blocked for now, and Black still has the ...g6 break for later on.

11 exf6?!

Another risky decision, as now Black gains a strong centre, as well as good squares on f6 and d6 for his pieces. Considering 'supposed style' though, some would say this is a natural decision. Julian is opening the position which should favour his 'tactical' style, while not assisting Keith's love of grinding out endgames.

11...gxf6

Now the break ...e6-e5 is something that White must always keep an eye on.

12 ♗h3 ♗d6 13 0-0 e5

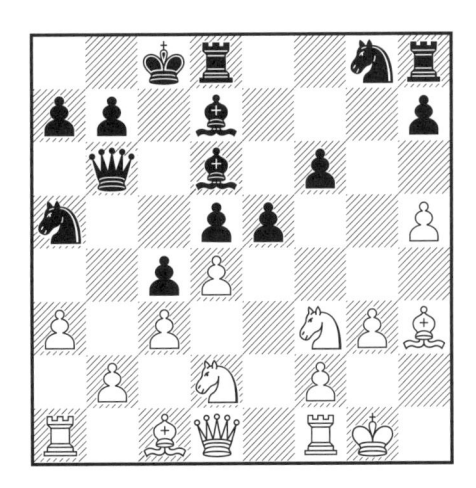

And here it is. Keith grabs the centre and opens up some lines towards White's king.

14 ♗xd7+ ♖xd7 15 ♖b1

White must create some counterplay on the queenside, so he aims to break with b2-b3 or b2-b4.

15...e4 16 ♘h4 ♘e7 17 b3 ♕c7 18 bxc4 e3!

Breaking open the fragile dark squares around White's king.

19 fxe3 ♗xg3

Something has clearly gone wrong for White, but it still requires a great deal of energy to finish him off.

20 ♘g2 ♖g8

Line them up boys!

21 ♕e2 ♘ec6

Beginning a very logical regrouping, which is something you will often see in

Keith's games. The rook on d7 wants to switch over to g7.
22 cxd5?
This is too much. White should play 22 h6!, preventing Black's intended plan.
22...♖dg7!

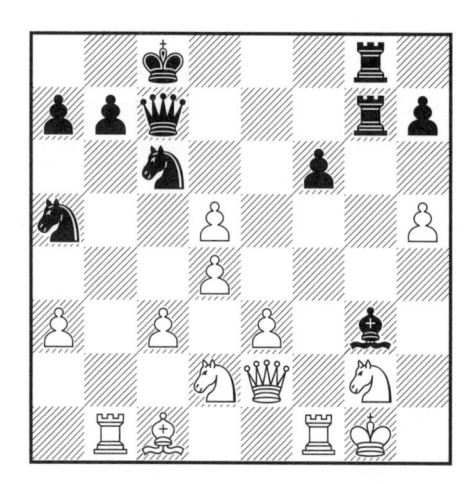

Not wasting any time defending, as the attack will come first.
23 ♘f3
23 dxc6 fails to 23...♗h2+ 24 ♔h1 ♖xg2 25 cxb7+ ♘xb7 26 ♕xg2 ♖xg2 27 ♔xg2 ♕g3+ 28 ♔h1 and now the brilliant 28...♗g1! leads to a winning position.
23...♕f7
Sacrificing to speed up the attack, but 23...♕d7! was even stronger. The queen would be tremendous on h3.
24 dxc6 ♕xh5
Can White survive the attack?
25 cxb7+ ♔b8
The threat of ...♗h2+ is quite stressful for White.
26 ♖b2!
Accurate defence, covering along the second rank.
26...♕h3
Edging ever nearer...
27 e4
There was nothing better, and this move at least gives White the option of developing the bishop from c1. We now have a very strange position as White doesn't enjoy a great number of moves, whereas Black can improve his position and it is quite strange just how safe the black king is on b8. If Black can ever get his last piece into play with ...♘c4 then it will be the end for White, but ...♘c4 is only possible if White

moves the rook from f1 to the wrong square.
27...♖g4!

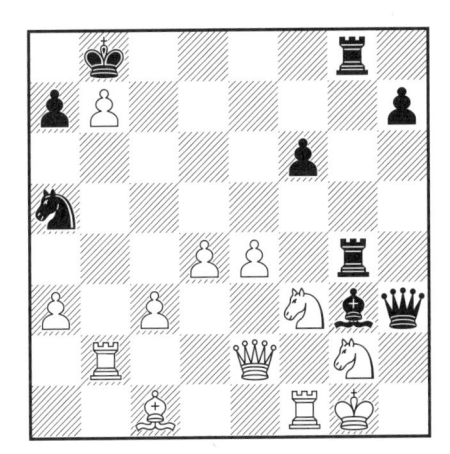

A very nice and aggressive idea. The rook is heading for h4, when neither of White's knights can capture it. White must now be very accurate.

27...♘b3?! was an interesting, but strange and ultimately incorrect idea, hoping for 28 ♖xb3?? ♗h2+. The main problem is that the knight doesn't actually do much. It tries to get back into play, but after 28 ♗e3 there is nothing better than 28...♘a5. Meanwhile 27...♘c4? doesn't yet work due to 28 ♕xc4 ♗h2+ 29 ♔f2! ♖xg2+ 30 ♔e1 when the rook on f1 defends White's position and he is winning.
28 e5?!

Instead, 28 ♖d1 is a semi-waiting move that aims to give the white king the f1-square to run to. Yet it is a big mistake due to 28...♘c4!. Now this idea works: for example, 29 ♕xc4 ♗h2+! 30 ♔f2 ♕xg2+ 31 ♔e3 ♗f4+ 32 ♔d3 ♕xf3+, as White no longer has a rook on f1 defending everything.

As such, we might wonder about 28 ♕d3!?, aimed at meeting ...♖h4 with ♘gxh4: for example, 28...♖h4? is no longer correct as after 29 ♘gxh4 Black, surprisingly, has no good discovered checks, as shown by 29...♗h2+ 30 ♔f2! or 29...♗f4+ 30 ♘g2 and wins, and especially White's brilliant idea, 29...♗xh4+ 30 ♘g5!! ♕xd3 31 ♗f4#. Instead, 28...♗h2+! is the correct approach: 29 ♔h1? (after 29 ♔f2 ♖xg2+ 30 ♔e1 ♖xb2 31 ♗xb2 ♖g2 Black is better due to his ongoing initiative) 29...♗c7+ 30 ♔g1 ♖xg2+ 31 ♖xg2 ♖xg2#.

Last, but by no means least, 28 ♖e1!! is an amazing computer defence that I would be surprised if any human could find. It is not at first even clear what the point of this move is. After 28...♖h4 29 ♘gxh4! White survives with a winning advantage: for example, 29...♗xe1+ 30 ♘g2 or 29...♗xh4+ 30 ♘g5! (a hard-to-see defensive resource) 30...♗xg5 31 ♕g2 ♗e3+ 32 ♖xe3 ♖xg2+ 33 ♖xg2 and after the dust has

cleared, White is better. Instead, 28...♗c7! keeps the balance, and if 29 ♕f1 ♖g3 30 ♘g5. Don't ask me what is going on, while the computer typically displays '0.00'.
28...fxe5

Simple and good. White is now lost.
29 dxe5 ♘c4!

A very nice way to win. The last piece joins in the onslaught.
30 ♖c2

After 30 ♕xc4 the easiest route is 30...♗h2+ 31 ♔f2 ♖xc4.
30...♖h4!

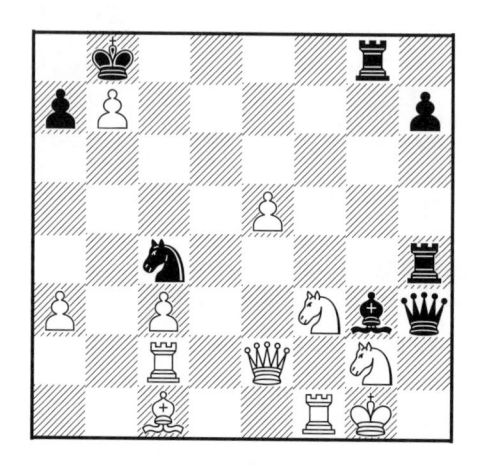

Beautiful.
31 ♘gxh4 ♗f2+!

Put that in your pipe and smoke it!
32 ♔xf2 ♕g3# 0-1

A brilliant attacking game by Keith. Had you not known who was playing the black side, you wouldn't be criticised for guessing someone like Tal, Shirov or Kasparov. I have always found it strange how people assume that players who prefer endgames cannot possibly play well tactically, and visa versa. The fact is that both these skills must be possessed by any self-respecting grandmaster. A very common way to win is to gain an advantage through tactical means, which then needs to be converted in an endgame. A glance at a number of Shirov's games will show just this.

We now come on to a move of Keith's that I believe ranks up there as the move he has played that he is most proud of. He has shown the position after 33 ♘b3 to numerous strong players asking them, "What should Black play?". As far as I know no one has found the correct answer with their first guess. Maybe you can do better, or at least work your way through understanding why the move played is such a strong one?

Jacek Gdanski – Keith Arkell
European Club Cup, Budva 2000

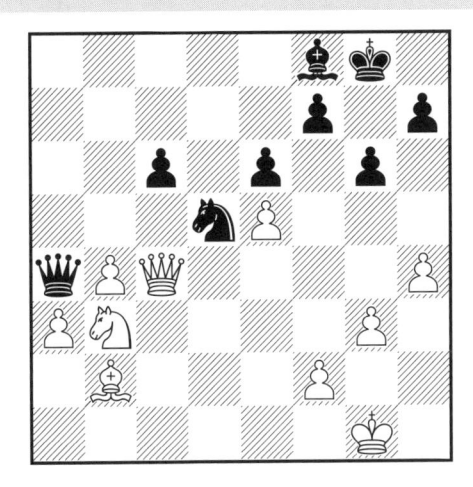

Keith is a pawn down and any 'normal' move or idea would leave him struggling without much chance of survival. The move that Keith really wants to play, that would give him active counterplay, would be 33...c5, but that idea fails here, so Keith goes about preparing it in a brilliant way.

33...g5!!

The main idea behind this fantastic concept is that after hxg5 Black will be able to play ...♕h5+ in some variations.

33...c5 is only refuted by 34 ♘xc5! ♗xc5 (or 34...♕d1+ when both 35 ♕f1 ♕c2 36 ♕c1 and 35 ♔g2 are very good for White) 35 ♕xc5 ♕d1+ 36 ♔h2!. White is winning as Black has no more checks or ways to create threats. That is why he needs the h5-square for his queen.

34 hxg5?!

White gets confused by Keith's highly imaginative idea. It would have been wiser to have not accepted this gift. Indeed, 34 ♕d3! would have been a clever reply. The idea is to put a stop to ...c5, as now ...c5 can always be met by bxc5. By moving the queen to d3 White has allowed the b-pawn to move, as it is no longer pinned. After 34...gxh4 35 gxh4 c5!? (anyhow!) 36 ♘xc5 ♗xc5 37 bxc5 ♔f8 White is better, but his king is still weak and the combination of queen and knight could always threaten White's position.

34...c5!

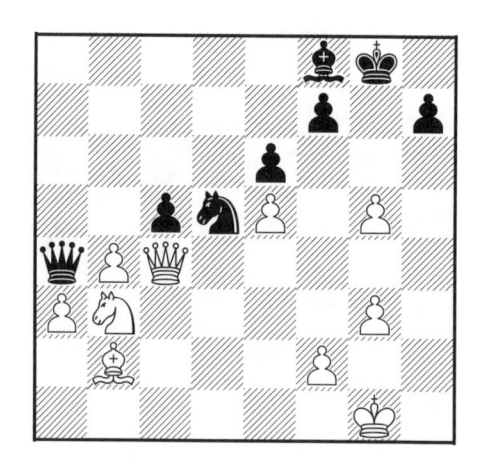

We will shortly see how 33...g5 made this idea possible.
35 ♔g2

35 ♘xc5 is clearly what White wants to play, but Black is now drawing after 35...♗xc5! 36 ♕xc5 ♕d1+ 37 ♔h2 (or 37 ♔g2 ♘f4+!!) 37...♕h5+ 38 ♔g2 ♘f4+!!, which reveals the amazing idea behind 33...g5. Black obtains a draw by perpetual check: 39 gxf4 ♕g4+ 40 ♔h2 ♕h4+ 41 ♔g2 ♕g4+ 42 ♔f1 ♕d1+, etc.
35...cxb4 36 axb4 ♕a2! 37 ♗c1 ♗xb4

It is time to take stock. White is a pawn up, but Black is incredibly active. White's extra pawn is also of little value as it cannot be used to create a passed pawn or any other kind of threat. As the computer confirms, the position is now equal.
38 ♕c8+ ♔g7 39 ♘d4

Trying to bring some pieces towards Black's king, but everything is defended.
39...♗c3! 40 ♘xe6+

White decides to force the draw. After 40 ♘f3 Black should centralise his queen, with 40...♕b1 41 ♗f4 ♕e4 when it is White who should be thinking about forcing a draw.
40...fxe6 41 ♕d7+ ♔h8 42 ♕e8+ ½-½

A lovely save by Keith. The idea of 33...g5 is something quite unique and special.

I have had the pleasure of facing Keith over the board on numerous occasions. You will never get a firmer handshake and broader smile then when sitting down at the board opposite him. It makes a nice change from the countless 'wet kipper' handshakes that I have encountered over the years.

When playing a good friend, over the board it is a gladiatorial battle, but as soon as the game is over the winner should take the loser for a well needed drink.

Simon Williams - Keith Arkell
British Championship, Torquay 1998
English Opening

1 c4 c5 2 ♘c3 ♘c6 3 g3 g6 4 ♗g2 ♗g7 5 d3 e6 6 e4 ♘ge7 7 h4

Well, what did you expect? Now Keith ignores me, electing to meet the wing attack with central piece play.

7...♘d4 8 h5 ♘ec6 9 ♘ge2 d6 10 ♖b1?!

I am not sure about this; aiming to play on both the queenside and kingside is rather optimistic. Better would have been 10 ♗e3 with the idea of ♕d2 and ♗h6.

10...♖b8 11 f4 a6 12 ♘xd4 ♘xd4 13 ♔f2!? g5!?

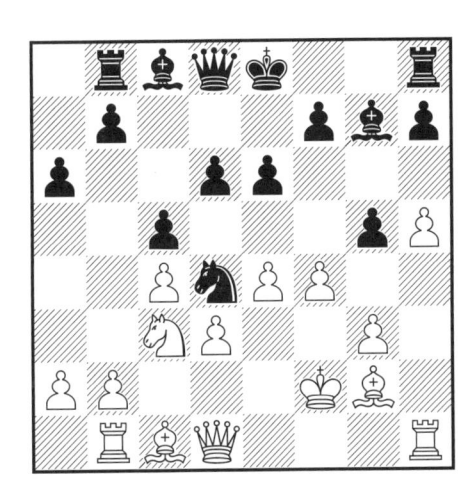

Keith's favourite move again. You should always watch out for the ...g5 advance when playing him! This advance greatly surprised me at the time, but it is a normal positional idea in certain structures. Like in some Sicilians, Black plays ...g5 to divert my pawn on f4 away from controlling e5 and the dark squares in general. This is very aggressive play from Keith, rather than the more restrained 13...b5.

14 fxg5 b5

Black starts active operations, and why not? It is not easy for me to come up with a constructive plan.

15 ♗f4 b4!?

Another rather surprising move. Keith closes down the queenside, for now...

16 ♘e2 b3 17 a3

One idea behind Keith's novel idea is that my knight on e2 has become a target for some tactical ideas.

17...e5! 18 ♘xd4?! exf4!

Beginning an attack against my dark squares.

19 ♘c6?!

Things normally go wrong for me when I start to get greedy, but it takes a great attack from Keith to put me away. 19 ♘f3 was better to try to defend.

19...♕xg5!

Here come the big boys! 19...fxg3+!? was another strong possibility.

20 ♘xb8

In for a penny, in for a pound. 20 gxf4 would have held off for longer, but matters are far from pleasant for White after 20...♕xf4+ 21 ♕f3 ♕d2+ 22 ♕e2 ♕xe2+ 23 ♔xe2 ♗g4+ 24 ♔f2 ♖b6. Black has a large advantage here, largely due to his excellent dark-squared bishop.

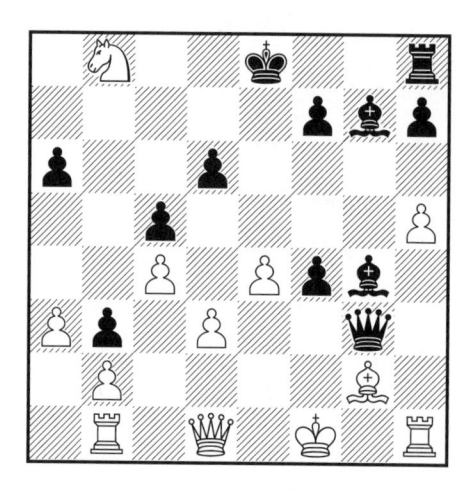

20...♕xg3+ 21 ♔f1 ♗g4

Black's pieces flood into my position like a tidal wave. You give Keith a chance to sacrifice and attack – and he will.

22 ♕d2 f3 23 ♘c6

An attempt to bring my pieces back to defend, but it is to late.

23...♗h6!

The bishop joins in with deadly effect.

24 ♕f2

There is nothing better, as if 24 ♕xh6 ♕xg2+ 25 ♔e1 ♕e2#.

24...fxg2+ 25 ♕xg2 ♕xd3+ 26 ♔f2 ♗e3+ 27 ♔g3 ♖g8 0-1

A powerful attacking display from Keith and by this point I had seen enough. I do believe that I may have just about been old enough for Keith to have at least taken me to the bar for a consoling drink, being the gentleman that he is.

Index of Opponents

Bradbury	*97*
Bruno	*107*
Byrne	*145*
Certek	*63*
Ernst	*82*
Franklin	*113*
Gdanski	*155*
Granda Zuniga	*142*
Groves	*125*
Hebden	*40*
Hodgson	*149*
Holland	*56*
Houska	*60*
Ilfeld	*77*
Koneru	*36*
Kosten	*22*
Kotronias	*28*
Kulaots	*51*
Ledger	*72*
McDonald	*139*
Milliet	*47*
Palliser	*89*
Panzer	*121*
Orr	*118*
Rodshtein	*32*
Spreeuw	*86*
Suba	*12*
Sugden	*134*
Toma	*102*
Vachier-Lagrave	*17*
Wadsworth	*68*
Ward	*93*
Webb	*130*
Williams	*157*
Zak	*44*
Zakarian	*111*